Hit the North

Hit the North

Jamo James

Lamojamo Publishing

Hit the North
By Jamo James

For Sara

Part One – Love Lies Low on a Long Road Travelled

Travel Hotel, Lancaster; Summer 1989, nearly eight in the evening

In the evening the smoky room of the Travel Hotel darkens, with its walls and low ceiling the colour of coffee, stained in places, like the nicotine on Max's fingers.

"Faced with this crushing injustice, the best form of defence is attack."

Billy watches the shapes of the words released in smoky bundles, murky speech bubbles from his friend's mouth. Behind him the sun dipping over the distant brown hills fires low orange rays on to the sequinned backdrop of the stage to their left; gold and silver discs about the size of two pence coins that quiver and glitter in the flattening light. One night each week this is a graveyard for aspiring comedians; a red velvet curtain on an arced rail pulled to expose failing stand-up routines on a tough Northern circuit. But tonight's entertainment is different. Billy has squinted at the glitzy backdrop all day without really noticing it. Now the light coruscating at angles off the moving sequins reflect his thoughts; shimmering, torrid, confused.

Since their arrival in the morning Max and Billy have sat and drank in the same place in their ill-fitting suits with little to show bar wet lettering from newspapers and beer mats marking the table surface. A large, brimming ashtray chronicles the time spent in the room and their contribution to the air quality. It's been emptied twice by the time the evening's main event is about to commence.

The room, in need of a makeover with a low stage that fills the space on one side is getting busier. Opposite the stage the arena splits into two levels, the upper forming a circular space enclosed by a bay window where they sit. This offers the best view of the stage and a short cut to the bar. The windows are dirty on the outside, flat panes with bubbled centres draped in grey net curtains within. The surrounding Lancashire countryside stretches into the distance and behind it the last of the day's light.

"I'll get another," Max says, standing.

Billy closes his eyes, but the light show continues as he waits for his travelling companion and partner in crime to return from the bar. He feels a small surge of relief when he does. Max is by now unsteady on his feet. Her sets two gin and tonics in stem glasses down on the table. A long day of drinking and both men are jaded, their conversation as exhausted as their attire. Billy's is a charcoal grey wedding suit, scratchy in the heat of the room, his thin, pale skin reddening at the collar and cuffs. He's worn it only the once before he left, on his big day, some years ago, before the ensuing breakdown of his marriage. Inevitable some say. That final act of failure, the *coup de grace* happened some weeks before and now he's wearing the thing again. It had been special; now it's pock-marked with cigarette burns, alcohol stains and tears, as well as other deposits of a two-week binge funded by a longshot horse called Kalamazoo. His friend's outfit is tight-fitting, grey and shiny, equally blemished and torn in places. It had been Daniel's, his late brother, older by two years and up the chimney as long. The trousers ride up to a line below the midpoint of his calf for he is taller and broader than his sibling had been, and the jacket is tight across the back and shoulders. This brevity pulls the sleeves up short, stretching the stitching and exposing his dark-haired arms as he smokes his cigarettes. He sniffs at the shoulder, an habitual tic to salvage remnants of the lost.

The two had arrived hot and dry at the Lancaster Travel Hotel, hitch-hiking on the dusty road with an immediate need to slake a thirst. The clattering of the shutters rising at the bar gave premature hope before the tender refused alcohol so early in the morning. They ordered coffees instead and took their drinks to a table near the entrance. Gold Blend in Pyrex glasses. Two sales reps had done the same and sat at the tall bar tables awaiting their appointments, checking their watches and diaries laid out before them.

"I'll talk, you show the right page," the sleepy one insisted. The other was nervous and drank his coffee noisily, clicking the top of his pen, in out, in and out. A sign on the wall above them explained that coffee was *gratis* for paying residents. Next to the sign was a small poster advertising the evening's guest speaker and a photograph of an elderly lady with coiffured hair and a steely, serious stare: Dame Elaine Kellett-Bowman, the Conservative MP for Lancaster. The theme of her speech; *Family Values: Their role in The British Revival.*

Billy peered at the poster from his tall chair at the tall table and read with interest.

"Who's she?" Max asked following his gaze.

Billy rubbed the back of his head as he read. "A right-wing politician," he said. "Not nice."

Max blew across his coffee to cool it and watched the froth shudder against the rim of the cup. "How so?" he asked.

"A hate-merchant," Billy continued. "A peddler of revulsion."

"Go on."

Billy turned away from the poster to face his friend. "There was a firebomb attack on a gay newspaper in London last year. She thought it was justified; said that any attacks on gays were an understandable intolerance of evil."

Max stopped blowing and the small storm raging in his cup ceased, the scum mark around his cup visible as the foam receded. "Jeez!" he said. "Was she behind it?"

Billy shook his head. "Maybe," he said, "who knows? If she was, she covered her tracks well. She certainly approved of it."

"Jeez," Max repeated.

Billy continued; "She doesn't have to pretend or hide behind her ignorance; she can tell it as she sees it, protected by money and suffrage. She's comfortable in knowing her knee-jerk tirades against anyone seen as deviant will find favour in many quarters."

"Evil!" Max agreed. "Middle name Misery!"

"*As evil as can be,* Elvis!" Billy replied. "She likes to speak her mind freely but doesn't like it when others do the same, especially if they're of a homosexual persuasion. You can pretty much guess the content of tonight's speech on *Family Values*."

Max had pondered this for a while and stirred more sugar into his coffee. "Marriage being the cornerstone of society?" he offered. "Something you should know all about."

Billy ignored this comment and continued. "She'll be lecturing and moralising that this is the case, and that hetero-sexual marriage is the institutional glue that binds a coherent civilisation together. You know the routine."

Max raised his eyebrows. "Hmm, I think I do," he said. "And I don't like the sound; let's hit the road Jack."

Billy drained his drink then shook his head, his cheeks puffed with coffee. He swallowed noisily. "No," he said. "We can't just walk away."

"Oh, sure we can."

"No, we can't! We have a duty. We have a moral obligation."

"A *wha'*?"

"A responsibility to free-thinking, repressed people the world over. The pent-up struggle of the dissident goes on."

Arms folded Max leant further towards his friend, hunching over his coffee, stretching the already strained stitching of his suit and pulling the fabric into small wavy lines. "Maybe for you radical, anarchist types," he said. "I say she's evil, so don't you mess around with her."

Billy sighed. "I'm afraid that's not an option. Ever heard of Pastor Niemoller, a man of the cloth trapped by the Nazis in 1930's Germany; *"First they came for the Jews and I didn't speak out because I was not a Jew..."*

Max leant back again and sipped his coffee more diligently now, the correct sweetness and temperature achieved. He unfolded his arms and sighed. "I see...," he said frowning. "So what are you going to do?"

"We can't allow people like this to spread their bile and do nothing. Somebody has to make a stand against this rampant repression. I don't know what, but we've got to do something."

"Something?"

Billy nodded. "Yes, something. Let's sit and drink and think about what we can do about this situation. Let's see it as an opportunity."

Max groaned and slid his empty cup onto the saucer. "Ok," he said. "Then let's get a drink; I mean a proper drink."

They took newspapers from the racks by the bar and moved to the window bay pondering their impending tryst with blue blood. A short time later the barman removed the towels from the taps and they'd ordered lagers and gin chasers and bought two packets of cigarettes from the machine. They drank their first drinks of the day and smoked cigarettes, then returned to the bar, consciously making little or no commotion and doing nothing to draw attention to themselves. The clientele was comfortably transient. They set up camp at the table, surrounding themselves with newspapers, ashtrays and footstools and continued to drink and smoke, avoiding any lingering eye contact with anyone who came through during the day.

"So, what are you going to do?" Max had repeated at some point in the afternoon.

"We," Billy said. "We are on the road together, remember?"

Max's eyes narrowed. "What are *you* proposing *we* do?"

"We need to make a stand, somehow."

"Like, placards?"

"Something more direct."

"Spin beer mats."

Billy folded the paper and put it down on the stool beside him. "Take this seriously."

"It's hard."

"This MP is a part of this hideous right-wing establishment who force their own vile opinions on to everyone, whether they disagree or not. Family values, the British revival, tight-lipped, buttoned-up *Brits as Top Dogs*, moralising and lording it over everyone else, pining for the days of Empire. It's the same thinking that did for your brother—"

Billy stopped short and winced, for Max's features abruptly darkened, his dark eyebrows shrouding his brown eyes. "I mean...," Billy said. "I know you don't talk about him."

"Just stick to the plan Amigo, whatever it is," Max said barely audibly through clenched teeth.

"The plan is to stop her in her tracks, prevent the event from going ahead. We'll stand and heckle when she's in mid-flow; grab the mic and tell it like it really is."

Max looked up and rolled his eyes then snatched his pint from the table, downing the last mouthful before reaching for the chaser.

"You won't last two minutes," he said. "This place'll be full of fanatics and security will be everywhere. We'd get roughed up and turfed out and hung up by the lynch mob from that Yew tree out front. If you're a serious radical as you claim to be you need a proper solution."

"Such as?"

Max swallowed the gin in a single mouthful and pursed his lips at the bitter taste. "Torch the place," he said.

Billy snorted. "Oh, sure," he said.

"You'd be wiping out a large percentage of these vermin in one fell swoop! The world would be a better place without them as you say. Make it so!"

Billy stared at Max, his familiar face. They'd known one another for years from their hometown, casually at first, from earlier schooldays, then to acknowledge in pubs. Recently they'd become closer, thrown together in low paid warehouse employment before choosing to leave it behind and travel North instead. Since that time, their friendship had deepened, intensified and for Billy their connection had revealed his friend well enough, but now he was not sure by how much.

He laughed nervously. "I can't tell whether you're serious or not?"

Max smiled a gentle smile and his eyes softened and lost the hardness that had emerged at the earlier mention of his brother. "What do you think? We both said we wanted adventure when we left home. Leave that all behind, cast it out and seek a better way." Max stood up. "Well, here's your opportunity to create a vastly improved world; one that's shorn of every one of these right-wing motherfuckers."

"You're nuts!"

"Here we are in our suits looking like straight office nine-to-five types, so we'd fit in just right. It's the perfect set up. No one would suspect it was us. Think about that and I'll go and get more drinks for added fortification."

With that Max had left to return to the bar once more leaving Billy at the table tearing small corners off a damp beer mat with the impression of having many more questions than he had answers.

And so the early evening, the sun casting its intense light and the place is beginning to swell with expectant punters. The car park beyond the bay window fills with vehicles, their drivers and passengers alighting and making their way across the gravel and into the lounge bar. Talk and laughter is loud and increasing in volume. People are at the tables where the salesmen had sat earlier in the day and stood at the bar, a row of people three deep in places so the room has an entirely different aspect, a separate venue altogether from the one they'd become familiar with in the day.

Max, emerging from the crush of stockinged legs and strident spirits carries two more large gins, one in each hand and another packet of cigarettes in his mouth.

"Why are you smirking?" Billy asks, as he drops the cigarettes and places the drinks down on the table.

"It's funny," Max says. "Us being here surrounded by these people. I never in my life imagined I'd be here; half cut and dressed in a suit. And look at us, look at these suits."

"What's the matter with them?" Billy asks.

"They're all wrong. You look like a gangster, and I look like I've been up before The Beak."

He sits down and wipes the backs of his hands across his thighs.

"And that's funny why?" Billy whispers. "We're supposed to be in blending in with this lot; you said we fitted in." He jerks his thumb over his shoulder and lowers his head as he speaks, his words emerging from his mouth with more of a snarl and a flash of his teeth than intended. Taking a deep breath, he licks his teeth, their momentary exposure revealing something he hasn't wanted to; has given something away.

"Okay, okay," Max says. "Jesus, take it easy. You're the one who wants to hit this place. Just keep your cool and relax." Rolling his eyes, he slides the drink towards him and takes a deep draught then scoops out the lemon slice and drops it in the ashtray. A puff of fine ash rises settles around the table. "Don't be so nervous if you want to get away with it. You're going to bring attention to yourself."

Billy's agitation manifests itself as a constant writhing in his seat. "Get away with what?" he says leaning forward but staring at the table. "We haven't decided on anything. You can't be serious about torching the place."

Max smiles, a wayward crooked smile that reveals the black gap of a tooth missing at the side of his mouth. "Why not?" he asks.

Billy's eyes widen with incredulity. "Because it's the craziest idea I ever heard of."

"Where's the courage of your conviction?" Max asks evenly.

"I have convictions, but I don't want to kill people. I don't want to end up in jail!"

Max dips his head. "I said relax, or you'll draw attention."

Billy leans forward too, clutching at the sides of the table with both hands. "We've sat here for hours and haven't organised anything to speak of apart from your ludicrous pyromaniac idea," he hisses. "Relax and take it easy?! Jesus, how can I relax surrounded by a bunch of Neo fucking Nazis and a crazed fucking arsonist?"

"You have a better idea?"

"No, no I don't. But yours is just absurd!"

"No Plan B means Plan A must be activated. Faced with crushing injustice, the best form of defence is attack."

Billy shakes his head. "Max," he says. "I'm a libertarian; that means I *like* my freedom. And I like you, we've become good friends over the last few weeks since we've been on the road together. I like the lifestyle of freedom we've had. I don't want to throw it all away."

"We won't get caught."

"We've been sitting here for hours getting pissed. A hundred people have come and gone and seen us to bear witness. It's totally insane! And that barman; I'm telling you he is giving me the shivers whenever we go and order more drinks."

Max arches his neck to adjust his view over and beyond Billy's shoulder. "What of him?" he asks.

"There's something about him. I don't like him."

"He's just a kid," Max says.

"He's been on duty since this morning, and he suspects we're up to something. I can see it in his face, every time we go to the bar; he's got an odd expression in his eyes every time I look at him."

"What are you talking about?"

"Like he's curious about us being here. I can't look him in the eye anymore. I don't like it, I'm telling you, he knows!"

"Take it easy," Max says again. "What does he know exactly?"

"He knows *something*; he knows we're up to something."

Max replaces his glass on the table and leans into his friend's ear. "Just stay calm and keep drinking," he says in a lowered voice, scanning the crowd in his peripheral vision. "Adjust your balls in your pants and take a deep breath. Nobody knows anything. The place is filling up nice and steady so don't get all worked up. Don't get so nervous that you can't look the barman in the eye or that *will* make you appear suspicious, are you with me? Here, have another cigarette."

Another cigarette thinks Billy, the answer to most things. He lights it and takes a sip of his gin and murmurs Max's phrase again; *Are you with me?* It's one he often uses. It has a dual meaning; *do you understand me*, as well as *are you on my side,* the implication being that if you don't understand him then you're not on his side; and if you're not on his side then you are against him. Since they'd been on the road together Billy's learned there's never much middle ground with Max. Now he sees in him a different light; a crisp, even calmness that paradoxically unnerves him more than when he's exhibiting his usual recklessness. This exceptional coolness weighs with Billy's own panic as the audience grows in size. He sees the swell and its composition with a mixture of alarm and morbid curiosity: young, lean and athletic, healthy-looking men with long, foppish hair and golden auras, well-groomed and in striped shirts. They are accompanied by equally ruddy women, sipping white wine Spritzers and teetering casually on heels, shifting their weight from foot to foot, making dints in the carpets lounge and on the parquet flooring near the stage.

Amongst them are the country types gathered in small rural groups; middle-aged people, thick set, plain dressed and flushed; the men with panelled pint glasses and women of sanguine appearance, pastel patterned dresses and flat sensible shoes. And as the audience assembles Billy identifies a third, to him more baleful element: the elderly, well-to-do landed gentry. As he sees it this last stratum are the most menacing; the hunting fraternity, the privileged set, barristers and judges, businessmen and factory owners, the well-heeled and comfortably moneyed, a lifetime captaining industry and meting justice, part of the throbbing moral and wealth-creating trunk of the country. Tanned faces, bright eyes, thinning hair and polished nails, firm words softly spoken, well-practiced in the vocabulary of influence and control. They're relaxed, content, purring with significance, wealth and authority, an intoxicating, high octane mix of wealth and power that intensifies both his anxiety and his loathing.

"Oh God," he says. "They have a terrifying look of serenity."

"Who have?" asks Max.

Billy waves his upturned palm across the table. "These people; the wealthy, these haves. It must come naturally when you have money and power."

"Easy," says Max. "You're like a rabbit in headlights."

"They're so superior," Billy continues, oblivious to the

censure, "at ease with the *status quo,* with the state of affairs and happy to be here amongst their loaded brethren. They're all here aren't they, all blue strata represented, well-dressed, confident and keen, happy with their lot."

"And us," Max says. "In our suits."

"I don't like it Max," Billy replies.

"So, we'll do something about it."

"I don't like them, but your idea is madness!"

With each passing minute towards the eleventh hour of the Dame's arrival Billy feels his anxiety jump a notch. A boiling sensation has gripped his stomach, a feeling that Max's nonchalance only serves to intensify. He reproaches himself for his inability to formulate a plan of action to counter Max's outlandish idea. Infuriatingly Max taps his nose and keeps his counsel whenever Billy speaks of it. And nothing else has emerged out of the miasma and bravado of the drink. Instead, time has slipped by, alternatives have faded, his own scheming more nebulous with each drink while Max remains insouciant throughout and Billy more frustrated with himself for not framing anything sooner. By now a circular pattern of thought has formed, the end product being that of Billy staring at the gold and silver discs behind the stage and biting a clenched knuckle red.

Max puts his hand on his knee. "Don't look so nervous," he says. "Stay there, stay cool and don't move. I'll get another round of drinks. One more should see us fine."

"Then what?" Billy asks.

Max stands and looks down at Billy but says nothing. He sees the fear in his friends face as he moves away. "Don't panic," he says leaning into him but looking around him. "You start fidgeting about and eating your hand like that and people will get suspicious."

Billy grabs his wrist. "What are you going to do," he hisses. "I'm not going to be a part of it Max. I'm going to walk away."

Max snatches his wrist from his grasp. "That's the kind of behaviour I'm talking about," he says. "Just don't do anything to bring attention to yourself."

Twisting a path through the crowd stood before it, he moves to the bar. Billy watches him as he stands amongst the throng waiting to be served. His appearance is relaxed, peculiarly debonair in his preposterous-looking suit, a curious trick Max carries well. Billy looks down at his. They had worn suits because it was Max's idea they could hitch lifts easier if they looked smart. Billy reluctantly packed his wedding suit. He concluded it must be even tougher for Max dressed in his brother's suit. But there's no way of telling now as he sways and smiles without regard for his threadbare attire smoking his cigarette and spilling the ash, nonchalantly chatting to the barman who's been on duty all afternoon.

Billy sees the barman smile again, guardedly as before, judging the misfit swaying before him as he has done all afternoon, glancing over his shoulder at him once again. He quickly averts his eyes and in doing so feels the panic rise again, squeezed out of his griping stomach and upwards into his chest and throat. It feels like a weight in his chest, flat like a tombstone, something firm that needs to be pushed away, either hacked up or forced back down. The new arrivals entering the bar scan the room for acquaintances, lingering on

Billy with his pale face and his mouthful of knuckle, probing him, seeking out signs of familiarity or recognition. The noise levels grow with laughter and chatter, as the outside chill and the smell of it is brought in on coats, wafts with their removal as fresh ice clinks and the drinks flow. And although he's been drinking solidly since the middle of the morning Billy feels peculiarly sober and the sudden acknowledgment of this fact is sobering in itself. It's nearly eight in the evening. He needs the toilet but the thought of entering the fray to get there appals him. He crosses his legs and lights another cigarette instead, extinguishing the one still burning in the ashtray.

By the time a hush descends with the imminent arrival of Dame Kellet-Bowman, Billy sees Max has been served another two drinks and is stood with them in each hand talking effusively to a young woman standing next to him. She tilts her head from side to side, politely shifting away from him, avoiding his inroads. Oblivious to the contagious cessation of chatter Max's single voice continues over and above the hush of the many as he sways at the bar, spilling the drinks with exaggerated gesticulations, turning heads. She leans further back, covering her mouth, a polite cough and a double hand movement from her mouth to her neck. People next to them petition for silence and she steps away from him and into the harsh light of the wooden panelling above the bar, emphasising the makeup on her face, the unevenness of her skin and her rising anger, harsh in the bright light across her bright red mouth. Her hand moves again towards her throat and a diamond ring sparkles.

Billy sees a number of people around them becoming

agitated at the distraction from the main event. At last he moves to intervene just as the doors at the far end of the auditorium open and at this the crowd begin to applaud and cheer the entrance of Dame Kellett-Bowman. Billy takes his cue but loses sight of his friend. He quickly scans the room and with a single step from the dais diligently works his way through the crowd, eyes down traversing the bar to where Max had stood.

But Max is nowhere to be seen.

Manchester's Hulme Estate;
Late Spring 1989

Elsa Kelly steps out of her flat and on to the balcony to light another cigarette, grateful for the coolness of the night air and the concrete railing cold against her forearms. The random largesse of perpetual heat inside is clammy, excessive and unwelcome at this time of the year. It makes her prickly and irritable and smoking indoors for respite is out of the question with the baby in the bedroom and her mother's breathing failing by the day. These moments on the balcony offer brief relief she savours, though marred as it is with portent from both ends of life. SOS, SOS, like semaphore, thin dashes of strip lights and dots of door lights blaze on each balcony of the tower block opposite, lighting the night sky and casting the whole area in a fizzing fake brightness. She's always found it comforting in a modern life sort of way, even as a kid, growing up surrounded by adults. Of late she's begun to perceive religiousness in its radiance, a connective beam linking the dark divine space high above to the courtyards and crescents below, the earthbound territory where wholly ungodly activities are conducted each day and night; drug runs, fights and muggings, the relentless struggle with poverty and wired wanderings of the lost or indifferent. Despite her Catholic stock the idea of a greater power is something she's never really considered, but the possibility is increasingly seeping into her daily thoughts, especially so in the evenings, at these times, standing on the balcony with a coffee in one hand and a cigarette in the other. Was it the birth of her baby that's provoked the stirring of a dormant contemplation of faith? Or is it just the reflective nature of smoking now she has to light up on the balcony and study the yonder world, such as it is. As both events coincide there is no telling which.

What is beyond any doubt is that right now, her baby boy Marley is her total preoccupation, the single fixed point around which her whole life revolves. The possible sound of him crying causes her to hold her breath and with it the inhaled smoke, released gently into the night air, blue turned to grey once certain that the sound is not of him stirring. The noise must have come from elsewhere, somewhere down below from the Estate with its wayward people and their disreputable activities, a world away from the powdery purple purity of Marly in his cot. What will he grow into and how will he harden in years to come as calcium deposits strengthen over gummy softness through nature and necessity? She glances across the silvery concrete and its black recesses, sees the flash of an empty beer can dropped from one of the balconies and thinks of Nelson, Marley's father who left her at six months pregnant. He's probably down there right now somewhere on the Estate, sprinting the decks or dealing in Sir Henry Royce, he too a world away from Marley and his innocence. What was it about so many black men around here that made them want to leave? Something in their blood, in their heritage; something to do with their history of slavery and emancipation, the desire for freedom and the need to be un-tethered? She never thought she'd offered him anything else, but maybe the prospect of baby chores, the tether that was childcare did not equate to the kind of independence Nelson craved. For her there was no inconvenience at all in these daily duties but for men, for Nelson it must have been different. But he hadn't stuck around to tell her his thinking and if only he had explained his feelings, explored himself he might have eventually felt differently.

A distant sound, a faint *plink*, the beer can hits the ground and the figures on the balcony opposite turn away.

Elsa turns away herself, back to the flat. She stubs out the cigarette in the plant pot by the door, adding to the others that makes a strange sculpture in the soil still supporting the stub of a Yucca. Inside, back in the heat and the unique human smell of her family and mealtimes she glimpses her mother through the half open door in the front room watching television before checking on Marley. The blue green rays from the screen flash against her glasses; a comic robot, mesmerised and motionless, lost in space. *Wish You Were Here.* Television; the great subjugator, the Opium of the People.

In the back room; Marley, lying motionless on his back, his lips slightly parted and hands on either side of his tilted head in a posture of surrender, a capitulation to sleep. A white crocheted blanket pushed to one side, made by Mrs Smith their neighbour in the adjacent flat, commissioned and paid for by Elsa's older sister Samantha wanting to give her something special when the baby was born but possessed of no knitting skills of her own. The gesture had made Elsa cry, something that frequently happened during the first weeks of Marley's life; her emotions all over the place, the eliciting threshold shot to pieces. The sight of the blanket, the feel of it still has the effect even now. Lachrymose with its touch she quickly pulls the soft wool over her son's legs and body and gently touches his forehead with the tips of her fingers, sensing his heat and his life as she does at all times, even when he sleeps, even when she's not near him. His eyelids stir, a myriad map of blue and purple veins flickering briefly then rest once more, the faintest sigh emitted from his viscous mouth, a miniature impossible perfection of a life. His father would not be a witness to any of this and although the sigh is intrinsic, the result of a physical function (like the smile he breaks into when he fills his nappy), you can't help but attach greater substance to it and fall in love with him as the baby he is and the person he will one day be. Even Bad-Assed Nelson, *Night Watchman* Nelson in his more tender moments would have appreciated this and could have valued it. Not Marley, too young and unknowing, but his father was missing out and they have never even met; the father and the son, a two-way thing. She breathes her own sigh and at that moment feels sadder for Nelson than she does for her baby for what he'll never be a part of and never really know. Stick to what you know Nelson, play safe!

For Marley! The Health visitor had pressed her and with all the documentation of new born immunisation, vaccinations, screening, routine reviews, growth and weight records and charts all initially written as *Baby Kelly*. Although Elsa named him Marley from the beginning her mother didn't like it because, she said it was too much of a *black* name, had too much of a Jamaican association when it was one of them who'd ran out on her and her baby and left them to fend for themselves. Not racist, just truth, she said. Of course, he had left but she liked the name Marley all the same and the boy had West Indian blood in him whether her mother liked it or not. There was no disputing this, no denying the fundamental truth; Black and Irish; a double helix of persecution, you'd have thought Kathy Kelly would have related to that, but her mother could be an intransigent boot at the best of times. Still, despite her mother's notorious governance Elsa could give as good as she got too. She had her mother's drive, and this was in *her* blood, like it or not. Marley was his name. Besides Nelson would have liked it, so it was kind of for him too, in case he changed his mind and wanted back in.

He would have to hurry. They were due for resettlement soon and the City Council had them near the top of the list now, or so Mr Hughes the nice guy at the office informed them when they saw him last; soon they would be out of there. But then he'd been saying that for a long time now. Mike, he insisted. She liked him and it was clear he was fond of her too, the way he lit up when he saw her, brightened then reddened and became shy and inelegant when he spoke, stammering, losing his thread. He was doing his best but was working against the system as well as for it, trying his best for her. He joked she would miss it; he meant the Housing Office, not the Hulme Estate as she thought. There would be no nostalgia. She was glad to be on the list, ready to move away from the place she'd called home for most of her life. The Estate had had it; crumbling, inhuman, ridden with cockroaches, notorious now. The people who'd replaced those already rehoused revelled in its bad name and their ill repute. All they wanted was to party and get wrecked, just as she had herself in her younger days, in her heyday, so she couldn't reproach them for it. But she'd grown up and moved on and now the greatest change of all had taken place, the birth of her son Marley. Moving on was physical and emotional too.

She hated Manchester and loved it. The tough-love accents of those lives lived on the same streets with no horizons above the moors and no dreams beyond them; the same accent that made her yearn for the place if ever she was away from it and picked it up on the breeze. Solid, down-to-earth, unfussy, dependable; all those Northern cliches, habitual euphemisms for life's unadorned truisms like swathes of the country being left behind to wither on the vine and decay through Tory neglect or mishandling. The Hulme Estate had it in bucket-loads. Those poor old folks with little but pride being pushed and pulled around, grateful to be top of the list to exit the same Estate they entered only a decade before.

Now give me the chance, Elsa thought. Let me go with my family to move on out.

Besides, the people coming on to the Estate were different now. They were demolishing the place gradually, from the inside, doing the work of the bulldozers. Hulme, experimental in its inception, always unique had become a law unto itself with the squatters, the Baggies, the punks before them but still here, party heads and drug gangs who created their own reality with minimal interference from the outside world. Nobody on the outside cared what happened. They'd been abandoned and left to their own ways to deal with things. They could not cope. The people in one of the flats in William Kent with a sound-system as big as the room had knocked the wall through to the next flat one night to get more people in and the next day the one after that for good measure. Communal living: others had done the same. Some of the walkways were so loose they would collapse with force and she worried that anyone could fall through to the ground below or be killed by falling masonry. No one spoke out anymore. Besides herself they were no longer interested, not the people on the Estate, too high, oblivious, or the authorities outside, ignorant and indifferent. She speculated that the residents of Hulme were unwitting participants in a great social experiment to see what would happen when people were left to fend for themselves and create their own way of life; Lord of the Flies in the North of England with adult characters, without impingement from the greater authorities and nourished only by a seemingly unlimited supply of cheap speed and E injected in from God-knows-where every day. So, they came here to live, the entire underworld of the country and beyond attracted to the twenty-four-hour parties and the drugs on demand, unsuspecting and never grasping the real truth that they were voluntarily rounding themselves up, imprisoning themselves in a giant crumbling cell and ridding the rest of the country from where they came from the trouble and chaos they caused. A silent crucible of containment. The cops called it *kettling*.

If it were true it was a brilliant strategy of social control. The police did not need to enter except on occasions in numbers to identify and snatch a victim, then quickly withdraw in tactical formation like Roman Centurions with shields and helmets. The bin men were braver. The anarchists proudly proclaimed it as a police no-go area, not knowing and never thinking that this was exactly what the police wanted. Others arrived on the Estate with trepidation. The health visitor Margie, a timid girl from Eccles who came to check on her and Marley and quickly ran in to her flat and sprinted out again and Elsa would watch her from the balcony as she ran to her car and fumble her keys and drop them in flap and panic until she was inside the safety of the vehicle before bouncing away. These comic flights made her laugh unsympathetically because she was accustomed to this life on the Estate. But it was no place for her young son and although it was how she'd spent her own childhood she wanted better things for Marley. She had instinctively come to see things had to be different now that she was a mother, and she welcomed the change, and it couldn't come soon enough; she owed this to her son. She didn't want him getting involved in the kind of things she'd seen and done, a viewpoint she might once have thought as hypocritical, but now, since Marley, just natural.

Elsa pulls the bedroom door to. It bounces back with a familiar knocking that causes it to wobble because it or the frame or both are twisted hopelessly out of shape. At least left ajar like this she concedes she can hear if Marley stirs, his natural clucks and sighs a hair trigger for her reactions. In the room next to his her younger sister Freya, still in drab school clothes despite her mother's instructions to change hours ago, lying in crumbled pleats and inky blouse, reading as usual with the torch held with reels of Sellotape to the back of a dining chair next to the bed, slanted to the correct angle for spotlight brightness. Freya needs maximum light in the absence of the glasses she also should wear but refuses to on account of the anticipated berating from school friends. Some friends! Buried deep in the text of *Camp Sunnyside Friends; No Boys Allowed*, only a hunting horn would break her concentration.

Elsa closes the door behind her, this one compliant to a snugger fit, to spare Freya her mother's scolding.

Thus commences her nightly rounds, the brief visits, peeks through the jambs, the checks on health and general welfare that begins as usual with her mother sitting before the television, which now takes in Marley, the process slowed with the hours just staring. On to Freya *(Our Freya, Who art in Bedroom)* and then out of the flat, checking the bowls behind the front door for cat food and water for Chairman Meow and a right turn to the flat next door and to Ivy Smith with her son Martin who has lived there since Elsa was a small girl. Martin had stayed with his mother all his life and is still there at the age of thirty something, getting on for forty. He is slow but not stupid, more bland and uninspiring, stubbly, flabby, harmless, no match for the Estate. Ivy cares for him and Martin for her in a reciprocity that has never matured beyond his early adolescence.

He opens the door, dressed in a maroon T shirt speckled with grease stains that will never wash out, jogger bottoms and raggedy slippers. He smiles but says nothing and gestures her into the flat. Elsa can remember a time when he had his own language up to the age of around ten or twelve, a tongue that only he and Ivy spoke, two more than Latin she joked. It had clicks and croaks and whistles as well as short-tongued attempts at English words. Elsa came to think of it variously as normal, then strangely exotic, then just plain weird as she grew older. Eventually with the aid of a speech therapist the language (like Latin) died though the temptation to cluck her tongue or whistle at him whenever she faces him never declines, unlike his language. She sees him most nights and silent beckoning with eyebrows and pulled cheek indicators are the lingua franca.

Bottom wobbling in baggy pants, he pads through the hallway, it's walls leaning inwards slightly at the ceiling and prods open the door to the living room with a slippered foot where Ivy sits watching television in a synchronised positioning to her mother in the adjacent flat, save for the cup and saucer resting in her lap.

Ivy looks up and smiles. "Hello love. How's the baby?" she asks. The question is asked with a head wiggle and simultaneous neck and shoulder movement that causes the tea to slop from cup to saucer.

"He's good, thanks," Elsa replies. "How are you? Do you need anything?"

"Tea?" Martin asks, a customary question she usually declines. Elsa shakes her head, tonight no exception.

"Nothing thanks," Ivy says, returning her attention to the television screen. "Any news?" she asks indolently.

Elsa contemplates this open query for its true line of enquiry; possibly her mother's health or results from the hospital following her latest bout of bloody coughing; Nelson's whereabouts, the likelihood of his return and therefore Elsa's general state of wellbeing; or further reports of the problem they'd been having with a volatile local junkie called Tulip who'd been springing some of the inhabitants on the balconies of late, jostling them for money he knew they didn't have.

She shakes her head, offering and seeking no further elaboration.

"I'll be off then. Knock on if you need anything." It's usually Elsa who knocks of late, to turn the television down when she's putting Marley down. Sometimes they can't hear the raps on the wall for the sound of the set and she sends Freya round instead.

Elsa steps back out on to the balcony and right again to the flat next to Mrs Smith's which has the word *Occupied* neatly penned on the white door in thick black felt at eye level. At this door, yielding only to a secret *rat-tatt-ratta-tatt-tatt* knock a pretty pale face appears at the metal chequered Perspex, then the sound of slide bolts unlocking within and Tamsin emerges from the darkness. Tamsin, quiet and unwell, agoraphobic and anxious, who is desperate for help with her incarcerating affliction but is too fearful to reach out to get it. There's nothing available anyway. She'd moved on to the Estate some years ago and has frozen in time and situ, too timorous to venture into the world of supermarket aisles and

Post Office queues never mind the runners and gunners of the Estate. Poor Tamsin never stood a chance, would have become balcony fodder if it hadn't had been for Elsa's mother who recognised the signs and had the time and forethought to look out for her. She'd been like a lost little girl, silently shaking her head beneath her long, blonde hair, her eyes and nose red, her words whispered and giving no clues to the whereabouts of family or friends. Like a silent wraith she simply appeared in a swirl of wispy vapour that formed her delicate disposition. She remains a mystery still but could not have been left abandoned to the Estate and Kathy Kelly had decreed that she needed caring for. And that's exactly what had happened. She had become a part of her family of sorts, like a forgotten daughter or sister, brought in from the cold and included in everything they did from shopping errands, tenants meetings, appointments with Mike Hughes at the City Council to get her on to the rehousing list along with the others, and of course Elsa's nightly visits.

Tamsin opens the front door. A faint smell of beef fat emerges.

"Hi," she says and smiles a beautiful smile of pale lips, smooth silvery skin and perfect white teeth that makes Elsa want to stop time and frame her and show this image back to her to prove what a beautiful young woman she truly is in the hope that it might in some way help her overcome her illness. So ethereal is she, Elsa wonders if there would even be a reflection if she held a mirror to her.

"Hi Tammy. You ok?" she asks marvelling at her mercury face.

She nods her head. Her hair is naturally white blonde; split at all ends and lit up by the balcony light shimmering overhead, so she has a ghostly appearance, not ghoulish, but like an angel against the background of the dark hallway. Her scalp is pink and visible through her hair.

"Do you need me to get you anything Tammy?" Elsa asks.

Tammy shakes her head sending a fizzing white shock in motion around her.

"Sure?" Elsa continues, resisting the urge to lean down towards her and speak to her like a little old lady, though in truth that is how she looks until you see the smooth, youthful features beneath.

Tammy nods vigorously. "No, I'm good," she says, and her hair falls across her face again and she eases back into the hallway to the comfort zone, the shelter of seclusion. Eye-contact for Tammy is excruciating, anything that might expose or illuminate her sanctum of inner disquiet. Annie Anxiety Nelson used to call her. Elsa once asked her if she ever missed others' company and the question elicited a painfully shy display of tics, twitches, stammering and breathlessness so the subject of companionship was never again raised. Discussion was whether her beauty and purity, the gentle delicacy was untouched by handling of rough advances, or whether something unspeakable had happened in the past that had forced her withdrawal. She would never know.

Elsa smiles, tries but fails to make eye contact. "You just holler," she says finally, as Tammy's relentless head shaking continues and the narrow upright strip of the portal to the world outside is already contracting before she finishes her words; "if you do."

"Has Sam come back yet?" Tammy asks finally with diminishing volume of an answer already known, the same question every time.

"I'll let you know if she shows."

The door clicks gently shut and Elsa hears the sound of the numerous locks sliding and latching inside, locking her down, working from top to bottom then up again, five in total, the last the deadbolt at hip height slipping across with a solid clunk, finality like an exclamation mark on the whole routine.

Elsa sighs, and as always there's a downward sensation born of the utter inadequacy in her dealings with her neighbour, knowing there is little she can do by saying words of comfort or encouragement to her. Words are entirely empty and therefore futile. The nocturnal routine of making sure made some headway, demonstrative at least. The only real prospect of any kind of salvation for her, or for any of them for that matter lies in the hands of the City Council and its ever-growing rehousing list on which they are all waiting, desperate to be rehoused, drifting sluggishly to the top like the froth of a scummy pond floating slowly to the surface.

She smiles at her own analogy and the mention of Sam, her sister who left the Estate and headed North some time ago. She breathes in the pungent air of clammy concrete and turns back towards her flat and back into her own world.

"How long is this going to take," she whispers to herself,

then half smiling, starts singing; *"We gotta get out of this place; if it's the last thing we ever do...."*

Travel Hotel, Lancaster;
Summer 1989, turned eight
in the evening

The Wedding Present. It's apt. There's rice in a pocket too. How did it get there, in the inside of his jacket? The registrar was a sour-faced woman who sucked her gums over acid brown teeth and made it clear there should be no confetti because it couldn't be swept from the gravel. They laughed at that. Everything was funny that day, nothing could detract from the special occasion. By the end of the day they'd laughed and grinned so much their cheeks ached. And all the guests too. In the end they threw rice bought from the Coop, staggered the short distance to the pub next to it and drank the place dry by time.

Billy rubs the grains between his thumb and fingers, recalling how it was on that day. It's a memory that saps him. He'd found other things too that made him baulk; a card for a place setting with a name he can't remember, a phone number with an 0782 dialling code. He fingers them again, then quickly discards them for fear of the memories they evoke. He closes his eyes and drops the seat behind him, and slumps back on to it.

So desperate to avoid eye contact with the surrounding crowd, he'd kept his head down and headed for the exit. But to get there, a small throng of men stood in the way, blocking the aisle in their desire to get a sight of the speaker as she entered the room. He didn't fancy his chances going through or around them, they were baying, literally barking before her. He felt the heat rising from his neck to his face, a Belisha combination of fear and anger and frustration. Instinctively he'd turned back towards his seat and then turned again as he realised, with relief the lavatory door was right before him.

In the toilet cubicle there's brief sanctuary, elicited by the bolt snapping in its casing. He feels sick. The solidity of the ceramic tile and laminate cubicle, its hollow hush and sparseness brings a quick and welcome sense of reality from the hours spent in the bar that have addled his thoughts and created a significant absence of truth. Alone in his cubical world he considers his options. Max has vanished and his only real choice is to walk away from the gig right now, when the chance is right. With it he will carry the silent disappointment at the disparity of his conviction and action, his own ineptitude and the unwitting curse of a lunchtime drinking session.

He drops the seat quietly, the cubicle a vicarious extension of his inner thoughts that any noise might betray. With heavy heart he hears the muffled but generous applause and a lone whistle from the auditorium as Dame Kellett-Bowman enters the stage and takes to the platform. The applause is long and rapturous, and Billy thinks of Max out there somewhere amongst the maelstrom, having abandoned any pretence of sobriety. The microphone whistles again, a wave of gentle laughter, an early addition of mild humour perhaps to win the crowd over before the meat of the discourse. A further smattering of applause and the speaker commences, her rasping words resonating, though unintelligible from the toilet seat box.

Billy stands and stares at the door. He wants to slide out of the room and out of the building but knows he cannot abandon Max. He knows too he is culpable for suggesting the idea of wrecking the gig in the first place, even though it's spawned his untenable proposal.

He sighs and sits again. He sees the words again, scratched out at eye level on the door.

The Wedding Present

It's just a statement, the band, not even; ...*are great*, or ... *wasn't what I asked for!*

Billy's thoughts drift back to it once more when someone enters the room and he hesitates, catching his breath, everything on hold to allow them time to leave before he gets out to the throng to find his lost companion.

A lit cigarette: the sound of the flint and wheel of the lighter rasping once, then a second time in the hollow tiled room and the smell of tobacco and then the cubicle door is kicked.

"Hey," a whispers voice. "It's me."

It's Max.

Billy opens the door and Max stands before him, the cigarette vertical from his bottom lip, the smoke spiralling into his watery eyes. He's holding the rolled-up newspaper they'd been reading and beneath it the lighter, gliding the flame back and forward around the end of the newspaper.

"The Guardian," Max says. "Best thing for it."

Billy stares, wide eyed. "What the fuck are you doing?" he hisses.

"What does it look like?" Max hisses back.

"You can't torch the place Max!"

Max grins. The serenity has gone, replaced by a dark and savage look in his eyes. Billy recognises it, has seen it before, a crazed look, a loss of shape and control, eyes seemingly moving in opposite directions in his head, independently of each other and with no cranial control. It usually follows consumption of alcohol and is around this point of excess he smiles a twist of his mouth that exposes his teeth on one side and the gap on the other where one is missing. It makes him look crazy, simultaneously dangerously mad and of riskily limited intelligence. For the first time in the light of the cubicle Billy can see that he's really drunk.

"Come on" he says, shaking his head, his eyes widening and rolling around even more than before, up and over that makes Billy think of a one-armed bandit where the handle's pulled the wheels in motion, all focus gone. "Let's see it through. Let's put a stop to this show. You're right about those bastards out there; let's give it to them. They're all bigoted Tory scum. You know that. I know that. So, let's stop messing about and just get on and do it! For once in your life put all your fucking preaching into practice, your pent-up frustrations, the talk,

talk, talk, always the bloody talk, talk. Stop playing at it Billy and let's do this thing!"

Max spits the last words between clenched teeth, snarling with quivering lips vibrating the ash from the end of his cigarette.

Billy lurches forward and grabs his wrist with both hands. It's an instinctive move. The flames flicker between them. "You've got to be joking me!" he says.

Max waves the torch, the flame rolling over the pages. "Oh yeah?"

"Well get sent down you fucking lunatic; it's arson, it will be murder. At the very least it's criminal damage on a massive scale if the place goes up. We've been here all day; we've been seen by the barman and all those others, you've just been talking to them for Christ's sake, they'll recognise us straight away—"

"If they live to tell the tale!"

Billy releases his grip and steps backwards. "Listen to yourself. Jesus Christ, I knew you were a crazy Max, but this is just—"

Max cuts him short by putting his hand over Billy's mouth and thrusting the burning torch into his hand.

"Be quiet or someone will hear you."

"I can't be a part of this," Billy mumbles through his friend's fingers. "I'm leaving right now!"

Max puts the palm of his other hand against Billy's chest to prevent him moving any further forward. "Stop," he says. "We're not going to torch it, you fucking dummy! Look above your head; there's a smoke detector! They're connected to the sprinkler system in the building. I've checked it out. We're going to rain on their parade."

Billy stares upwards and sees the silver disc of the smoke detector next to the light. He looks at Max, who is smiling and nodding sagely. He looks up again. Relief rains down over him from his head, streaming through his arms and into body and down into his legs, hot salvation that feels deliciously ice-cold. The sudden physical release weakens him at the knees, and he grabs at Max's arm for balance.

He begins to giggle.

"Brilliant," he blubbers. "That's a brilliant idea! The sprinklers, yes, Max; *brilliant*!"

"Yeah?! So give me a hand."

"Of course, the sprinklers. You twat, why didn't you... yes, sprinklers."

"Come on," Max urges. "Grab this and wave the flames under it. I'll guard the door and make sure no one comes in."

Billy is soaked by a continued rush of elation, a sense of silky euphoria, born of the fact that the idea doesn't involve personal jeopardy or mass murder and that their clueless afternoon's session has actually thrown up a plan that's actually feasible and practical. It's so obvious to him now and he laughs loudly, not knowing if Max has harboured this idea all this time and has been toying with him, pulling him along and playing with his anxieties. He doesn't care, it doesn't matter now.

But what does is the sound of the silence being broken, split by the echo of a slide lock snapping open, a single report that ricochets around the room from another cubicle situated around the corner of the white, grey and gold tiled space; a cubicle that has all this time been occupied. A movement, the drawing of air like a vacuum and from behind the wall a large man of middle age appears, dressed in a dark woollen jacket and beige, casual slacks, slowly, deliberately emerging into the halogen light. He walks leisurely forward until he stands squarely before them, the last step taken like a Sumo wrestler about to engage his opponent, his jacket fastened by a single button stretched high and wide over his stomach. He pushes his thumbs into his lapels and drums his fingers on his chest, a stance of self-parody, as though he's been here before, or if not, adopting the posture he considers fitting. The man's head rocks slowly at an angle and he has a glint in his small, dark eyes and a smug, determined look on his face shiny in the down light.

Billy stares aghast. Hope evaporates as quickly as it had arrived as he comprehends the figure standing before them, bristling with latent have-a-go heroism. He knows by the arrogant smile steadily forming across his face that this man is absolutely thrilled by what he's witnessing, to have overheard it all, now unable to conceal his delight at having caught them in the act. Billy can see that to him standing there, he and Max are the sort of social degenerates his diet of Daily Mail fodder has been alerting him to for years and can picture the headlines and photographs beneath, shaking hands with Kellett-Bowman, a national disaster averted. And here they are, the real deal standing before him on his own doorstep, in the heartland of his own habitat with his kith next door in significantly large numbers while these two punks stand before him attempting to burn it all down around them.

Billy and Max stand motionless, gawping. Red embers of misspelt newsprint float upwards and return, drifting around the room like hot black snowflakes. Billy's mind and limbs are stone as he hopelessly retraces the utterances the man will have heard, his own verbal fingerprints all over the scene. Unable to move or do or say anything but stare at the ruddy figure before them, rocking back and forward on the balls of his feet he looks on in horror, failing to think of any excuse, any mitigation, anything that might get them out of the situation.

"Well now, —" the man says. He has a faintly Scottish brogue.

That's when Max punches him full on his nose, quick and hard from a squat position. He follows through and sends him reeling right back into the cubicle from whence he came. Dropping the flaming torch he follows the back-peddling man back into the cubicle and goes in for a second hit. Billy hears the man groan with the mushy thud of the second strike.

"Max! Let's go!" Billy shouts and turns to run. Max follows, but not before a final check, just to make sure he's out, before calmly closing the cubicle door.

They move quickly out from the toilet and down the side of the auditorium. Billy scampers ahead, elbowing his way through the room aiming for the exit signs at the far end that will take them into the foyer. Dame Kellet-Bowman is in full flow from her elevated perch. She's small in stature and her voice is harsh and shrill. The microphone stand next to her is taller but she has a hawkish gaze and a gripping intensity as she delivers her message to the audience. Spectators mutter complaints as Billy pushes past but Max, more measured in his exit drops back instead. He sees his friend tipping chairs over behind him as he nears the exit, a desperate attempt to obstruct potential pursuers. He does not look up to see if The Dame has seen them from her vantage point of the raised stage where she stands. He hears that her speech does not falter and doesn't know or want to whether she's detected the commotion but that, like any good orator continues with her address regardless. Max has his eyes fixed on the green exit sign with the white man running above the door directing their escape into the foyer, and below it Billy, focussed and committed.

As Billy races out into the foyer and towards the front doors the man behind the reception desk shouts for him to stop. Two other men sitting near the door get to their feet and step out of the auditorium following the commotion, but Billy has gone by the time they enter the lobby. All three peer through the glass doors into the darkness outside at the escaping figure when Max appears in the foyer from the auditorium and stops abruptly.

They turn to face him.

He's breathing heavily.

"Where'd he go?" Max asks, catching his breath to disguise his panting and a hard beating heart thumping within his chest.

The two men glower back at him then quickly back over their shoulders towards the exit. Both turn so they're standing square on to him, a muscle and bone barrier to the freedom of the night. Max arches his head left and right, trying to see past them at the running figure beyond. "Did he get away?"

They peer at Max. "He's gone," says one. He's suspicious, Max can see but resists the urge to bolt.

"What happened in there?" the other asks.

Max shakes his head and shrugs, perching on his naivety. "That guy ran out behind us," he says. "He knocked my drink from my hand; it went all over my wife and business partner. My finance director's gone to get a cloth."

Again, they turn to stare out of the glass doors to see if they can see the offender, but Billy has gone. Max stands and holds himself back and one of the men, the more gullible turns back to face him.

"Are they ok?" he asks.

"Who?"

"Your wife and business partner."

Max nods. He can feel the blood in his ears, outside and within. "Yeah; they're getting themselves cleaned up in the toilets," he says. "I'd better go back in and see to them. Come on, I guess he's gone now. Let's go back in."

He lingers, maintaining his observance and then to his surprise and greater relief, the two men dutifully move on and return to the auditorium.

"Wait a minute," the receptionist says to Max. "I know you. You were with that other guy today; you were in here earlier drinking with him."

Max sees a combination of recollection and recognition straying into his features. He's young and generous in a fresh-featured way and has a red spot on his forehead he's been picking at behind the reception desk. The blemish is angry against his pale features and Max feels an unexpected if fleeting sympathy for him. From his face, the turned down mouth, creamy skin and watery eyes he can't tell whether or not he's about to hit the panic button.

The truth of his association identified Max can muster nothing else but a smile.

"That was for Daniel," he says; "My brother," and calmly turns and walks away.

Outside, he walks along the pavement then onto a track that leads down a bank parallel with the main road, the direction he'd seen Billy running, stopping briefly to light a cigarette and inhale deeply, filling his lungs with smoke and dampness from the chilly night air. Soon the noise of an ambulance roars by on the main road behind him, its sirens wailing as it goes by and Max walks steadily on and into the night.

Glasgow, Summer 1989

The postie's savvy enough to know he can score on the rounds of the Estate and the letter arrives late Saturday morning. The Glasgow postmark and the black loops of Sam's hand indicate a problem to be addressed, the only time she ever seems to write these days. With the imploring missive in hand beckoning her North, Elsa sits on the balcony and smokes. The pattern is as familiar as the handwriting on the envelope and she lights a fresh cigarette with the old one and considers her options. The text brief over distressed paper provides a phone number and a time to call. She makes her way to The Spinners for the rendezvous, the only pub on the Estate with a working phone. Under the Perspex hood she dials, a call from one public phone to another. The receiver is off on in an instant. The subsequent conversation, distorted by sobs and the cord twisting in her sister's fingers informs Elsa of an intermittent relationship, not new, but complex and difficult nonetheless. An affair with a Frenchman who Sam lives with, made all the more twisted by his on-off relationship with another woman in their big, open squat with its mix of transient residents and their equally ephemeral relationships. Sam talks and weeps in waves of lucidity and absurdity while Elsa listens, comparing her older sister's emotional naïveté to her own. Elsa just wouldn't entertain that relationship, though less harshly acknowledges her own situation of single mother-hood. Then the receiver is wrestled from Samantha's hand by another needing to make a call and her fading words are a petition for Elsa to make a mercy dash to be with her.

What choice does she have?

Her options are shaped by priorities. There's Marley in the cot and her COPD mother wheezing up flights of stairs and along skywalks to their flats. Elsa has taken the familial respon-sibilities of her care, not begrudgingly but with the practical-ities of her mother's ill-health to consider. The natural thing would be to decline Sam's request, to offer apologies or to urge her to stay with them in Manchester instead. It would be a chance to get away from the squat and its complicated open affairs of free thinkers and pursuers of liberty. But Elsa knows it's unlikely Sam will put further distance between herself and her lover despite their tempestuous relationship. Besides, as the moments pass from the abrupt ending of their telephone conversation, Elsa begins to see it as an opportunity, a chance to get away from the Estate and escape to Glasgow if only for a few days. Ostensibly it's to assuage Sam's tormented relation-ship but it's also to forget her own travails in caring for her immediate family and neighbours. She's been wedded to that intensity for months, and now with her own son too, she's not even ventured out of the Crescents. As Sam's entreaty echoes to her own footsteps in the damp stairwells, it seems that the decision has already been made, subconsciously and with escalating certainty. With it too she feels an unexpected shudder of something memorable, which could be excitement at returning to Glasgow, a pause from her considerations and the well-trodden patterns of fatherless baby, sick mother and vulnerable neighbours. As centred as she is with her new-found equanimity and accord with motherhood, Elsa Kelly still likes to have a good time.

But the baby. She knows the squat from previous visits and it's no place for bairns. It's on both of them, and though she's unwilling to break the intimacy of her devotion, she'd never relax with him in the house. Later, talking it through with her mother, Kathy cautions against her going, then accepting her will, the folly of her taking the baby. She agrees to lend the money for the coach journey to oil the decision Elsa's already made to herself.

So Elsa takes a bus from the Estate to the motorway junction, so she can hitch to Glasgow. Instead of the coach ticket she buys gin with the money and watches the Manchester skyline receding, her fear of parting mingling with the joy of hasty departure. Still, uncertainty comes in waves, as do moments of composure, elicited by deep breathing and a persistent reminder that this is her decision. She's in control of this journey and the baby is best left in his Granny's care and not subjected to the casual sketchiness of random characters. With the enduring paradoxes and chaotic feelings she feels a compulsion to reach into her bag for the gin meant for her and Sam that evening. She pulls out a photograph of Marley instead and stares at it until she can no longer do so without her eyes tingling hot. She returns it, sees a woman opposite watching her with a countenance and smile that seems to suggest another's maternal understanding; a mother, woman and sister and that smile is what she needs to gather her composure. She overcomes the volatility of her burden for the remainder of the journey, is lucky, and gets to Glasgow in two straightforward rides, heedless of cautionary tales of single women thumbing for lifts. There are enough travellers on the roads these days and the junctions are busy and safe.

"You don't want to hear about my woes," she says to Sam as they sit together, referring to herself as a collective that are many and pressing. She knows Sam has enquired as a prelude to her own plights.

Sam hunched on her bed and oblivious to the cold of her room casts a haunted, doleful expression at odds with the spikiness of her tribal tattoos and silver piercings. Elsa strokes her forearm with the backs of her fingertips and nips her skin. It's a childhood thing, emollient. She's fascinated by the block-inked skin raised by goose bumps. Tearless, Sam screws her raw and swollen cheeks below her eyes with the heels of her hands. Her full lips pucker and shine, like prawns Elsa thinks, ready for peeling.

"He's such an arrogant shitbag," Sam says. "He intellectu- alises love but never delivers; it's so frustrating."

"Why persevere?" Elsa asks, not unreasonably she thinks, though doubting rationality rarely survives in times of tender hearts. She's familiar too with Sam's history of liaison choices. Elsa met Belzaire the French lover on her last visit to the house in Denbeigh Street a year ago. Sam had recently moved there and was instantly taken by the free spirits at play and by the gregarious older Frenchman in particular. Elsa, on seeing her sister smitten, had urged caution. She sensed then that involvement with Belzaire would be difficult and his terse interaction with her during that time suggested he perceived her hunch.

"Cast your gaze wider and find someone else," Elsa urges. "You're a beautiful woman, and you could have anyone."

Sam raises her eyes and stares at Elsa, delighted but unconvinced by this notion. Then tears emerge and Elsa takes her shoulders and pulls her close, tight into her neck, anticipating the calming warmth of her body to transfer into her sister's cold inky flesh.

Sam sobs, silently shaking.

Holding her closely in her arms Elsa remembers the first time she'd had tattoos, on her shoulders then, and told Elsa about the feel of the needle driving the ink under skin, the sensation electrifying and how addictive it was. She planned to get more. And now she's inked all over, strange, dark, geometrical blocks and broad lines and with piercings too, more each time they were together, new ones she proudly exhibits, the fresh marks the best she conceded last time, the ones that still had the blood and soft scar tissue near the surface. Elsa can't understand her need for them, it's as though she's trying to blot out the original person. But Sam refutes the notion; they are enhancements she says, the way others accumulate material things, belongings or wealth. Those things that would never be for her; she's made different choices instead, bodily choices, the one thing you come in and go out of this life with.

Those choices, Elsa thinks, are what makes her unique.

What she finds captivating about her sister is that she herself has no such feelings; a naturally beautiful woman who chooses to mark herself permanently, a curious mind but flawed, her failings perhaps being the most endearing part of her. The squat with its beguiling parade of misfits and artists, intriguing and simultaneously infuriating, like Sam herself in a way, fascinating company, but in small doses. At one time Elsa herself would have launched into this kind of world and had done so at various times but it's no longer for her. Now she has her son to care for and when she thinks about him, the emptiness of missing him thuds inside her like a giant hollow bell.

She feels a momentary panic that catches her off guard and Sam withdraws from her embrace and stares at her curiously sensing its physical manifestations.

"Are *you* ok?" she murmurs through thick lips glistening with snot and saliva.

No. No, I'm not. I need to be with Marley, my boy. I need to be with him right now, to feel his doughy skin and reassure him so he knows that all's well, that Mammy's here and she will never, ever leave him. The magnitude of his absence becomes briefly all-consuming, an anxiety attack that surfaces and winds her, sucking the air from within her, then submerging with a deep breath and a calming appreciation of this being what motherhood is about. Her own mother had told her to be prepared, to understand at the birth of her son just how deeply she would fall in love with him.

So it proved.

Elsa lightly brushes her sister's cheek, a curative touch

intended for them both. It's been a matter of hours since she's held Marley then handed him to her mother for safekeeping before leaving. Despite knowing there will be just a few days away from the feel of his sweet breath against her cheek, his absence from her arms is unspeakably painful. The hurt is conveyed to Sam through physical contact, and both hold each other tightly, watery eyed, missing their male company in two very different ways.

They pull back, regard one another and through the blurred focus and residual warmth of their embrace begin to giggle.

"What the hell are we like," Sam says.

Elsa pulls down her sleeve and dabs at her cheeks. "So tell me more about Frenchy," she says.

Sam takes a deep breath, expanding her chest to prevent further tears.

"It was fun when at first," she says. "You know, sex was great, made me feel wonderful, like he had no time for anyone else in the house but me. Now he's just getting his kicks; nothing more. And then there's Bernie Frichs."

Elsa frowns. "*The other woman*. Does she know?"

"She must do."

"Are they an item?" asks Elsa. "Has he told her about you?"

"She knows," Sam says. "All sorts of things happen in the house; people come and go and not much goes by without someone knowing something."

Elsa knows how it is. Although the house in Denbeigh Street is smaller than she remembers it, it's still as complicated. A large Victorian building with dark hallways and landings around each flight of stairs, a termite mound of passageways and rooms on each level. It belonged to a wealthy family connected to ship building who declined along with the industry. Now it's in disrepair but still standing. The open doors at the front of the stairways allow in sunlight which floods huge illuminated wedges that cut like wire into the darkness of the hallways. They light up sections and cause deep shadows in the corners and doorways that are decorated with stucco work, old and in need of repair. Elsa arrived in the afternoon, the sunlight smoky and hazy and the smell of cigarettes, dope and incense permeating the glittery air, visible and swirling in the defined segments of light. The house has a shabby and decayed feel of former grandeur, a long-lost opulence through which a vague noble dignity remains in rooms with ornate fireplaces of half burnt coals and logs that smoke in the sunlight but give out little heat.

"Has Bernie said anything to you?" Elsa asks.

"Not in so many words," says Sam. "We share an art space at the top of the house, but don't really talk. She' too focussed on her painting, self-contained with all that stuff going on inside her brooding head. Who knows what she's thinking?"

Elsa sighs and looks around at the room, the spine broken literature, the Angela Carters and UK Le Guins, the Henry Giger posters falling from the wall. Then her sister, lethargic and forlorn, caught in a fix between love and lovers.

"Do you love him?" she asks. The enquiry is returned with dejected silence.

"Does he love you?"

Sam stares out into the gloom, black and silver like the

negative of a photoshoot. "He talks about love as a concept, an idea, as though love is hypothetical and not real."

"And how is it for you?"

She sighs. "I don't know. I'm not sure what I know anymore; Belzaire, this house, the people who live here, it all feels so unreal at times, like an abstract impression of life. Everything is just theory, nothing is real."

Elsa takes Sam gently by the hand and stands, silently lifting her until gradually, reluctantly she's upright before her, smaller than herself by a couple of inches, enough to pull her into the crook of her neck. She squeezes her sloping shoulders, physically moulding her into a more cheerful posture. She pushes her chest and lifts her face upwards, holding her once more as much to maintain her bearing as to ensure her sense of solace.

"Let's go downstairs and make some tea," she says. "The world's always better with a cup of tea. And after that," she continues gripping Sam's clammy hands tightly, "let's get pissed! The world's even better with a bottle of gin!"

Elsa remembers the kitchen too from her previous visit; the heart of the house with a constant coming together of people around a large wooden table at its centre. The building had electricity then, free from a meter tapped with magnets before the Board had sussed the scam and disconnected the lot. Now light and heat is from candles and gas that diminishes the convergence no less and gives the room an air of solidity in the fading natural light of the day, where little else matters beyond it. Sitting with others at the table Elsa finds it a comfort, helping forget her anxiety over Marley for a while at least, the way she had visualised it.

Others, mostly women are preparing food. They work diligently chopping vegetables and grinding spices, then bring two huge pots of stew to boil at the stove. Elsa and Sam help out by rolling thin Chapattis made from flour and water, dry-fried and piled on to plates in the middle of the table for imminent diners. The food has been put together from hand-written recipes pinned next to the stove where ladles, knives and pots hang from hooks under shelving that border the walls of the kitchen. One of the pots on the hob is heavily spiced; the second milder with a hint of the sweet, gingery seasoning of Red Lebanese; *Finger Licking Good*, as the recipe is called. Elsa smiles and sees too that Sam's mood has lifted, absorbed by the physical work, the conversation a diversion from her torment. Others join around the table throughout the afternoon and into the evening; John, a shaven headed Glaswegian with a nasal tic who Elsa struggles to understand, and Murray who she remembers from last time, younger and fresh-faced with springy, wavy hair that leaps from his head like a cliff top sloe bush. He bounds in and his bright and mischievous eyes settle on her momentarily, an inkling of recognition.

"I remember you," he says, "from before..."

"Before what?" she says, then more amiably; "Elsa; Sam's little blister; smaller but no less irritating."

Murray laughs and grateful for the prompt turns to his partner Rachel and the two men who have entered the room behind her, travellers just off the road, both in need of a bed and a wash. Rachel pulls out chairs and passes spoons around the gathering and the two newcomers swoop to eat almost as soon as the two blackened pots are brought to table where the surface is charred at either end from previous offerings. Other moths join the flames, emerging from the gloom, from the surround sounds of the house, from who knows where, hovering, circling, bringing various additions to the table; bread, some wine and beers, fresh tobacco and candles to keep the light burning and there is chatter and hilarity born of the company and the satisfaction of the finished victuals.

Elsa squeezes Sam's hand, a gesture reciprocated, and sits at the table as the others gather, happy that she's achieved her aim of pulling her sister out of her grief. Sam sits too, now more relaxed, almost liquid in her movements and Elsa admires with mild envy how she can turn on the appeal in the presence of those she feels the need to.

Then voices from the other side of the kitchen, where the doorway leads from the dark side of the house heralds other arrivals; a stern and unsmiling man called Lawrence, involved in some sort of argument with the person who's followed him into the kitchen. The former has the humourless look of a seasoned campaigner; short grey black hair cut back over his ears and a ponytail that falls short of his collar. And behind him, sauntering into the kitchen Belziare, the *bete noire*. Elsa recognises him and follows his entrance into the room as he takes his seat at one end of the table, a large hirsute man, older than the others who moves unhurriedly and pulls out a large bottle of Retsina from inside his jacket as he manoeuvres himself into position to eat. She glances at Sam and sees the tip of her sister's tongue flashing rapidly, toying with the sleeper in her lip, a snake tasting the air, the only change to her demeanour.

"Fear and greed, Belzaire," Lawrence says. "Know what makes your enemy tick."

Belzaire, stood opposite says nothing at first, preoccupied with cutlery for the meal.

Lawrence continues; "That's the only way to beath The Capitalist." He pushes his worn-out black cap with a metal red star badge to the back on his head. His beard is vertical grey lines like stair rods he habitually strokes as he talks, running his hand over his chin and down his neck, fingers ingrained with dark lines around his nails and knuckles. He speaks with a short tongue, the *W* and *R* a combination letter like his name and his intonation is of a lecturer's; didactic.

Belzaire, hunger seemingly salient, fishes for his seat behind him. Elsa feels an urge to put down her spoon and place a hand on top of Sam's, a physical reassurance against his presence but she's as yet untroubled by him. Instead Sam leans catlike into her; "*Here we go again*," she whispers.

The stern man's invective continues: "Sharing wealth frightens them the most. Their greed creates their fear! The fear of losing their money, the fear of it being taken from them for reallocation. The fear of a world where they can't amass more. Advanced Capitalism, as preached by Thatcher is rooted in Feudalism and Mercantilism and any other *ism* you care to name, but it has the same principle of enriching the few at the expense of the masses."

He finishes his sentence with a rising inflexion and at

greater volume, as though awaiting the sound of applause. Again, he smooths down his beard, tweaking his Adam's apple between thumb and forefinger as a finishing flourish to his comment, an exclamation mark in a hand movement!

The others at the table, less than a dozen eat and bob their heads, grunting noises of agreement and rebuke at the discourse, or gratitude for the meal, the sounds indiscernible. Belzaire is yet to respond but chews noisily, breathing through flared nostrils. Elsa observes him, and someone else nearby, a pale, black haired woman of slight build, who has joined them almost without notice, slipping into a seat near to Belzaire. Sam nudges her elbow and so, without words of explanation, she understands this latecomer to be Bernie Frichs, Belzaire's other lover. Elsa glances at her sister and nods by way of returning her understanding.

"Capitalism presents the *allure* of modern society, with commodities to buy for a better life, produced for the purpose of consumption, to perpetuate the system. So, the cycle continues. The rich get richer and the poor even more so, but the theme of aspiration is what's promoted, desire fuelled by envy. What kind of model is that?!"

"Merci, ma belle," Belzaire says in a deep, dark voice as bread is passed.

So, the walrus awakes, Elsa thinks. He is an artist and a thinker – his terms – known to spend hours staring out of the window at the Glaswegian rain, ruminating, smoking heavy tar and drinking tea. A Parisian built like a strongman with broad shoulders and a thick neck over which wild black hair cascades. His hirsute face set in a recurrent scowl and the shadows around his jowly features give him an air of menace until he smiles, at which brightness lights up his face and his white teeth beam from behind his beard like sunlight through storm clouds, the latent warmth, Elsa presumes that so attracts her sister.

He reaches up to the shelf behind him and takes down a collection of vessels, one by one; beakers, shot-glasses, wine glasses and tumblers, and pours the Retsina in unequal measures, spilling the liquor between the glasses as he does so, clumsily distributing them, shedding more of the liquid in the process. The act of dispersal is more important to him than the amount itself. The drinks go around until everyone has one and offer their thanks variously.

Belzaire raises his head from his distribution. "Listen to him," he says, turning to Bernie Frichs, pointing to his object with the base of his beaker and a jerk of his head. "He talks like a Situationist." His voice is deep and rich, a robust French accent although his English is good.

Bernie flicks her head, her black hair falling symmetrically and gives a little snort of acknowledgement, the sound of a knife against a whetstone. A double act, Elsa thinks.

Accustomed to the lone sound of his own discourse, Lawrence, wide-eyed and open-mouthed briefly stops before regaining his stride. "Not at all my gay Parisian," he says, recovering his thread. "You Situationists seek to perfect the right moment for the revolution. I'm saying that the moment exists for us right now, and that the vehicle for change is the Proletariat; the workers."

"You think Billy Blue Collar is any more altruistic than Willy White?"

Thin laughter at the table; not Belzaire, whose delivery is laced with scorn.

"The workers are the material producers," Lawrence continues untroubled by the derision.

"The revolution is in everyday life," Belzaire replies. "It exists all around us."

Lawrence smiles and strokes his beard demonstratively, an explicit picture of discernment. "*The revolution is in everyday life*," he repeats, not with mockery but more in contemplation. "And that sounds like one of your pamphlets."

Belzaire grunts. "It is, you Scottish peasant," he says.

Elsa watches the two sparring, intrigued by their positions and their beards in motion, but it's Murray who speaks next. "That's racist," he sings, conceivably not for the first time; this altercation perhaps less rancorous than previous.

Belzaire stops and turns to him. "And Feudalist also?" he asks.

"Yes," Murray replies, smiling behind his straight face. "That too, I'm afraid."

"Oh," says Belzaire, groaning and wiping his lips on paper towel then folding it back to work his fingertips, before placing it to the side of his bowl. He clears his throat and begins;

"The worker of the West will not ever return to pittance pay and fourteen-hour days. The revolutionary movement is a discredited corpse in the soil if it is to evoke this as a catalyst for change. Strident gains have instead been made. The worker would be insane to renounce that and nobody in their right minds would buy into it. It is a fallen method of change that is advocated by vanguard politicians who profess to know best but who do not live in the real world but one that is made of doctrines, tomes and late-night kitchen table discussions. But the poverty of daily life exists yet. Tyranny and brutality are no longer necessary because the cities of illusion have been built for us all to work and to live in."

"The illusion of power," Lawrence says.

"The illusion of participation," hisses Belzaire. "The Western Worker will grunt and push and heave until the small changes are made where his position, his demands are accommodated. But nothing fundamental ever changes! The stevedore he is Tantalus; the middle management service provider she is Sisyphus. The fruit will always elude their grasp. Their toils are quite literally fruitless. A boulder of such magnitude they try to shift cannot be moved without considerable force. And so, they expend the requisite force, but they will never drive it to the top of the mountain because when they are almost at the summit, *lo!* it stretches further away. The state of the art moves on. Just when you can afford to buy your new car, the latest model is released but now it has a new light cluster, electric windows and a *sunroof*! The washing machine has an LED panel display instead of a knob! *Bah!* And so, the illusion is maintained, with subtlety and stealth, no longer having to resort to the lash and stick and chain of dark history. The golden commodities that line the stomach and cushion the fall is the drug that soothes the pain but shrivels the insides with little more than cold comfort. The realisation is tantalising close, but just out of reach, so as long as the illusion of attainability remains then the great confidence trick is maintained."

"And this," chimes the harsh voice of Bernie Frichs, "is the Society of the Spectacle."

It's the first thing she's said since being at the table and she says it with an imposing, easy conviction at which all around including Lawrence are instantaneously confounded. He, like the others are fixated by her tone and by her implacable authority; remarkable from such a diminutive figure.

Elsa notes it; the change, the momentary hiatus in their exchanges with her simple words; her command impressive. The atmosphere abruptly shifts, a stone thrown into a lake, before slowly settling again. With their bellies full she sees how the others watch the proceedings with care; their interactions, the manoeuvrings and posturing, vying for positions of intellectual prowess. The men particularly seem instantly captivated by Bernie Frichs. Though small in stature next to Belzaire's bulky profile, she has a striking Teutonic appearance; thick, dark hair cut severely short; smooth, white skin, pale lips and piercing black eyes that demand attention as she speaks. The two together make a formidable team, Elsa thinks. Sam's involvement with them is all the more difficult. Elsa is suddenly fearful for her sister.

As though sensing her fascination Bernie stares at Elsa and for a moment locks into her gaze, seemingly detecting her scrutiny and Elsa finds herself averting her eyes, as though her own curiosity is prurient. She turns instead to Sam with a surge of protection and also despondency for her, to think that this is the person with who she vies for Belzaire's attentions. Bernie is a woman of considerable prowess, the artist and sculptor from Frankfurt whose hands are covered in paint and white plaster. She's older than most at the table, neither shrill nor loud but possessed of a beguiling presence made more substantial by the brevity of her words laden with insight and warranting attention once uttered.

The whole affair between her sister and Belziare is tawdry to Elsa. She sees how Bernie considers each person in turn, as though challenging a response, the blackness of her pupils dissolving beneath a horizon of thick eyelashes so that only white crescents below the black pupils are visible. It's a lunar inverse, wholly magnified by the thick lenses of her black framed glasses that make her eyes seem too large for her otherwise small face.

"*Precisement!*" says Belzaire who pulls an inglorious smile, observing the others with amusement by their captivation.

Elsa watches Bernie remove her glasses, slowly and deliberately polishing them with her sleeve. Naked eyes, Elsa sees they are clear and brilliant, more so without the glass, flickering in candlelight.

She's like a bug, Elsa thinks, with its antenna in continuous motion while her head and shoulders and torso remain upright and perfectly still. She senses the tension between Bernie and her sister, mindful of the underlying issues between them, guessing that others are also aware. There's silence, a pause.

It's Rachel who breaks it. She suddenly jumps to her feet with the screech of her chair along the tiled floor, all flowing silks and long hair.

"Fuck politics! It's all you ever go on about," she says, kicking her heel to topple the chair fully over. Her shock of red hair explodes with the violent movement of her head, bright makeup and flowing multi-coloured dress. Block plastic jewellery and henna latticed hands flash as she wheels her arms.

"Revolution again. You're all so fucking dull," she shouts. "Every night the same old talk. Change the music! All the talk is the revolution, the bloody revolution; talk and talk and talk some more."

At this, others cheer and bang their hands on the table.

"You're always yakking about it, or devolution or evolution! Always some kind of 'lution."

Elsa sees her mouth something to Sam, a prompt for encouragement, a signal.

"Here here," Sam says, banging her glass on the table.

Rachel grabs an armful of unlit candles and throws them to Sam, a faltering dance with jerky, exaggerated outstretched arms.

"Revolution time again," says Sam, now standing to catch them, lips curling with her counterblast.

"It's not the *so-lution*!" Rachel adds, placing a hand on her hip and pushing it to one side, cocking her head the opposite way to make an S line of her body, the physical shape of her professed boredom.

Suddenly energised Sam stands erect beside her friend. Her silver piercings are visible when she opens her mouth, the sleepers in her cheeks filling her dimples shaped by her smile. Her muscular arms shadow in the candlelight.

"So, what is the solution?" she asks.

"Vive la evolution!" Rachel shouts, holding a burning candle high above her head. The hot wax spills down her hands and wrists, small rivulets flowing then cooling over the flesh where they harden and crack against her skin. Without flinching she grabs a blanket from the back of a chair and throws it over a shoulder, then clutches a folded newspaper to her breast in the crook of her arm. She climbs onto a chair and pushes out her chin and stands still and silent until Sam speaks again.

"Equality!" she shouts, in tune with her housemate's outburst.

Rachel shakes her head.

"Fraternity?" Sam asks.

Rachel furrows her brow, indicating her body with a wide, expansive sweep of her arm. The gesture runs from her shoulder to her hips with the newspaper in her hand. She nudges a hand beneath her breasts and pushes them forward, grabbing the makeshift cape slung around her and holding it forward, emphasising the attire.

"Of course she is *Liberty*!" shouts Belzaire.

The rest of the room breaks into applause as Rachel smiles and nods vigorously at them. She straightens her back, pushing her face upwards and the candle higher, the flame still lit above her head, close enough to the ceiling to form a blackened circle against the whitewash. The wax flows unabated, now further than before in long white lines like alien veins.

"Liberty, Fraternity, Equality!"

"And *REVOLUTION*!!"

"Aah, no... no, no; evolution!"

"It's like revolution without the R!" she says.

"Without the *aaah!*"

Rachel jumps down from the chair and throws the folded newspaper over her shoulder. "And here sit the masses," she says; "The rank and file, their strength in numbers."

"All ranked and filed away."

"In neat little boxes; a sight to behold!"

"To fight in the streets if they may be so bold!"

"Or just from the kitchen that's quite far enough thank you!"

"Smashing the system with spliff and Retsina," says Sam, replacing the burnt stubs with fresh candles within the kitchen alcoves.

"And lots and lots of guff!"

"You're too kind," says Lawrence.

"Down with the system!" Sam continues.

"Down with the state," her friend replies. "Smash it to pieces, but please be careful with that Molotov around the Benefits Office."

"Fight the good fight; the everyday struggle continues."

"Each and every day; until Thursday, as that's Giro Day."

"Until the day of the Giro!" She screams; "THE GIRO, MY GIRO! WHERE'S ME BLEEDIN' GIRO GAWN?"

"Have you lost your pooch my dear?" says Sam.

"No not my dog," says Rachel. "He's a dog on a rope and I need him for protection."

"An doggy called *Giro*?"

"No, no. My Dogger is German Bight!"

"Oh, I see. And tell me this," Sam says as she moves around

the table behind Bernie Frichs, gripping the back of her chair with both her hands.

"I wonder, does this German bite?" Sam rocks the chair gently, her muscular arms toned in the candlelight, the long black lines of ink flexing and contracting in her forearms.

Elsa watches aghast, but sees Bernie stiffen. A flash of light winks at her from Sam's pierced lip in the candlelight. She hears it tapping against her teeth. Bernie does not move, and Elsa sees her chiselled mask of stoicism, no flicker of mirth that might shade her impassive features; no disclosure of her willingness to participate. Only her eyes shift sideways, staring at the silver ringed fingers of Sam's hands at her shoulders.

Elsa sits in silence, as do the others, intrigued, enthralled and gripped by the performance being played out before them.

"Well...?" Rachel asks, continuing her flight of illumination.

"Well?" asks Sam staring down at the smooth jet-black bob of her nemesis.

"Does the German bite?"

Sam pokes her finger towards Bernie's mouth then quickly retracts it.

"Frau Frichs, zee German's bite, for sure," she says then stands and releases her chair from her grip. Bernie lurches with the movement but quickly resumes control of her posture and with it raises her eyes and fixes her gaze firmly at the centre of the table, an effort to rebalance. Once achieved she stares once more at those around the table, the recovery of her composure a necessity. It's a control thing, Elsa supposes, from which she is once more able to challenge the others.

Turning to Lawrence her head to one side, Sam says; "The German bites and the Scots Pine." Then quickly returning and directing her question to Belziare, she says in a dry, sly voice; "But what does the French Fancy?"

She pulls Belziare back and grabs his legs from under the table dragging them towards her, sinking down to balance on his knee in one swift, lissom move. She crosses her own legs on top of his and leans her face into his thick black mane and strokes her fingers through his hair, the shiny silver of her ringed fingers flowing like metal fish swimming through a jet sea of hair.

"And does the French kiss?"

"Oh my," Belzaire mutters and closes his eyes allowing his head to loll backwards, forcing his wiry beard to protrude high into the air.

"Monsieur?" Sam whispers, her ear against Belzaire's mouth, pushing her tongue inside of her cheek so that the silver sleeper bulges out against his chin. "What is your fancy?"

Belzaire snaps his teeth. *"Je veux mordre ta cerise,"* he hums quietly.

"Well?" says Rachel. "What does he say?"

Where before there had been laughter and bursts of applause, the others are now silent, watching intently the mini drama unfold before them.

Bernie Frichs sits upright in her chair but is as straight as she can be. The movement brings about a shuffling from side to side with her head rocking and no further elevation. She folds her hands together on the table and stares out in front of her until at last she turns to Belzaire, and says, "You already have, Schatz."

Suddenly Lawrence laughs out, loudly and forcefully and the others join him, banging hands on the table once more, the tension abruptly broken though a tautness remains across the room, the residual sting of a snapping elastic band. Warped by laughter and their role play the brief performance has disturbed something, the looks, the glances, the avoidance of eye contact.

"If I were you my friend," Lawrence says to Belzaire leaning across as he rises from the table, "I'd mind my Alsace-Lorraine!" He raises an eyebrow and pulls a half smile.

Behind him, Sam looks to Elsa, a mischievous smile across her face and Elsa slowly shakes her head and doesn't know whether to applaud her sister in admiration for the vaudeville act she's just witnessed or admonish her for the trouble she's clearly courting.

It's just as Sam likes to do, as Elsa knows she always does.

Oh my sister, she thinks to herself as she reaches across the table for another drink; *what fire do you play with here?*

The Marsh Estate, Lancaster; Summer of 1989

An hour of pensive searching the pathway. Wolf whistles and bird calls ring out in the scrubland that snakes between the road and the river. The undergrowth is dense with brambles and buddleia and dog rose sprawling over the uneven track, creating a damp, matted barrier through which only riverside animals can punctuate the vegetation. Eventually Max and Billy meet again. Billy smokes a cigarette on a concrete block, the remnants of industrial buildings sunk into the land reclaimed by the riverbanks. He recognises Max by his tall frame, his broad shoulders hunched up to his ears in the gloom. He inhales quickly, with a surfeit of nervous energy. The stubs of I beams and sub structures of demolished buildings rupture the surface of the concrete, rust orange in the diminishing light, the oxidising a luminous process. Max emerges silently through a dark mass of hawthorn and into the dusky light reflected from the water. The darkness of the liquid Lune flows wide and silent before them and Billy flinches when Max appears and makes to leave before he figures it's him.

"You made it," he says, exhaling audibly. "Thank God for that."

"Are you ok?" Max asks. In the darkness he can sense Billy is edgy and jittery, his long limbs fidgety. He feels oddly paternal towards him but doesn't know why; it was his idea that got them into this mess.

Billy eases. "I'm ok, what about you? I heard the sirens from the roadside. I thought they'd caught you. The cops..."

Max sits next to him, levering him along with his elbow. He takes a cigarette from the packet in his pocket and plucks the one Billy's holding to light it. "I'm ok. And I'm here!"

"But the sirens," Billy says. "I heard them..."

"That was the ambulance you heard," Max replies. "I followed you as you ran."

Billy turns to face his friend. "But you weren't behind me."

"You were keeling chairs behind you."

"Shit," Billy murmurs, "I'm sorry, I was in a panic. I..."

"Well I made it, evidently here I am. We got away."

Billy laughs, a high-pitched release of anxiety, incredulity and delight, all chewed up into a squeal that sounds like one of the riverside creatures in the undergrowth.

"They must have seen us though," he says, recovering composure.

"Yep."

"They'll give the descriptions to the police."

"Probably."

"That's not good." Billy shakes his head. "You don't seem bothered."

"Well, what can we do?" Max counters.

"They'll be looking for us Max. The guy you punched heard you talking about burning the place down." There's a fluctuating tightness in his body, rising and falling in his neck and shoulders, a sensation that should have signalled release but won't let go.

"We won't get caught," Max says wanting his affirmation, not its detachment but certainty to recreate something; confidence, trust. He wants Billy to calm the fuck down.

"Why didn't you tell me what your plan was?"

Max thinks on it, briefly. *Why hadn't he said something?* "Well, you were getting all edgy," he concludes. "I thought it would make things worse."

There's dust from the concrete between Billy's fingers. "But the guy you took out..."

"Collateral," Max says unhesitatingly, knowing the question is due, having thought about it groping through the scrub trying to find his friend.

"He was—well; thank God you got out and you made it here. I was convinced they'd caught you, the mob, that crowd in there..."

"You showed a clean pair of heels," Max says, unable to clear the image of Billy throwing chairs behind him as they made their escape. "I didn't know you were so quick."

"But I was thinking about the guy you took out. You don't think..."

Max draws long and hard on the cigarette and breathes out with equal vigour. "He's alive," he says, reining Billy's ultimate fear. "He won't feel much right now for sure, but he'll still be walking this earth when he comes to."

"But still—"

"But still what?" Max growls abruptly. He wants Billy to keep his voice down and show some composure or at least acknowledge his culpability in their predicament and the action he'd had to take. "You think we could have talked our way out? You think he'd have listened?"

Billy sighs. "No, but I didn't know you were going to take him out."

"I did what I had to, in the circumstances."

He sits down again and turns to face his friend, pulling up his legs, the surface cold against his thighs. Max's profile is sharp in the fading light; the dark stubble around his chin, the hook of his nose, his thick curly hair, black as the night in the falling light. The red glowing end of the cigarette momentarily lights up his face with each long draw; his nose and cheekbones and the hood of his brow, a sparkle in his eyes. Billy hears the sound of a fish or something, a vole or rat breaking the surface of the river deeply sliding before them. A breeze comes off its surface and up the bank towards them, disturbing the night air, taking their smoke away with it.

Max flicks his cigarette before him, its embers spinning out into the night air, disappearing in the undergrowth. He turns to Billy, acknowledging he has to show poise if it's to rub off on him.

"You sure you're ok?" he asks again.

Billy nods. "I guess. It's just that, I've never seen you like that before Max. I've never known you so violent."

It's been some two weeks Max and Billy have been on the road together. They've had some wild times since the win on the horse, the catalyst to their departure, culminating in mayhem and a few situations with other revellers, all heavy drinkers, some more than themselves. They've been embroiled in drunken arguments and indiscretions and one particularly intense disagreement in Liverpool over a poker hand and the discovery of marked cards. Billy's seen Max pissed and mouthy and reckless yes, but never violent. He always seemed to know when to back down but Max's reaction in the Travel Hotel has shocked him, not so much by the punch, but by what happened next, moving in again for an unwarranted second and third. The initial hit gave them time to escape; a quick blow from speed-of-thought, grotesque but impressive. A fat man stunned and stumbling, the obstacle cleared decisively. But the second was wanton. Then another. By then it seemed more like an assault and Billy had had to call him off.

"Well, there's a time and a place and that was one of them," Max says. "It's not my usual thing but isn't that what we wanted from our newfound life on the road; the unusual, the unfamiliar, some sort of adventure? That's what we agreed, right?"

"We wanted something different from our lives," Billy says meekly.

"And that's what we've had up to now, thanks to Kalamazoo."

"Yes," Billy agrees. "But that money's gone and now we're in the shit."

"And I thought you were some hardnosed revolutionary," Max says smiling. He lowers his voice and speaks quietly, more mellifluously. "It had to be done," he says cupping the back of Billy's head. "You wanted a stink for the Dame and that's what she got. Now let's move on, ok? What's next?"

Billy smiles at last. "I need to make a phone call," he says. "And I need a drink."

Walking on, the scrubland gives way to industry around the marsh of the river with rigid Palisade fencing, some of it broken in parts. The wind picks up where the river widens and begins to merge with the sea and the fencing rattles where it's loose. Beyond the railway line lies the Marsh Estate, the dwellings brown stone and terraced and the streets cobbled, and they walk through the quiet streets until they find a pub and with it a sense of solace. Sounds of laughter and music drift from within and a microphone set too loud beyond the lounge door and frosted glass. They enter the place and surge through the sudden wave of noise and damp heat in a meandering course to the bar to order drinks, the atmosphere a protective wrap around them.

At the bar Billy's head spins with the surroundings, the abrupt shift in ambience; the noise, the heat against his face, the sense of enclosure. He holds up a hand and asks the approaching woman if there's a phone in the pub he can use, and she hands him one from a shelf beneath the bar. He dips into his pocket for change.

"That's ok," she shouts over the music. "It's on the house." Large and tanned all over he sees through a baggy, sleeveless T shirt a glowing colour of spray tan and thick gold jewellery around her neck. Her smile has warmth and Billy's glad of it; it gives him a faint belief of acceptance, of being back amongst his own, empathy for a stranger in her bar.

"Thanks," he says.

From his pocket he takes a furry piece of paper and gently unfolds it to a list of telephone numbers and addresses. Taking the phone he whips its cord over the beer taps to the end of the bar where it's marginally quieter, carefully placing the piece of paper on the bar towel before him so the split liquid won't blur the ink any further.

"Where are we?" he asks a woman sat in shadows on a tall stool at the end of the bar. Even sitting he sees how tall she is with long legs and torso. She wears a white blouse and a pencil skirt and has thin, bare legs, mottled skin that reminds him of corned beef. She turns to face him, her pale face and grey eyes penetrating heavy black mascara and long black hair falling over her shoulders like a General's epaulettes. He's captivated by her briefly before she speaks. Her interest in him is passing, then gone, her eyes moving quickly beyond him before she responds to his question.

"It's the Victoria, on The Marsh," she says, her voice low and even, a suggestion of intrigue and annoyance: *why are you asking? Why are you bothering me*?

"Thanks," Billy says calmly, sensing a shift of sorts, an imbalance that arises from within by her emergence from the shadows before detecting the whistle of Max's breath in his ear next to him.

"Oi," he says, punching his side. "What's the plan?"

Billy turns to him, smiles. There's a sour odour to his breath.

"Who are you calling?" Max asks.

He jabs the numbers on the keypad. "A cousin; Mannie

and his wife Becca," he says. "I'm hoping they can put us up for a night or two."

Pressing the phone to one ear and his index finger into his other Max watches his nail whiten with the stem of the blood. "We're in a storm and need a port. Get some drinks in; it's been a while."

Billy's cousin Mannie, his wife Becca and two of their friends walk into the pub some twenty minutes following the phone call. Mannie is tall, Lancastrian with a rich curly accent and hugely exaggerated features; long chin and a large nose slanted to one side. Skewed in the same direction they appear straight as he talks with his head tilted in the opposite direction to rebalance his appearance, a product of formative years of torment. Small sunken eyes therefore always peer sideways, set in a pale face pelted with freckles distinct enough for a Dalmatian; a red gash of a mouth exposing brown, irregular teeth. His slow, carefully enunciated words are backed by the mannerisms and genuflections of a mime artist; a long neck, bobbing head, angled elbows and twisted wrists. This comical appearance is counter-balanced by his drab attire; brown trousers and brogues, an over-washed and faded T-shirt with a small hole below the left nipple beneath a brown jacket with stains on the lapels.

He takes Billy and holds him by his shoulders at arm's length to get a good look at him, like an art dealer holding a painting.

"Good to see you cousin," he says, his voice low, rumbling deep from within like distant thunder from far off hills. He pulls Billy towards him for an embrace that's both formal and theatrical, then away again to show him off to the others, an unexpected movement that unbalances Billy and forces a squeak from his throat. "Becca; you remember our Billy."

Becca steps forward from behind her husband and kisses Billy on both cheeks. She bobs her head and smiles for a long time before speaking. "Yes, I remember. How are you Billy?" she asks.

Billy remembers her fine features; a delicacy of looks that belies a sonorous voice and big personality. She is distinctly different in appearance than the last time he'd met her, which was also the first. Then, with her first child he recalls her as mumsy with a bulging white throat like of an exotic bird. The baby, about six weeks old had wailed the whole time; a speck of life with a voice to match its mother. Now she's lost weight, and it's changed her appearance and with it Billy's recollection of her, almost a different person. She wears an open necked shirt and a tiny cross on a chain midway between the top button and the deep dint in her neck. It shifts as her sinews flex when she speaks. She is markedly dissimilar to her husband; petite and well-proportioned and Billy wonders now as he had then just how this mismatch of aesthetics had occurred. He figures that in the case of their union the laws of opposing attraction have clearly applied.

"I'm good," Billy says. "How are you?"

Becca smiles and strikes out her bottom lip, the affirmation of her wellbeing sufficient; too busy inspecting him to be distracted by words. The cadence of conversation falters and Billy has an urge to widen his mouth and eyes, push his face into hers just to elicit a response.

"I met you at my twenty first," she says eventually. "That's, God, nearly seven years ago now?"

"That's about right," Billy says, and suddenly feels a pressure of years, a deficit of filial maintenance.

Mannie, leaning forward and extending his long arms pulls Billy around and beckons the others; "This is my cousin: our Billy. And his friend…"

"Max," Billy says.

"MAX!" Mannie shouts excitedly. "And this is Helena; and this is Leonard."

Our first three contestants.

The two eagerly shake hands with Billy and Max, Mannie's apparent enthusiasm infectious. He signals the woman with the gold jewellery behind the bar who crouches and resurfaces with a bottle of expensive whisky, setting out glasses and pouring the whisky for all before returning the bottle beneath the counter. Mannie takes Billy to one side, his hand lightly directing him by the elbow while Becca remains with her friends and Max with them.

"Here," he says, "for my mother's sister's only child; for old time's sake!"

"Thanks," says Billy and dutifully breathes in the aroma before tossing it back.

"How've you been?" Mannie asks. "And what brings you out this way?"

"Okay," Billy says, trying to appear unaffected by the events of the night and his cousin's unusual face. His features provoke forgotten recollections and he sees now that Mannie is studying his own face too, seeking out some unspoken truth in his features.

"Good," Billy continues, a higher grade this time.

The heat of the whisky forces his lips up over his teeth.

"It's a surprise to hear from you after so long. You sounded breathless on the phone. Is everything ok?"

Billy frowns, then quickly tries to disguise it. The question brings forth a flash of red and white in his mind that the whisky cannot subdue; bloody crimson ribbons arcing against hard ceramics and silver chrome; the stunned features of John Bull in the bright lights of the Travel Hotel toilets. He tried to stay on his feet as the blow had forced him to back-peddle, a sudden switch from the self-righteousness beaming to the dazed expression on his face. His mouth had twisted and eyes rolled like spinning dials.

His lights had gone out.

Billy reels himself at the memory then gathers his thoughts, guarding against unwitting disclosure. But he's troubled by this image, a mental imprint that refuses to leave.

"I was shouting over this music," he says. "I could hardly hear what you were saying. We need a place to stay for a few nights, if you could see us right. We've been travelling and sleeping rough and to be honest we just need a shower and a decent bed; maybe a hearty meal if you can stretch to that."

Mannie grimaces and glances briefly over Billy's shoulder at his friend Max who's standing with the heel of one hand against the bar, his fingers wrapped around his pint glass, gesticulating with the other hand, talking into his wife's ear.

Leonard and Helena stand on either side of him with looks of serious concentration on their faces.

"Sleeping rough? *Okaaay*," he says slowly, unravelling the knotty situation. "No call ahead and we haven't seen you for years. That seems a little odd don't you think? But what the Hell, I guess we can probably do something. *Mi casa es su casa*, and all that."

That saying, Billy hates it; often said but rarely with conviction. Every time Billy hears the aphorism the words sound hollow, as they do now. His cousin Mannie makes it sound like a quote from a film. "For sure," Billy says, equally even.

"What brings you this way all of a sudden? And what's with the suits?" He touches Billy's lapel with the back of his hand.

Billy quickly calculates the number of times he's seen Mannie. The previous occasion of his wife's birthday aside they've been distant cousins brought together fleetingly by the occasional marriage and a great uncle's funeral when they were younger. They've never been close, nor are they likely to be. Billy guesses Mannie feels this too and senses the winding course he's about to steer around desperation and expedience will be an arduous one.

"We've been on the road for weeks," he says, "moving on, meeting people, seeing what's what. It's the luck of the road. We had a win on a horse and that just seemed like... serendipity, like it was meant to be. The time was right to leave home, head North, look for I don't know what, adventure, have some fun, you know..." Economy; enough for Mannie to go on.

"Right," Mannie says, shaking his head slowly. "What's wrong with Midwich?"

"Midlands Industrial Decay With—"

"*Inadequate Council Housing*!"

"You remember." Billy's surprised and faintly moved. "Well?"

"In the coffin; no chance of work and generally shit."

Mannie's head moves further to the right and his eyebrows veer down beyond his errant nose. "Okay," he says again, only this time with a smear of humour emerging at the corner of his mouth. Billy can't tell if it's with irony or because of Midwich handle.

"Right. And how's...?"

"Jackie?"

"Yes, Jackie!"

"We've parted."

"Oh dear; I'm sorry to hear that," Mannie says, his words sincere.

"Don't be," Billy reassures him. "It's for the best; for both of us really."

"Oh," Mannie says and averts his eyes, looking to the floor as though this reality is difficult for him. "She came with you to Becca's twenty first."

Billy nods. It's a statement but some element of it has dejected Mannie; Billy's wellbeing, Becca's dear recollections of her special day or something deeper, a more lasting impression Jackie had made?

"Yes, she did." Simple affirmation, wholly appropriate.

"How long had you been together?" he asks after a time.

"Seven years, married for five. We grew apart. She wanted different things. It wasn't going anywhere but she seemed happy with that. I wasn't!"

"I see," Mannie says.

Billy doubts that he does. He isn't sure he does himself so offers this as an explanation, a reason for leaving, a mantra, as much to echo to himself as to Mannie.

"Jackie was happy to just accept things. She didn't want much more than a house to call a home, a steady job, two weeks in the sun, a car, our dog Wanda, the surrogate child. Beyond that she wanted little else. Her horizons were... different to mine."

Jackie. Oh Jackie. Where did it all go wrong and was it ever right? Somewhere along the way they'd dropped the baton and never picked it up again or even notice it had gone. Billy closes his eyes and sees her face, hard and bitter in the swinging kitchen down-light struck in rage. Her face is swollen from the tears of his declaration of his intended departure. He hadn't expected that. He didn't anticipate the anger or the force of enmity she felt towards him. Afterwards he felt a fool for being so guileless, so inattentive in his anticipation. What had he expected? Naively he thought she wanted it too, or maybe hoped that. He figured she would readily agree to their separation because it was so obvious this moment was about to happen, and both had been walking that path clearly sign-posted for so long. They'd drifted for years. It seemed so clear to Billy that he assumed it was the same for Jackie. And this assumption felt like his instinct, his own gut feeling, as hard as metal. The separation, it would be a joint undertaking and she would shrug her shoulders and at last acknowledge to herself the things she'd known in the depths of her heart for so long; that their lives were diverging and that somewhere along the way their marriage had gone stale and was heading nowhere. They'd grown so far apart in the years they'd been together he thought, wrongly she would understand it. It seemed to him that their breakup was just inevitable; almost a formality and she understood that too.

He was wrong. It didn't change things or his feelings, but he was wrong about that.

He looks at Mannie who shifts uncomfortably; with the news of the split or Billy's openness about it, he can't tell.

He was wrong and yet he was right too; right about his deep feelings, his emotions, his judgements, correct but wrong in their execution. Of this he knew he was as certain as he could be. They never talked about it. He never talked about it. So why should he be so surprised that she accused him of springing on her that he wanted no more of the relationship? Why had it been a shock to him that this had hit her so hard, that she'd failed to notice the telling signs? Had he expected her to be aware of these things? With his certainty he should have brought the notion out into the open and discuss and make it tangible by it being out there rather than some vague set of ideas and feelings floating within him. And maybe the truth was that he wasn't so certain about his desires and needs himself. Maybe he didn't understand himself or what he really wanted. Perhaps he wasn't so sure?

But he was. He knew it really, even if he hadn't formalised them into the palpable notions she said he owed her.

"I see," Mannie says again and once more averts his eyes, as if this is painful for him too. Billy guesses it's his way of expressing sympathy. "So, you left her." Another statement of fact, the truth of it. Put so plainly it sounds accusatory.

"Yes," says Billy and feels the need to explain himself; "The whole thing got messy after I told her."

The truth was it had erupted into violence, flashing vehemence he had so comprehensively failed to foresee. Then they had talked, standard parley overdue. Billy's position: that between them their common bonds had unravelled, and neither could muster the effort to reconnect and to some degree Jackie acknowledged this. A little.

"Love is a thing of the heart and not of the head," Billy says. "If the love is no longer there, it can't be engineered back in by thought or intellect."

Mannie bends his already twisted mouth to a shape of compassion. "That's very profound," he says.

Billy smiles. "Jackie said that," he says. He's sure about this because he remembers it being shrewd and he agreed with it. He'd been taken aback by her insight and wished she'd demonstrated more of it. If she had then maybe things would be different between them; maybe they would still be together. He considers telling Mannie that but somehow it sounded trite in his own head in these circumstances, a little too sentimental and he's not in the mood for that; doesn't want to be sucked into that place. The whisky and the Bowman gig have seen to that. And his recollections of her saying it is a piercing rod painfully straightening his body, her new-found insight making him sit up and question himself and whether he's missing something in her he should have taken more time to seek out, as he had at the beginning, when he was sure he loved her, just as now he's certain he no longer does.

It had confused him, then and still now. She so rarely demonstrated such perception, but she did possess it. She had it within her but seldom revealed it. But the more he thought about it the more it began to irk him, her failing to use it or show it, the latent intuition idling and wasting. She had become too passive, the effort too much to employ.

"Did you argue?" Mannie asks, recovering eye contact, adapting.

"In the end, yes. It didn't get us anywhere."

They had talked as she demanded; the quick, clean break never an option. Jackie with her long black hair that fell about her shoulders and over her large breasts and trickled like treacle between her fingers as she ran her hands through her hair with the anguish and consternation of what he was saying to her. Her makeup ran and the bright nail varnish on her painted nails chipped and bitten. She made him explain himself to her; he owed her that at least, she insisted. He conceded. And as he did his thoughts and feelings for her became more real, more substantial, like an egg in a pan, transforming from runny and translucent into something hard and definite that could be rolled around, held and pressed and squeezed in the hand. In this way his thoughts became more tangible. The more they talked the more certain he was of his feelings. It was almost cathartic, and he realised the paradox that the object of his conflict should also be his sounding-board and that ironically, the more he talked to her about their failing relationship, the further from her he felt.

"We talked," Billy says explaining his outer thoughts, reticent about the deeper. "In her opinion if you constantly question your happiness you'll never discover it."

Mannie sighs. "Maybe there's some truth in that," he agrees.

Billy quickly downs more whisky. He wants to feel the pain of the hot liquid burning his throat and into the core of his being. He isn't minded to have his deepest emotions squeezed out of him or his motives questioned. The plain and simple fact right now, as it stands with his cousin before him is that he just needs a place to rest his head for a couple of nights, for him and his mate, comfortable being an added bonus. The whisky is doing the trick and then there is fire inside him, a molten centre.

And now this woman sitting at the bar behind the crazy features of Mannie's warped face has become Jackie. She's sad and there's beauty even in her grief. There is beauty in her contempt for him as she looks directly at him over his cousin's shoulder, sneering and full of scorn, disappointment, sorrow and a box full of things she'd rather keep locked away, beneath her bed with other valedictory items from penfriends and late grandparents. Now her husband belongs there too. She can see where he is and what he's doing. She knows he is wrong, even when he says he's right. Then she turns away again and Billy's left standing remembering. She has long black hair, at least.

More whisky from behind the bar at Mannie's behest,

generously poured by the woman with the golden skin that merges into her Sovereigns and the nine carat chains that draw the eye line down a steep V towards her breasts and Billy rallies again.

"And what if you don't question it?" he says. "What then?" This question is meant to be rhetorical, he's eager to put this one to rest, no longer prepared to explore the idea with his cousin and seek new angles of it but to deliver its coup de grace. "Acquiescence is not an option for me. It never will be Mannie."

"Yes," says Mannie. "I remember that sentiment when we last met."

Billy looks into his cousin's eyes. *Is he siding with her*?

He remembers that too, more clearly now, recollections creeping back, wild dogs to a carcass. They had talked for a long time; a drunken late-night conversation slouched against the hotel bar when others had gone to bed. Jackie had been with him that night, the night of Becca's birthday. Billy and Cousin Mannie left to chew the fat, smoking cheap cigars and drinking anything; pints, shorts, Sambucas and Malibus while the sober barman had continued to pour, entertained.

Billy recalls how strait-laced his cousin had been and how argumentative he'd become when they were alone and fluent, no longer the restrained host on display at the beginning of the evening, squinting and slurring, his hackles quick to rise. They'd talked about all sorts; politics, marriage, relationships, babies, music and agreed on little. Mannie seemed determined to test. Even through his own drunken haze Billy recognised his deliberate hostility, arguing at every turn for the sake of it, his weird features contorting uglier with every drink.

Unwisely Billy had pressed on regardless, explaining his desire to change things and live life differently, disappearing down all sorts of holes, trying to explain his addled thinking to his cousin who thought him juvenile and idealistic. Subconsciously Billy had buried this ugly episode but as Mannie stands before him now he realises part of his reservation about calling him up were from the smothered memories of that night.

And now Mannie, drunk again, beginning to loosen up and showing early signs of that hostility again. Billy's conscious that the drinking should not get out of hand again and watches with disquiet and mild curiosity when Mannie gestures for more whisky. He lights a cigarette, offering one to Mannie, who refuses. "Well, that's all done now," he says. "We've parted. I've left her. I've left home too."

Mannie does not pursue it either. "Got wheels?" he asks presently.

Billy shakes his head. "No; no money. We're calling on the kindness of others, relying on their good nature."

"Compassion for humanity, eh?" says Mannie.

"Something like that," Billy replies.

"Much around?" he asks.

"Some. You get lucky or work out the best place to stand. There's salvation through kindness, sometimes through boredom or necessity or relief or just by chance. There are the usual chance encounters; nice guys, loners, normal, bored, chancers themselves in a way. Then we've been dossing on sofas and floors; friends and friends of friends."

"Where are you heading," Mannie asks. "What are your plans?"

Billy shakes his head. That word; *plans*. "Anywhere; and nowhere, wherever the road takes us. It's a deliberate thing we agreed to have no specific destination; seems freer that way. The lack of transport seems to be instrumental in that. We're happy to throw ourselves in and see what happens; leave it to chance. We're in the hands of the Gods, or the fates or whatever it is that's going to spirit us away. Turns out we've mainly been heading North."

Mannie shakes his head. "I can't understand that myself, but I suppose it's your choice. I mean what the Hell it sounds awful."

"Sometimes," Billy says and feels a sudden, deep-seated provocation to justify himself and though he has no intention of doing so, he can't scratch away the itch either.

"What about your friend?" Mannie asks.

"Max? We're on the road together. I've known of him for years, from afar, just seen him around a few places but nothing more; enough to nod and say hello. Then recently we were both in a job together, warehouse work and that's where I got to know him properly. We worked together and then he was laid off. We've become close friends in the last few months.."

Mannie raises his eyebrows and Billy marks them as antennae of his presumed understanding, an indication of his knowing. "Getting down with the workers, eh? A part of the proletariat," he says.

Billy flinches. "That's very cynical," he replies with a little laugh.

"Well, cynicism is healthy. You said that the last time we met. You are an advocate, remember?"

So, he remembers that night too. Though wilfully trying to master it Billy is spiked by his cousin's challenging tones and feels his own shuddering rancour, the surfacing needle of justification jabbing within him. He keeps himself in check not wanting to give any reason that might cause him to change his mind about his *casa*. "You remember well," he says, a little too coldly despite his efforts.

"So, what happened to your job?"

Billy smiles and takes another sip of whisky. If he's right about the challenge he's determined not to take it on but tell it like it is, factually and with composure.

"Max was asked to leave. The work was drying up and the gaffer didn't think much of him anyway. So, I call him up a few days later. I'm all alone, staring at the walls and Jackie has gone. I've moved my stuff out of the house and sleeping on sofas. We've been apart a few weeks and the rawness of emotions is beginning to subside. At first I don't want to go out but then I think there's nothing left, and I've got to do something. My life needs to change; I have to discover a better one. So, I have a plan. I tell Max to meet me in our local pub. I insist. I tell him I have a proposition. So, he meets me and during the night I convince him we have to get out of the place. We need to have an adventure. What is there to lose? He's lost his job and the one I still have is shit; a shit job paying shit money. Modern life is shit. It's over between me and Jackie so there's nothing to stop us leaving. And so we hatch a plan to hit the road and leave the place."

Mannie smiles uncertainly. "Like a couple of hobos" he says.

Billy looks down and wipes ash off his sleeve. Looking at the state of his suit he can appreciate why he's said it.

"It all made perfect sense," he continues, "to leave the mundane, unfulfilling existence behind; to see if there's a life more rewarding; and Jackie was the catalyst. Then by some crazy twist of fortune we come into cash. Max in his own unique way takes the newfound spirit of rashness to heart and goes and puts all his Giro on a fifty to one at Uttoxeter. The horse is called Kalamazoo and Max has a hunch about it."

"A sixth sense," Mannie says. "What was behind it?"

Billy shakes his head. "He didn't know why and the name Kalamazoo, the place means nothing to him, he just has this notion that it's going to win. So, he bangs the money down on the nose. The whole lot, seventy odd quid. What a gamble! And *kerpow!* It comes in! That's over three monkeys each."

"You got lucky."

"In the end, yes." He doesn't think of his breakup as fortunate. "The old boys in the bookies slap us on our backs, send us on our way and we take off. Everything seems right. Outside of the bookies the sun was shining, the gamble's paid off and we have money in our pockets. We don't have to go to our shit jobs anymore, at least not for the immediate future. Max is willing to split it 50-50. Fuck it, he says, he regards it as *our* money so let's just enjoy it together. Our decision to take off is blessed. It's the right thing to do. We're justified.

I'm leaving Jackie and the bad blood between us behind. Max doesn't have anything to keep him there either, no family to speak of apart from his mother who he never sees. So, we hit the road and we have a ball. We spunk the money pretty quickly. We go to Liverpool, meet up with some friends, hit the boozers and the clubs and spunk some more. We chance the Casinos and roll out in the small hours down. But we've had a great time in the process. There's wine and women and good times."

Billy knows Mannie has never done anything like this in his life and is never likely to and it's satisfying to tell the unadulterated story. He's verging on embellishing for added spice, maybe throw in a few sordid details about the wine and the women. The story is true and doesn't need much exaggeration and Billy notices his cousin throwing all this information around in his weird-shaped head and that he's not entirely comfortable with it. Disapproval? Curiosity? Jealousy? Billy doesn't know which but is unapologetic and presses on with the tale.

"Well, that was a few weeks ago. We left Liverpool and headed further north, an address in Blackpool, a friend of a friend of someone we met after an all-day drinking session; you know how it is?" He's on a roll. "No one's home when we call and the fund is running dry. After a couple of nights of phone calls in pubs and trying to make friends for a bed or at least a sofa we hit the road again. This time things are slower. We're not as cheerful anymore because of the shrinking pot and there's a sense that the good times are coming to an end. And so we're on the road heading North again; only this time we're skint. The money's gone. That's it. That's the way it happened. I say to Max that my favourite cousin lives here on The Marsh Estate and as we could do with a bed for the night, or maybe a couple of nights, I decide to call you up. And here we are. Now, what about you? Are you still working at the Council?"

It's intentional of course; switching from tales of high rolling to enquiries about Mannie and his armchair local authority job as some sort of housing officer, he can't remember exactly. It's a challenge back; *beat that!* He knows he can't, but also that he wants something from his cousin and because of that he doesn't want to lord it over him too much. The question is how far his cousin will go to make him sweat.

Mannie dutifully responds to the direct question without passing judgement on the story he's just heard. He breathes in deeply then looks downwards, sees something on the floor that bothers him then kicks it away with his toe. "Yep! It's steady, but it's a job and that's what's important these days, with Thatcher and the family and all."

"How are the kids?" Billy asks.

Mannie looks up again. "Growing; one at school and the other will be there soon."

Billy's silent, deliberately waiting for further information, knowing it won't be forthcoming. The silence is uncomfortable. "Planning for more?" he asks eventually.

"Two's plenty, thanks. But what about you?" Mannie asks, restoring the order of his focus. "What are you going to do now?"

Billy shrugs. "Don't know. Sign on. Try and find work."

"Will you go back?"

Billy shakes his head. "I doubt it," he says, then forces a movement to express nonchalance. Behind it remains a defensive parapet that doesn't fit well. He's desperate to secure a place to stay for the night and now he has a faint niggling feeling, a notion that in the cool night beyond the heat of the room with the crashing band and his adversarial cousin the townsfolk are waiting; a lynch mob, an armed pack from the Travel Hotel, hunting with pitchforks and burning torches. He swallows and closes his eyes then is surprised to feel his cousin's fist punching his shoulder.

"It's not for me but each to his own, eh?" he says and with these words his expression shifts. "You haven't changed Billy. Let's drink to that," he says, smiling broadly and banging his hand on the bar for the bottle once more.

Billy feels the warmth of blood and whisky. He accepts the drink, rolling the liquor around his mouth and this time the fire is soothing.

"You're a good skin," Mannie says. "You're family and you're always welcome, you know that."

Billy touches his glass. "Thanks," he says. "That's good to know."

To his surprise Mannie moves to hug him, a brief embrace, stuttering, almost perfunctory, a sudden response to his own inner emotions, then with second thoughts. Billy responds. He can see Max laughing in his peripheral vision over Mannie's shoulder, still in the same stance, calm and comfortable at the bar. Released from his embrace and as though hearing his thoughts through proximity says, "Unlucky for you that your marriage didn't work out; for both of you. But if you it's not meant to be then it's not meant to be, is it? I got lucky with Becca and we're both happy together. One day you'll find who you're looking for."

"Thanks," Billy says. These are heartfelt words and Billy senses another hug coming his way but is interrupted by Max and Becca and her two friends, Leonard and Helena who step closer to them from the bar. Helena has her hand in Leonard's pocket, and she's linked her arm through the loop of his and clutches a glass of wine in her other hand which she sways before her as she speaks, indifferent to its containment. She's taller than Leonard with rosy cheeks, possibly coloured through drink, bright flashing eyes and a downy chin.

"Hey Mannie," she says. "You didn't tell me your cousin and his friend here are fugitives!"

Perplexed Mannie glances at Billy for a response and Billy feels the blood drain from his face, a rapid loss that washes away his strength with it and the stiffness quickly returns down his spine and across his shoulders; a hot lasso tightening around his torso.

"These guys are spunky monkeys," Helena continues. She has a sloppy mouth, a tongue unleashed, uncontained. "In my opinion they've got balls, doing what they did."

"What did they do exactly?" Mannie asks. Billy feels his alarm rising, replacing the blood that's drained from his head. The heat of back-washing whisky enters his mouth, bitter with something from below, a woody, sour taste. He looks to Max for explanation but Max turns quickly to watch the band.

Helena laughs a single high-pitched note that makes those around them turn their heads. She unhooks her arm from Leonard's and points a finger at Billy with a circular motion. There's fluff on her nail from his pocket.

"The fugitive is coy," she says.

"Helena," Leonard says, his voice low and monotone.

"Men of courage; making their stand against the evil-doers," she continues. "I'm with you guys all the way with. Man the barricades and fight back. Smash the system. That's *so* rock 'n' roll baby. That's so damned sexy!"

"I hear you sister," Billy says with another little laugh that reveals too much nervousness. He's trying to make light of what she's saying by playing it down, underselling whatever she might say next.

"Yeah, you hear me alright. I'm fine-tuned to the world around me too you know, and I don't care for what I see either. It's a world of first-hand loss and denial and marginali-sation and frustration and paranoia. It's the Age of Unreason we're living in." She turns directly to Mannie. "You know we don't belong Mannie; we never did and never will belong. You *know* it! Kick out against the pricks. Run away;" and back to Billy, "I'll tag along with you."

Billy glances at Leonard's dour features and wonders what he's making of her suggestion.

"What are you talking about Helena?" Mannie asks.

"The country's been invaded by aliens Mannie; can't you see that? They're faceless and unknown and they've made us all the same; eroded and worn smooth like pebbles in the sea and battered into tiny grains of sand thrown together. We're all beached unless we do something about it. Well, you know I won't hold any truck with it either Mr Fugitive."

Billy smiles. "The name's Billy," he says, hoping for some sort of deflection.

Helena offers her hand and Billy shakes it and doesn't let go. He wants to pull her away from the circle of people, pull her head to his shoulder and whisper into her ear to *shut the fuck up*.

Leonard's eyes roll and there's a clucking sound from the back of his throat; a familiar refrain for a frequent situation.

"I know there has to be more to life," she continues. "There just has to be. I don't know what it is, but I know I want it. Hey, we could go where you're going, wherever it is you're going, me and Lenny here. Your friend has told me all about you and your escapades. That's what I want too; a life of fun." She leans forward and her eyes widen, big eyes, Harvest Moon eyes where the pupils and irises merge into blue-black circles. "Smash the Government! Wreck their cosy little ball! Have a ball yourself!"

Billy steps back and lights a cigarette to the side, hoping his movement away from the others will be enough to lure Helena over to a more private conversation where he can talk quietly into her ear within the protection of the pub clamour. "Have you been talking to my friend?" he asks more quietly to add to the inducement. She takes a step towards him. "What did he say to you?"

Helena laughs and throws back her head theatrically then returns to her original position, back to the arena where the others focus in on what she's saying. "He's told me all about your little caper with the local politician tonight you naughty pair."

She smiles, an immature grin, that wayward mouth, a drunken smile that repels him.

Mannie turns to Billy with a look that urges a requisite response.

Becca moves forward and is about to speak but Helena retakes the initiative.

"And you are quite the An-ar-chist?" she says. "Mr Fugitive."

"*Billy*," says Billy.

Helena smiles then drains her glass of wine. "The life here's a slow death. Welcome to The Marsh everyone! Everyone wants to leave but nobody does! They should make it a film called *Escape from The Marsh*! It would have a cast of thousands and whenever it's shown in a cinema near you, they can just change the name of the place and the names of the cast and you've got your tailor-made British Film Industry Grade *A* British Film Grey Day!"

"Easy girl," Mannie says. "No more of the whisky."

Helena smiles and shakes her hair away from her face, blowing errant strands with a protruding bottom lip that makes them rise up before her face then fall back again on either side of her nose. "Mannie," she says, looking at Billy. "Mannie, you really need to be careful of the company you are keeping."

"Your friend Max says you're on the road looking for work," Leonard says abruptly as though he can sense Billy's discomfort and is also tired of Helena's monologue, her need for attention. "Where are you heading?"

Billy seizes the opportunity to redirect the conversation. He wants to embrace him and walk him away from the group within his clinch; thank you, *thank you*. "We're not quite sure," he says cutting through the circle and moving around to address Leonard. "North bound to somewhere. If you know of anyone work—"

"And right now the medium of your grand scheme is that great winding snake of tarmac known as the M6 Motorway," Helena interrupts. She's hard to shake.

"I gave your friend my brother's address in Glasgow," Leonard perseveres. "He lives in a shared place up there. You should look him up."

"Thanks," says Billy. "We'd be grateful for that."

"It's a kind of art collective, a political collective; you know, Marxists, Fabians and the like. It's a big place with lots going on. Look him up; you'd be welcome. His name's Murray. Murray Falconer. Your friend has his details."

"Thanks," Billy says. "Sounds interesting. Have you been there?"

And it's Helena again who interjects. "Murray the Little Brother. Sure, we've been there, sitting with his squatting friends, punks and anarchists and general dropouts. They're all proponents of individualism but all look the same, kindred strays all alike; vegetarians, dope smokers and abusers of other recreational drugs, always angry, obligated to non-doctrinal ideas born of heated yaddayaddayadda in pubs, deliberately obtuse and non-conformist to the degree of conformism."

She grins and leans forwards, rasping in a loud whisper; "By and large ineffectual".

"How do you mean?" Billy's eager to take the conversation down her lead.

"Their stance, wide-spread dissatisfaction, system-rejection and common paranoia; those birds always stick together, uniformly dressed and subscribers to genuinely shit music. They gravitate towards each other for protection like all the others out on a limb; the Gypsies and blacks and the Born-Again *facking* Christians."

"It's interesting," Leonard continues regardless, unperturbed. "You should try it. It sounds right up your street."

"Thanks," Billy says again. "We will."

He's certain Helena has at last been thrown off the scent, but Becca has said nothing during this exchange, displaying a mouth shaped to speak but uttering nought, rolling her eyes and rocking on her heels and balls of her feet like a schoolgirl waiting to jump into the skipping rope game. Now she makes her interjection.

"Mannie," she says sternly; more of a shout, a call to attention and Mannie duly obliges with bodily rigidity. Her face still has the fine features but now they are linear, and the delicacy has gone, replaced by a robustness that Billy knows comes with a booming voice. "Mannie, you might want to ask your cousin what he and his friend have been up to this evening," she says, then continues; "And why they've come here looking for a place to stay."

Becca's convivial demeanour has gone, and her soft features harden, a season skipped. Her head shakes left to right to give certain syllables greater weight; *been-up-to; why; stay*. They're the ones that carry weight, the important ones.

Mannie returns his drink to the bar. "Oh? What has happened? Go on," he urges, turning to face Billy.

Max, sensing trouble takes a step further away from the group. Helena smirks at him, flashing her eyes between him and the group and Billy observes her with disdain the deliberate toss of her little hand grenade in to the group. She's enthralled by the mess it's about to cause, eager to observe the fall out; whose limbs will fall where, who will survive intact.

"What did you say to them?" Billy asks Max outright.

Max shrugs and Becca is quick to engulf his slowness with her own rapid interjection; "Oh, he told us about the attack on the man in the toilets of the Travel Hotel."

"*What*?" says Mannie. "What attack?"

Billy rolls his eyes. "Hang on a minute; you make it sound like..., it wasn't quite like that. I know it seems... on the surface, it seems, it must seem like a random act."

"Explain," Mannie urges. His voice is calm and suddenly formal, a slip into his Council work voice. He faces Billy squarely with his body, his face still to one side, head tilted until his neck is squeezed into his shoulder.

"I'm trying," Billy says. He looks around at the inquisition; Mannie, baffled and intrigued; Becca, hard and impatient for Billy's version of events; Max, melting into the background, guilt and clumsiness about his movements receding into shadow; Helena, drunk, swaying and smug and Leonard, embarrassed and clearly uncomfortable with Billy's plight. He pulls Helena's hand back towards his pocket with a swift jerk, a demonstration of his disapproval, reasserting some correction, a show of a force she fails to anticipate, taking quick steps to redress.

"Tell Mannie, cousin. Tell us all the truth about tonight."

Billy clears his throat of the thick and dry film coating the back of his tongue but is too slow to respond.

"They beat somebody up in toilets of the hotel," Becca continues. Her lips quiver as she speaks, puckered red and glossy, an insidious jungle flower in her long and serious face.

"*Shit a brick*," Mannie says, raising his eyebrows and turning further to the side.

"It wasn't bad," says Billy. It's a lame commentary.

"How bad?" Mannie asks.

Billy, annoyed for prompting the obvious follow up rubs his stubbly chin with thumb and forefinger.

"Who was he?" Mannie sings the question, a tune of salacious intrigue.

"I don't know; a guy from the audience."

Becca picks up the story with apparent brutal relish. "This is what Helena is referring to, Mannie. They crashed the MPs speech at the Travel Hotel, beat up some poor guy in the loo then smashed the place up. Now Billy and his mate are here looking for refuge; in our house."

"Radical!" exclaims Helena, stridently.

Billy winces at the shrill caw of her voice. "We didn't smash the place up! And it wasn't planned," he says. It still sounds feeble. He's in a collapsing vortex of weak excuses, losing air and will with his lungs compressing.

"You assaulted him," Becca says, snorting incredulously.

"God," says Mannie. "Kellet-Bowman? What happened to peaceful protest? What about the non-violent direct action?"

"It was Max who...," Billy says and stops short of the denial of his own culpability because he knows he's as responsible. The blame, it sounds juvenile and unfair, and he regrets the words, not their veracity but the delivery, the speed to shift the thing he's led Max into, something they've both ended up embroiled in. He flicks a quick glance at Max, but it hasn't registered with him and he keeps his distance from the group again, physically removing himself; a family affair to him now over which he has no influence.

"Right so you can stay but he can't!" says Becca.

"No," says Billy. "Mannie, we just need a place to stay for a few nights," Billy implores, desperation rising in his voice. "Or just one night."

"No," Becca barks.

"Like a safe house?" Mannie says.

"That's probably over-romanticising it," Billy mumbles.

Becca pulls her husband to face her, her hands around his sides steering him towards her. "What if the police come looking, asking questions? You know what they're like! We don't want to be implicated in anything like this."

Mannie looks over again at Billy and his travelling companion.

Leonard steps forward again. "Look," he said, his voice calm and even, boring even, a welcome calming tone. "If you two guys are looking for a place to stay the night then we can put you up. We have a spare room. It's no problem, really it isn't."

Relief courses through Billy's veins. Leonard the saviour; Saint Leonard. He has genuine warmth, an avuncular demeanour as well as attire, kindly and sincere.

But it's Mannie who speaks again.

"No," he says. "That's kind of you Lenny but Billy is my cousin and we should be the ones offering him and his friend a bed for the night."

Becca throws her hands in the air and gasps loudly. "What do we say to the children when there's a knock at the door at two in the morning and the police are standing there? And besides, who was the victim?" She turns to Billy. "Who was this man you attacked? What had he done to you? Did you know him? Where did he come from?"

Billy silently shakes his head and declines explanation to her inquiry.

Becca continues, filling Billy's silence. "He could have been a local councillor, or Alderman or an aide to the MP, or some or other Tory Big Wig? They don't know who he was. You don't know who he was, do you? You know what these people are like Mannie; they're well-connected, they know people in high places. They'll be pulling all the stops to find your cousin and his friend! They could make your life difficult. They could make our lives Hell! You work at the Council for God's sake; you could lose your job!"

"Becca, calm down," Mannie says at last, and Billy is thankful taking Leonard's lead he brought his own equanimity to the conversation.

"Don't call me hysterical, Mannie!" Becca insists. She steps back and holds up her hands, her eyes closed, head shaking.

Billy sees she still has the heaviness in her white throat, and it vibrates beneath her chin as she shakes her head. "Do *not* call me hysterical!"

"I'm not calling you hysterical, honey. I'm just saying that we should be a little more rational here. He's my cousin and he's in a fix. One night, is not going to hurt anyone, okay?"

"We'll be gone by tomorrow," Billy says.

"He's my family," Mannie adds. The breadth of a blood trump card to play.

Becca stares into her husband's face and the hard lines, the linear, vertical creases fade by just a small amount, a barely perceptible diminution but enough to release the cold grip of resistance.

"One night only," she says at last. "Just one night, then you're gone."

"Sure," Billy says. "We will be. Thank you."

"One night!"

"Yes, only a night," Billy says. "Thanks, again."

Mannie breathes deeply. "Ok, so let's all have a drink, and everyone just needs to calm down a little bit, yes?"

Billy smiles, exhales reaches for his cigarettes. "Oh, yes," he says. "You don't have to ask a second time."

M6; Summer 1989

Across the North Lancashire landscape, Max stares out from a hexangular tower that rises thirty foot out of the service station next to the M6 like a giant thumb tack. The hexagon is a restaurant, one that should revolve to give the diners panoramic views while they eat their over-priced full English; hills and dales, the M6 North and Southbound, the sandbanks of the Irish Sea; sumptuous scenery to take your mind off the food and the price of it.

It doesn't rotate.

Early weekday morning and the sun floods the place more than the customers, its brilliance reflecting off plastic surfaces bolted to metal frames shimmering around the room, everyone squinting, all filmy chins and sleepy eyes. In this egg yolk morning light Max's gaze settles on the hedgerows aside the carriageway and the traffic flowing between, the route of their escape; the mighty M6. Inside the Formica pinwheel service station, the silent chewing and slurping of food and drink reminds him of the cows ruminating in the fields beyond. Around a dozen people sit eating in silence. One of them is Billy sat opposite, stubble about his face, broadcast with dry nicks, slurping tea and chewing on toast. He's lost in thought and Max observes him as he loads his own drink with sugar then empties the contents of a brown sauce bottle all over his breakfast, a fitting adornment for fare prepared so utterly without care.

The lack of shaving is part necessity, part intentional; one disposable razor between them rusted and blooded and used before the Bowman gig. They've binned it and opted for facial hair to try to alter their appearances in the forlorn hope of speedy growth. Max lights a cigarette; the last of the Bensons bought at the Travel Hotel and sends smoke billowing over the table in a thick grey cloud that grows in the sunlight like an algal bloom and settles in lingering strata around the place.

Billy coughs. "We need to go," he murmurs, lowering his head beneath a layer of smoke.

A young waitress next to them methodically wipes the tables with the care of a French polisher and Max watches her with a passing interest. He bites the nail on his forefinger and twists out the spur to use as a makeshift toothpick, then indicates his approval and extricates himself from the bolted chair.

Out in the sunshine the noise of the passing motorway traffic whines all around and a sweet, heavy tang of diesel fumes fills the air as they walk to the exit in the hope of hitching a ride out of the place. The morning is warm already, dry enough to bring the salts out of the tarmac on the slip road. Others are positioned here and acknowledge their arrival, graciously moving down to accommodate fellow travellers. It's road etiquette. Max and Billy take up their own position. They had left Mannie's house early that morning before the rest of the family had risen except Mannie himself who'd made them coffee and toast. Sat at the table they'd listened in silence to the local radio report of a serious assault at the Travel Hotel the previous night; police looking for two assailants, both mid-twenties, one medium build, dark hair and complexion, grey suit; the other in a black suit, six two, pale complexion, short cropped hair.

They'd looked awkwardly around the table at one another.

"That'll be you two then," Mannie said solemnly. "So on your way now, and good luck to the both of you."

Billy holds out a scrawled sign for *GLASGOW* and Max rolls a cigarette of tobacco and fluff from the corners of his pockets, humming a tune, then singing; "On the road again; goin' places that I've never been..." It's a thing they do, throwing song lyrics to match their everyday circumstances. Billy looks at him and shakes his head.

"*Willie Nelson*," says Max, idly noting the arcane graffiti of bored travellers, the in-jokes of close friendships cork-screwed over time out of logical meaning and humour:

GOD LOVES ME SAME JUNCTION EVERY TIME!

~~Skelly to Delhi - Around the world in 80 60 days~~

Dempsey is a Warlock

"You shouldn't have said anything to anyone," Billy says after a while. "The fewer people who know the better."

Max rejects the notion with a cluck of his tongue.

"Doesn't it concern you?" Billy asks.

"I thought they might be on our side."

"You were bragging about it?"

"I was telling it like it was."

"Where was your tact?"

He peers at Billy. "You shouted my name out, partner."

"When?"

"*Run Max run!*" Max squeals, waving his hands around his ears.

"But the guy was out cold by then. Surely he wouldn't have heard that?"

Max throws his head dismissively. "Who knows," he says. "It doesn't matter now."

"Shit," Billy whispers. "But maybe it does."

Max rubs the back of his neck with the palm of his hand. "Forget about it. Besides, there was something about your cousins and their friends, the way they were looking at me; hanging on to my words, like everything I said was interesting. It felt good. For the first time in my life somebody was actually listening to what I had to say."

"Now the cops are on us."

With the sunlight, Max picks out the details in his friend's eyes, the woody grain, the woolly fibres and rebukes him inwardly, mildly for being deaf to his justification, for spooking instead.

"Be calm," he says. "If the Rozzers come by you just eyeball them to show you've nothing to hide. Smile. Don't look down or at your watch or scratch your nose or turn away. That's an error, will make them suspicious because you look shifty, a bit suspect, not being able to maintain eye contact."

"We need to ditch these suits," Billy says through clenched teeth.

Max continues. "Rozzers know all the tell-tale signs;

averted eyes, facial tics, all that cod psychology shit they learn at the academy about who's trouble and who's got something to hide, even if you're not black, or gay."

"Thanks for the advice," Billy mumbles, then draws a long breath. "But we need to get away from here as quickly as possible. We need a decent sign or a travel bag or something to make it look like we're on the road for a purpose. We need kit bags like squaddies; they always get lifts."

"Relax," says Max. "We'll get there soon enough. Besides, it's madness that squaddies always get rides, when we all know they're really battle-stressed, sadistic killing machines. Most I've come across are crew-cut, volatile fuckers with a fondness for carnage. Beats me why you'd want someone like that in your back seat eyeballing in the rear-view mirror?"

"It's the uniform," Billy says. "They're easy to identify.

Max begins to hum; *"Arsehole, arsehole, a soldier's life for me; my piss, my piss, my pistol on my knee;"*

"And the shiny boots," Billy continues. "They complete the costume, implying whatever happens they won't be treading shit into your freshly valeted leather interior."

"Fuck you, fuck you, for curiosity; I'll fight for my cunt, I'll fight for my cunt, I'll fight for my count-ery."

Billy laughs. "You should know," he says. "Your brother was a squaddie."

In the dusty air and bright sunlight Max's face quickly darkens, a swift, scudding cowl of shadow bringing in the familiar squall at the mention of his brother.

"Yes, he was," he says steadily, deliberately.

Billy sees him, pensive and suddenly motionless, a man

who might have heard his brother's name whispered in the wind.

"You don't talk about him, Max," he says.

Max shakes his head. "I don't like to," he says. "He was led astray by the army, and now he's no more. You know that. And now I wear his old suit."

Max never talks about it and for Billy the details are patchy. He knows his brother Daniel had been killed by the IRA in Northern Ireland; this was common local knowledge often mentioned over fences and in bars. Billy had known of the family from the next housing estate and the story of his brother's demise was sufficiently newsworthy for press and TV reporters to descend on the house for several days. Local whisper conveyed the family bereavement and the subsequent difficulties they experienced; meagre details, rumours and hearsay, a core of solid truth caked in the fluff of indolent pub and checkout talk. Beyond the basics the facts were limited, descriptions vague. Though his knowledge of Max and Daniel is therefore scant, Billy has not been minded to seek out more. Max is glad of it, his unbridled sadness is a private matter to him and not for others, that enquiry he sees as prying for salacious detail. He likes that Billy hasn't overstepped that.

But standing together in an M6 service station, Max knows Billy is curious. It's not the first time he's seen him want to scratch that itch. He stares at the hot, shimmering landscape around them and the trembling fuzz of heat and dust and insects are like the details of the event; real and tangible but ill-defined, ones that flicker and tremble under scrutiny. Billy has collected this story in minor surges over time, retrieving random elements with little elaboration. Max's reticence is to do with pain and with trust; an unfamiliarity with the latter, a fear of it. He won't be pushed on it and his friendship with Billy has burned slowly and steadily over the past months with little mention of the thing that casts its shadow or of the darkness itself; just silent, noncommittal. Max erects it like a fence with trespassers' warnings all over it.

"Sometimes it helps," Billy says.

"We're men; we don't talk about feelings."

"Talking might help to let it go."

Silence. He knows Billy wants to help ease that pain but is wary of how to do so. Behind the distant manmade rasp of tyres on metal roads the birds sing in the trees and hedgerows and insects fill the air; nature all around, it's paradox; serenity in its perpetual industry. Max sits motionless. He's heard the prompt and waits to see if Billy repeats it. He doesn't and the thing remains, hanging silently in the air, lingering for some point in the future, or for now.

Max smiles. "A Provo got him," he says at last. "That's what you want to know."

"Where was he?"

"Crossmaglen near the border with the South, on a routine patrol with an RUC cop."

"When was that?"

"A Tuesday night in February, and it was raining. It always rains in Ireland, that's what they say."

"That's how it seems," says Billy. He wants to say more, to offer succour, but not fill the space.

"The bullet was a headshot. It got him just below his left

eye; just there." Max gently places a finger on the left side of Billy's cheek indicating the spot. Billy smells the sweetness of nicotine on his fingers.

"I'm sorry." A whisper.

"He was twenty-six, another soldier killed in Ireland is all there is to tell; so don't ask me again, ok? Let's leave all that behind."

"He wasn't just another soldier; he was your brother."

Silence once more and now there's a look in his eyes; an emptiness so striking as to contain a lifeless intensity. It's the familiar darkening, the shutters fastening tight as always, the lights diminishing. It's in his complexion and in his eyes, as though black blood, blood without oxygen goes straight to his head, bypassing his heart where the pain lies. His shoulders rise with the tension too, forcing his head to hang lower and shadow, so that the darkening is within and without.

"I'm sorry Max," Billy says, indicating sadness for this loss, and his regret of asking.

"Just don't pry..."

"Sure", Billy says. "I was just trying—"

"I know what you were just," says Max releasing the pressure from Billy's cheek at last and touching his face in the palm of his hand instead. It's an unexpectedly tender touch. "You're my good friend Billy, but now you shut the fuck up. Just get us the fuck out of here and get us to Glasgow."

Billy smiles. "Let's see if I can just do that," he says.

Max hands Billy the sign and sits down against the barrier.

"Hit the North!" he says.

Some moments later Max is lying motionless, slumbering

by the roadside. A while after that he awakes and looks around to find himself in the same place, takes the sign from his friend and swaps positions. Traffic passes and occasionally stops but not for them. People come and people go, come and go and with their departure and the slowly dropping sun Max has a sense that their passage out of Lancashire might take them on similar journeys, something favourable to both of them. They both need to escape and though it might be from the stuff in their heads, the physical movement helps. With the passage of time, marooned at the slip road he has a flourishing sense of optimism that comes from deep within, an unexpected buoyancy at odds with the things he's revealed to Billy. It's more akin to the process of travelling on a road, it being as much about things left behind as it is of finding new things and discovering new places. Motion towards and movement away come in equal measure but not necessarily at the same pace. In any given journey neither he nor Billy will ever be able to move from one place to the next without first going through something in between, something together.

Deliverance eventually arrives hours later that evening in the form of a forty-tonne articulated lorry that slides to a dusty halt on the slip road for them, then bucks and gallops out of the service station and glides out on to the carriageway. The darkening fields and hedges, barns, bridges and streams are dispatched to the past, diminishing in the distance, time and space falling behind them all together as they move onwards, the here and now being systematically consigned to the there and then. It feels good to be on the move again, out of Lancashire and heading north. The light fades fast in the west; vague flecks of dim illumination that could have been tricks of the eye, so tired were they from all the adrenalin. The day with the light dying in strips he sees beyond the hills like wet fingers dragged on a chalkboard, blue and black in the darkness and silvery grey in a twilight reducing to a blur of horizontal lines.

With the forward motion relentlessly carrying them along, propulsion so strong as to seem unstoppable, a question surfaces as Max drifts into sleep; what happens if they meet an obstacle they cannot overcome, a barrier so unyielding to stop them dead in their tracks? And what is the outcome if they met it on a means of travel too powerful to stop? Who will be the winner when the immovable object meets the irresistible force? Which one will succeed, which one the stronger force, for there has to be one? It's the conundrum that fixates him as he falls into broken sleep on the Northbound road to Glasgow with his friend's head resting on his shoulder and his breathing ringing heavy in his ear.

Denbeigh Street, Glasgow; Summer 1989

Sam licks two papers, one angled at 45 degrees to the other, pecks away at the block along the centre, rolls, roaches one end and twists the other into a product accomplished through years of practice. She smiles and triumphantly raises the final creation to the sky like libations to the Gods. She is a monochrome picture: white teeth, black hair, black lashes, pale face, silver studs in her cheeks and lips and sleepers in diminishing loops from her lobes to the top of her ears. Black, black clothes, silver jewellery around her soft neck and dark blue tattoos like vines creep from below, spreading along her body and visible upon her collarbone above the neckline. The ink on her arms is drawn in strong, angular lines, running vertically from her wrists to her elbows and from her elbows to her shoulders and they are in a block formation, with dots in places and small but perfectly drawn X's.

Achievement abruptly turns to doubt.

"Shit," she says. "I forgot. Are you still breastfeeding?"

Elsa shakes her head and grins but cannot conceal a wistful frown.

"Don't you want any?"

"I've lost the appetite."

"Wow," says Sam, as if the notion is unfathomable. "What else has changed?"

"Thankfully, no more leaking la-las."

Sam giggles and puts the joint behind her ear for later. "Well, thank God for that."

"If we saw more of each other, you'd know."

"Els," she says sulkily. "Don't..."

"I don't understand what keeps you here. Why not come back to Manchester, even for a short while."

"It's complicated," Sam says.

"It always is. So uncomplicate it."

She twists the rings on her fingers, the jewellery she's made herself, and says nothing, her sensitivity exposed.

Samantha often complicates things, she's mindful of this. She recognises Elsa's awareness of it too, a difference between them. She was raised in the belief imbued in her by her mother Kathy that life was ever thus and that an absence of difficulty usually implied naivety or even gullibility. This aspect of parenting was a result of Kathy's own tough Fenian upbringing. Categorically, Sam is neither naïve or easily fooled and will go to extreme lengths to demonstrate this, particularly where her mother is concerned. But the unheralded consequence of this stance is that Sam finds complications in life where none need exist at all. Where she cannot find them she will actively create them. And so it proves and has done so on many occasion with her choice of friends and lovers. Sam prefers difficult people and courts their complications, her inclination is the attraction of their flaws. They're just more interesting. She considers Elsa's opinion of this trait as from the luxury of her being the middle of three sisters. One day, she vows inwardly, they'll talk more about it.

For now, deflecting Elsa's challenge, she asks: "How is everyone?"

"Tammy asks about you every day. She misses you. Freya, Mam too; *I* miss you for God's sake."

"Mam?"

"Of course; yes, you have your differences, but still..."

Both Sam and Elsa have had their altercations with their mother; that was just the way of things. Now times had changed; Sam has moved away, and Elsa has Marley.

Elsa continues: "She's calmer now Sam. Maybe it's having the baby that's done that. I can call on her insight and that's like an unwritten rule. It surprises me how thoughtfully she gives it, without the usual bossy crap she used to mete out. It's brought us closer. I never saw that coming. And, she's not well you know Sam."

"How bad is it?"

"She's just about coping but it's not getting any better."

"I'm only a thumb ride away, if things get... you know."

Sam sees Elsa baulk inwardly. She doesn't know how serious the COPD is and perhaps, deep down she's too afraid to find out. She doesn't probe her sister too deeply.

They're at the table and still drinking with all the others following the routine with Rachel. Sam had rehearsed it with Rachel but the intention was for it to appear spontaneous. In this sense she's pleased with the way they made it work but can see it's somehow unsettled Elsa. Belzaire's sat in the same position, holding court with Bernie and one of the newly arrived travellers. Sam sees Elsa looking at him and knows he's the reason for her trouble. "Hey," she says, clucking her tongue to recall her sister's attention.

"The French guy Sam," Elsa says. "And Bernie..."

"It is what it is, Els. Relationships in the house are fluid. No strings acceptable, less conformist." Sam pulls the joint from her hair and lights it; fortitude. She's aware her words are injudicious to Elsa and knows too that Elsa considers her prone to having her head turned, a trait she can't deny.

As if circumstance somehow underlines this Sam turns to the person next to her, the other traveller, the one with the dark curls called Max and passes him the joint, deftly, between her little and ring finger. He accepts with a nod and a smile but is otherwise taciturn. Sometime later she rises to her feet for more tonic water from the shelf and deliberately brushes herself past him and sees Elsa mark it with uncertainty of whether this is the latest opportunity for *fluidity* or a chance to bait Belzaire sat opposite. She doesn't really know herself but Belzaire seems not to notice anyway. She senses Elsa's discomfort which was never her intention and sees her move around the table to talk to Murray which as Sam knows her sister is her subtle demonstration of disapproval.

Others around the table have splintered into small talk too and Sam pulls her chair in front of this guy Max and manoeuvres to engage him in a conversation of her own. Wasn't this kind of encounter the kind of thing she lived in Denbeigh Street for?

"Got a cigarette?" she asks.

Max duly obliges; a twist of tobacco wrapped in a king size cigarette paper.

"I've no other papers," he says passing the little package to her.

"I have," she says. "I'm Sam."

Max smiles. "Max," he says.

"I know; I heard. And tell me, who are you and how did you get here?" A game show question.

"Your friend Murray's brother told us about this crazy place full of beautiful people," he says drolly, just the right side of sarcasm.

"Now, the Fates have you here," she replies, and steady, stealthy connections are quick to form; silent bridging, communicated through a handful of words and more by positioning: her knees pointing straight at him, her body angled squarely on to him. She places her hands between her knees and the effect brings her shoulders forwards and between them her chest so that knees, shoulders, breasts and eyes are all unswervingly drawn within his vision. Hushed signals lie within her frame, her risen clavicles that form horizontal pools of darkness above and below thin chicken bones. The lines of ink on her arms are perfectly linear, no movement of muscle or sinews to distort their tapered angles. With the silver jewellery, the studs and sleepers emerging from her skin she is robotic; an android pose of metal and inky flesh, her pale face lit by candles like an angle-poise lamp positioned on a chair before him, ready to interrogate.

The effect is intimate, confining the two of them, sealing them from the others around the table. Her ridge and furrow shoulders work upwards and her head forwards, deliberately, physically barring the rest of the kitchen from her intimacy, attention drawn, all else out of focus.

Max finds himself acting as a receiver to this pointed positioning. He reclines in his seat though it's not comfortable to do so and the wooden slats squeeze his backside and pinch the bottom of his back. He tucks his heels under the seat of the chair and pushes his knees out wide, throwing an arm over the back of the chair and expanding his chest to match the width of his knees. Between the two people the result is of a plug and socket; male and female in which she is the male and he the opposite.

She sets about grilling him, inspecting him; where has he come from, how has he got there, how long has he been on the road, who does he know in the house, what are his plans, where is he sleeping? Max answers each of her questions in turn, diligently, dutifully.

"Punks and pie throwers," he says when asked what he knows of the others in the house. "That's who they said live here. Plotters and bombers, pamphleteers, subverters of ancient orders, crazy circus freaks. I'm quoting here."

Sam smiles at the description and looks behind her with a knowing look, confirming his description of the others. In doing so she catches Elsa's curious eye and for the briefest of moments hesitates before the reprieve of seeing her sister involved in her own conversation. She smiles warmly and returns her attention to Max. She has a delicate smile and Max tries to imagine how she would appear without the make-up and tattoos and metalwork; softer, less streetwise, more innocent he decides, warm eyed with a gentle smile. Animated, he regards her wide-eyed enthusiasm, a sort of wet-nosed puppy eagerness. The pierced pink tongue gives her a harder edge and he concludes that this is probably her aim; a natural look of virtue and inexperience she seeks to roughen or use to conceal an inherent shyness perhaps. He's known people hide themselves in this way before, but she hasn't appeared at all timid, quite the opposite she's straight on him almost as soon as she'd seen him.

She moves a fraction closer so that her knees are almost within touching distance of his and would have touched if his legs were not either side of hers. Sparks of electricity. The description of her and her friends has delighted her, as it would most if they were described as different; unique and interesting, a bit deviant.

"What do you do all day?" he asks her.

"I make jewellery," she says; wariness for the first time. She withdraws her hands from between her legs and holds them up before him, splaying her fingers and rotating them slowly so he can see the jewellery adorning her fingers and wrists from all angles. She has rings of heavy silver ovals on most of her digits. The rings are long and tapered, thick in parts, they're layered in flat pieces one on top of the next, spot soldered and decreasing in size, like physical models of isobars on a weather chart. Some have a rough finish, others highly polished that catch the candlelight. She wears sliver bracelets too; bangles of the same design; burnished surfaces, roughly textured irregular miniature panel beating he guesses is the intended finish. She inspects the jewellery herself as she twists her hands before him.

"There's a little workshop at the top of the house where I ply my trade; it's upstairs."

"Your trade?"

"I sell what I make. It keeps me afloat and means I don't have to sign on like everyone else does. Do you like them?"

"You're talented," he says.

"Thanks." She's pleased by the praise, the pleasure genuine. "There's more upstairs; do you want to go up and see?"

The question comes upon him, grows. Max hesitates then brushes it by.

"Why not sign on?" he asks.

Sam lets her hands fall and lays them flat on her knees. She sits up a little and the movement pulls her knees back away from him.

"I don't wanna. I don't agree with relying on government hand-outs; I'm too independent for that. I don't want to be at the mercy of the state. I want to make my own way and not have to depend on anyone else, including the Government for dole. Signing on is demeaning; standing in the queue for a Giro every two weeks with a spotty oik you knew from schooldays asking why you haven't found a job yet. Deliberate marginalisation; I just can't hack it. They moan," she cocks her head behind her indicating the others, "about the system but they're happy to suckle off it, like runts on a sow's tit even if the milk is thin and doesn't nourish. I'm not like that. I'm different."

Max smiles. "Yes, you are," he says. "It's quite a stand. That's why you sang about it."

Outside of Sam's frame he sees that Billy, Murray and Rachel and Sam's sister have moved into their own space, their setting, perhaps as a result of Sam's positioning, having seen and recognised the signs. Does she often make a beeline for newcomers or is this intimacy special?

Her satisfaction at him noticing her performance creates a wriggle.

"Make any money?" he asks. "From the jewellery."

"Enough to pay my way. Not as much as your win on that horse you told everyone about, but its steady."

"Kalamazoo was a once in a lifetime thing," says Max with dreamy reminiscence. "The winnings had to be spent in one go; it was shit or bust. We owed it to that horse."

"*Mmm...*," says Sam smiling. She toys with the hot wax at the top of the candle, squeezing the semi-pliable nuggets between thumb and forefinger, rolling them around then back into the flame. The fire flickers and sputters and the wax spills over the rim and down the candle with the displacement, pooling on the surface of the table. Beyond the lights Max sees Lawrence still talking, animated, stroking his beard in his longitudinal thoughts. Next to him the German woman Bernie, alone at the end of the table, the palms of her hands flat on its surface, eyes probing the room, settling individually on those present, her consideration detected in the fibrillating movements of her cheek muscles. She settles on Max beyond the flickering flames; just observation with no change in facial expression, the lingering look at his face until her scan complete and details logged, she moves to the next; to Rachel and then to Murray, then Sam's sister Elsa again.

"What about the others?" Max asks. "What do they do?"

"Like you say, *pie throwers and crazy circus freaks.*"

"What about Lawrence over there?"

Sam pulls her chair closer to Max and leans into his ear, conspiratorially. Closer to her face he can see how the metal jewellery emerges from her soft skin, breaking the surface of her flesh, a rupture with redness in places, cleaner in others, the ring in her eyebrow, the stud in her lip. The two silver balls in her cheeks sit flawlessly in her dimples, like pools of mercury in two downy depressions. They are perfectly symmetrical and give her face balance. Max imagines the sharp points inside her mouth scratching her tongue and teeth. She looks younger still, the closer she comes to his face where there is scar tissue in her ears from previous piercings, thin and red and pitted, only noticeable at close scrutiny. There are tiny capillaries in her ear, their patterns like miniature river deltas seen from the air.

"Lawrence is a thinker, a talker, another bloody talker, another man of words and little else. That's what they say about him; an armchair Marxist, all jaw jaw and nothing more more. He came here for tea one night and never left; just carried on living here even after the lights went out. He's something to do with the university, a lecturer or something; or maybe that's just pretence and he thinks he is. Cut through the political crap he's really a nice guy. He just needs to lighten up a bit, you know? Needs to get himself a good woman, like everyone."

Her breath is a combination of spearmint and nicotine, a tiny fleck of chewing gum floating around her mouth, surfacing occasionally, a shell in the surf. Max inhales her smell in occasional waves as she speaks into his ear, the stud in her tongue clacking against her teeth making a hollow metal sound like the bit in a horse's mouth. Over her shoulder at the far end of the table he sees Bernie still staring at them. Their eyes come together again, her pale face and little body still hunched in the same position he finds unnerving all by herself, alone on a limb.

"What about Bernie?" Max asks.

Sam leans back, briefly tilting her head back and pushing her tongue into her cheek, looking at Max, a mirror against Bernie's uncompromising gaze.

"Bernie? She's different. Steer clear is my advice to you; you don't want to mess with her; she's a strange one."

"How so?" Max asks.

Sam edges forwards and her animated eyes narrow, looking beyond him over the horizon of his shoulder. "She's a loner, a difficult woman. You saw her at dinner tonight; cold and aloof. Some say she has no family to speak of. Others that she's a killer!" She says it salaciously, her eyes widening again, more so with her disclosure.

"How do you mean?"

"She killed a man," Sam says quietly.

"No shit," Max whispers back. He flicks a glance over her shoulder again, but this time Bernie has resumed her lighthouse sweep of the room and her beam settles with equal intensity upon Belzaire who's talking to Billy and trading slugs of cognac from a hip flask.

"What man?" he asks.

"I don't know," she says. "A guy in Germany in the '70s. She was part of a terrorist group, the Baader Meinhoff.; those paramilitaries who assassinated their enemies, I think, so the story goes." Looking up Sam moves her head away from the closeness of her intrigue. "She went to prison. It could just be rumour I suppose," she says brightly, "but there's no smoke without fire is there? She's a private woman. She hardly ever speaks, event when we're working together in the studio."

"A killer! You work with a killer?" he asks.

"At the top of the house; it's the only place in this building with any kind of natural light so we share the space. She spends her time painting and saying little so she's no company to share a studio with. I like to sing or talk to myself when I'm making jewellery, you know, a relief from the concentration. I have the radio on. Belzaire works up there too sometimes, you know, he dabbles; he likes to mess about. I don't think he's as serious about his work as Bernie. She's so focussed. You look at the line that goes right up the middle of her forehead from between her eyes and her hunched shoulders; she gets her posture by staring at her paintings and concentrating so much."

"The paintings of a killer. And Belzaire is her lover?"

Sam shivers and quietens. Soon she says, "Sometimes yes, sometimes no. They have an open relationship; sometimes will share a bed together and sometimes with others. They never work together. Their artistic styles are completely different;

they never paint and talk. Belzaire wears a big smock and a pallet with a thumb hole, holds his brush up to his painting. His paintings are shit. He just looks the part. I think he's just playing at being an artist with the smock and his big beard. He gets paint in it. He plays with himself beneath his smock and lets me know when he's hard, casually but you know he's proud of it. He'll come over to give his opinion on a piece of jewellery and lean in closer so I can feel him against me."

"What do you do?" Max asks.

Sam raises her eyebrows. "I brush him off. He's harmless really. He gets bored, easily distracted, rolls lots of cigarettes and shares, stares out of the window and then paints a little scene on the glass. Then Bernie shouts at him: *the light, the light; why are you blocking the light?* and he wipes it off sulkily.

He'll study my jewellery for a while. He used to spend more time and giving me advice. Bernie doesn't like it. I do. He made me feel good, for a while. When you're the centre of Belzaire's attention he makes you feel special, like you're the only person that matters in the world. The problem is that in his world you're just passing; there are always others around the corner. I don't care; it's my art space really. They're just trespassers as far as I'm concerned."

"A terrorist in our midst," Max whispers, tersely.

"You want to come with me to see my space?"

The corridors that lead through to the stairs at the rear of the house are dark and dank, a damp sheen on the walls that glisten dully as they pass with the candles held out ahead of them. Those they're holding are essential to light their passage as Max instinctively cups his hand before the flame. The place has no electricity and the candles in the kitchen are not just for atmosphere. On each of the landings the candlelight is enriched by orange light of the streetlamps, the light flooding the landings with electric hues through the windows at each end. They walk up one creaking staircase after another, Max treading gingerly two steps behind Sam with the absence of light around him until they reach the top of the house where a double room has been knocked into a single space with one door boarded shut.

Inside the room is painted white, ghostly orange grey in the half light. It's a wide space that stretches from the front to the rear of the house and dips in the centre where a stud wall has been removed. At each end there are wide sash windows without curtains to allow light to enter the room, this space high enough to overlook the streetlamps below. Max notices sky lights in the roof too and through the grey and dirty windows he can see stars amid silver clouds bruised orange obscuring them in other parts of the planarian.

"This is my space," says Sam proudly, motioning Max to join her at one end of the room. Her voice has a closeted finality to it. She places the candle down on a large table and lights a number of others already there, fixed by pools of cold wax. There are off cuts of metal scattered on the table and the floor beneath it, a blow torch and soldering rods, G clamps and tin snips. Small engraving instruments like dental appliances are scattered about; scribe tools, dot punches, doming punches. On the walls are a series of sketches, large and bold in Hard Black, the first drafts of ideas and designs to be forged into jewellery. Above them are a number of pegs where necklaces and bracelets hang, rings and earrings Sam has produced, finished or yet to be.

Max examines them closely with the aid of his candle in a circular holder, picks up the jewellery and lets the pieces rest in the palm of his hands. He runs the chains through his fingers and holds them up, twisting them in the candlelight. Sam watches his face studying her work. Her breathing is long and even. A wheezing sound of the breeze squeezing through the loose windows blows through the room and the candle flames flutter throwing flickering shapes on the walls around them.

"Do you like them?" she asks.

Max turns his attention away from the metal finery towards her. She leans on her workbench with locked arms, so the crooks of her elbows are pushed inwards, almost unnaturally double jointed, her face turned upwards towards him. Square on he sees she has a wide jaw line, cheeks like the bout of a cello so her eyes, nose and especially her mouth are small and disproportionate within the frame of it. He nods in affirmation of his approval of the jewellery and gently returns the piece to the peg, butterflies in his hands. He turns back again to face her and she's not altered her position or her study of him as he does so. From somewhere in the depths of the house below them the portentous sound of drumming emerges over the whistling of the wind in the top studio. The rhythm is slow and deep and resonant, dark beats, the bass and the cadence heavy to reflect the night time, the snare replaced with deeper, lower pitches.

"Well?" Sam asks.

"Well?"

"What do you think?"

"I like them," he says.

Her eyes and small mouth in her wide face narrow further; strong yet suppliant.

"Is that all?" she asks, raising her eyebrows and arching her neck so her face tilts further upwards. In the dim light Max can see the faint and even pulse in her neck, heartbeats slowed to the drumbeats.

"They're really good," he says.

Sam's eyes widen. "Is that all you *like*?" she asks.

Her eyes are big and heavy in her moon face. Behind her Max can see a thin muslin curtain gently moving at the end of the room. It flows with a ghost like quality and through the grey-white surface and between the coverings he can see paintings; deep colours, blocks of colours that demanded release, as though the colours themselves are moving the curtain before them, craving attention. The paintings of Bernie Frichs, the works of a killer. Only Sam's white features demand more. The silence is burgeoning like the muslin behind her, a hush Max has no desire to fill with an answer. Her look becomes earnest, then with the continued silence, plaintive. Demanding it becomes painful to him, a familiar feeling he senses gradually in the pit of his stomach; reticence, not shyness, not caution and not desire. Intrusive and uncomfortable it hums and glows and the gentle movement behind her claims greater consideration than Sam with her wide face and imploring eyes and Max knows the distraction is expedient. It seems the veil moves to the beat of a single drum surfacing from the depths below accompanied only by a faint moan of the Scottish wind, the *blinter* they call it in these parts. It eases into the room from the outside night. The movement and the drumming and the wind conspire to draw him away from Sam and her jewellery before him and her striking, flashing features and immediate expectancy. The feeling is excruciating, and Max can scarcely acknowledge in his own mind why this is, knows he will step back from the edge but can neither leave the silence hanging expectantly nor explain himself to her.

He lowers his eyes instead. Metal filings and ash litter the naked wooden floorboards. When he raises them again it is not to her eyes. Her efforts of contact repel him further as she seeks him out, lowering her head for purchase, brow furrowed, her urgency impotent. The art of avoidance in a single square foot.

Then she accepts his distraction. "What is it?" she asks.

The liberation of words. "I... ..."

Sam sighs and her head drops for a while, her hair falling with the movement. Her head down she turns her face aside. "Yes," she says quietly, a word almost lost to the sound of the beat and rattle of the drums where with it there comes the sound of footfalls on the wooden steps from the stairwells.

Briefly her fists clench. The footsteps are slow and deliberate, suggesting the climbers are moving to the beat of the drums audible throughout the house.

Someone calls Sam's name.

Both she and Max turn to look at the doorway and see the dim, pirouetting shadows of candlelight and the footfalls that accompany them growing brighter and louder, bringing company from the lower floors of the house.

It's Rachel and Murray who appear in the doorway.

"Hey, why don't you—" Murray begins then stops at the threshold of the room. He bites his lip as he looks at Sam and Max together. "Sorry," he continues, "are we interrupting?"

Rachel pushes forward. "Come downstairs you two," she says heedlessly; "we need musicians," and she moves into the room with her hand outstretched towards Sam.

Sam reaches out and takes it. She walks backwards, defeated, dejected.

Watching her receding, stepping back towards the door Max can hear the blood rushing in his ears or it could have been the wind through the windows. Either way, the noise is like a vortex, time and space sucked out of the room along with her leaving. Her parting glance towards him is brief and wistful, a drag of heavy eyelids that fail to rise to a level for eye-contact, an earlier failed mission. She leaves the room and follows Rachel downstairs and Murray follows too calling back after Max to join him as he does, their footsteps quickly diminishing with the candlelight as they descend to the haunting sound of his heartbeats.

*

"Hybristophilia."

"What is it?"

"A condition, the Bonnie and Clyde syndrome; when a woman is sexually attracted to a man because he's a *badass*, violent and dangerous to know."

Billy leans closer. "You mean your sister?"

Elsa nods nonchalantly rolling cigarettes for them both. "Theoretically," she says. "Got a light?"

"Max isn't violent," Billy says defensively, then concedes to his recollection of their escape from the Bowman night. The look on Elsa's face, her rueful red smile and raised eyebrows darker beneath her blonde shock of hair gives him the notion that she somehow knows, that Max's tongue has loosened once again. In current company there's less of a problem with that, but who knows in future.

"You think...?"

She lines her teeth with her tongue. "They went off together, who knows to where? And I know Sam; her tastes in men are dubious at best, always goes for the wrong 'uns, the *troublesome* type."

Billy stifles another protective reaction to her assertion, instead accepting certain established truths.

"Where did you hear about that?"

Her head tilts from side to side, licking the cigarette papers. "You know," she smiles, studying her construction; "books, in libraries."

"Does it work the other way; men attracted to dangerous women?"

Elsa stares at Billy curiously then flicks her tongue again. "Possibly," she says, dipping her head towards the lit match cupped in Billy's hands. "Do you know your friend like I know my sister; are you as close? I was watching you two tonight; you seem to have the same intimacy between you, you know, a rapport, an intuition."

A quick and unexpected heat rises within him; that of affection being observed, coming as it does from the surrounding company, the kinship he feels, human and as soft as the candlelight in the kitchen. Most of all, he realises it's the warmth of being perceived by Elsa who has moved herself to sit beside him, her grey eyes having unobtrusively taken in the situation around her. He thinks this is perhaps a natural gravitation, a conventional one her sister and his friend leaving the fray together, the space to fill, both of them newcomers to the house.

"Am I right?" she asks, observation one step, confirmation the next.

"Yeah," Billy says. "We're close, and each day on the road brings us closer."

"Lovely," she says. "And you ride your adventures on the back of it."

"I guess so; that's a very lyrical way of putting it."

Elsa laughs, throwing her head back into shadows. "More lyrical than Marx and Engels over there," she says, pointing to those still arguing at the other side of the table. Then; "Or is your journey one of hardships to overcome?"

"How do you mean?" he asks.

"A quixotic struggle against adversity; *the impossibility of it all.*" she says placing the back of her hand against her forehead. She gives up on the point, then says: "So your Max and my Samantha; Bonnie and Clyde?"

"I don't think he's looking for complications," Billy says.

"Oh? What is he looking for?"

Billy pauses. "Companionship, camaraderie..."

Elsa's smile dims as though disenchanted by the seriousness of his response. She draws on her cigarette and lets the smoke float out of her mouth. "And you; why the road," she asks; "what are you running away from, apart from cops and Tories?"

So, he *has* talked.

"What do you know about that?"

Elsa plucks the cigarette from her lips and grins. "Beans get spilt," she says. "What about you? Who are you running from?"

She's direct and Billy likes that; it feels real to him, shrewdness but not without warmth.

"A five-year marriage on the rocks."

"Ouch," she sighs, "that must be hard."

"It has been."

"Children?"

Billy shakes his head.

"Bonus," she says brightly. "It makes things less complicated."

He says nothing further and after a time Elsa says, "That's the escape?"

"Sort of," Billy says, "but there's more."

"Tell me," says Elsa. "Tell me all."

Billy thinks. "Well, at times I feel, this will sound ridiculous; I feel alone."

To his surprise, Elsa becomes equally serious, quickly shedding levity.

"What about Max?"

"Not immediately; I'm speaking in the wider sense."

"Why?" she asks.

"You'll probably think this bizarre, but I just feel troubled; by the Establishment, a Government that's unjust and prejudiced but keeps getting voted in. I'm not part of this country, my home; that me and everyone else are at odds. I suppose what I'm saying is that at times it feels sort of isolating."

Elsa smiles, pours a large glass of warm gin and pushes it towards him. "Here," she says, pressing it into his hand; "If it's any consolation I know a lot of people who think like you. You are not alone. And something else," she continues, "It's really *very* endearing to hear a boy admit to his insecurities."

Billy observes her closely and sees her look that's sincere and solemn.

"Thanks," he says.

Elsa smiles, takes a sip of the neat gin and leans back with a tremor from its taste, the lightness returning. "What are you're looking for now?" she asks.

"A mixer," he says.

"There is none, so apart from tonic?"

The million-dollar question. "*For Light and Liberty!*" he says with a sweep of his arms, a public declaration.

The candle flame next to them flickers with the sudden motion, casting a dimmer, quivering light across her face so that she seems at once amused and puzzled by his proclamation. The aspect of her features changes again; softened, less angular. The effect is brief and disappears with her smile but not the lightness cast by it.

"Why those things?"

"It's what my old man had on his Union banner; *For Light and Liberty*. I've sort of adopted it as my own mantra;

for freedom and an absence of darkness or discovery of joy, or grace."

"*Eleutheromania*."

Billy stares blankly.

"It's another condition; the zealous pursuit of freedom, emancipation and liberty."

Billy smiles warmly. "You know so much," he says.

"*Whodathought*! Or is your *Light* simple luminosity?" she asks.

"Yes."

"Enlightenment?"

"Maybe," he muses.

"And what else?" She peers into his face, curious, eager to seek his truth.

"Possibly more than that; a place where we can be at one with everything."

"Ah, a Utopia?"

"The personal perfect world," Billy says languorously, revealing his own scepticism.

"Christ, you'll be searching a long time," she says without sarcasm, her manner Billy notes; composed and strong, thick skinned but not hard hearted.

"Yes, perhaps, but I have time."

"Know what Sartre said about freedom? That everyone has the freedom to be the architect of their own choices, and so we can't be anything but free. As such we are condemned to be free; condemned by freedom."

"You read Sartre?"

"*Yes, a mere woman!*"

"No," he shakes his head. "I didn't mean—;"

"I go to libraries, read books, read all sorts then leave love notes for the next reader. I'm an incurable romantic at heart, Billy."

"And do you believe that we cannot be anything else but free?"

"It's a curious theory," she says. "But if you're asking if I'm an existentialist, then no, I'm not. I believe that people seek freedom in all sorts of places. I think freedom starts in the mind and not necessarily in the physicality of being free to roam and wander. That seems rootless to me, more escape than discovery. For me, freedom and liberty are nothing without love."

"I suppose not," Billy says. "Is that your personal perfect world?"

"We all need love Billy, one way or another," she says, and Billy is struck by this, more by her delivery, its emphatic truth, like it's been there all along and he's just failed to see it or at least acknowledge it to himself, something you walk past every day and don't notice it until it's gone.

"Do you have it?" he asks.

"Yes, it's all around," Elsa says, "in many ways, though my world is far from perfect."

"Why so?" Billy asks.

"I came here to see my sister and for brief respite."

"Respite from what?" Billy asks.

She pauses before answering. "Stuff, you know, the usual issues; exes like you, family, home..."

"Which is?"

"Manchester."

"What's wrong with Manchester?"

She looks up and broadcasts another smile of warmth and surprise.

"You've never been to the Hulme Estate? If you have, you'll know what I mean."

"Rough," Billy says.

"Pejoratively speaking. It's...*interesting*."

"Euphemistically speaking. I've heard about it."

"Who hasn't," she says, a little forlornly. "Hulme makes this place seem like a picnic in the park. That's why being here is like a mini break for me."

"Not your average Butlins," Billy says. "Can't you move out; come and live here—;" He checks himself; it sounds ill-considered and doltish, the cooling glow of Elsa's smile suggesting as much. She draws on the last of her cigarette and drops it with a *pfizz* into an empty wine bottle.

"Unlike you I don't have the freedom of the road."

"It doesn't always feel free," Billy says again with mild censure, for it sounds petulant in a way and ill-considered for her not having those choices. "What stops you?" he asks after a while.

A pause of reticence or caution. "People; the ones I love. My baby son Marley, my mother and sister Freya. They all need me in different ways. They're all back in Manchester, my family and my friends, trapped and vulnerable on the Hulme Estate, surrounded by chaos. I have a mission myself you see Billy, but it doesn't involve running away. On the contrary it means staying with them, caring for them, sticking together until the Council move us off the Estate. That makes it sound like a chore, but it's not. They're the ones most dear to me and to be away from them would be inconceivable. You see, we've created our own community, in the midst of all the lawlessness, we have a miniature functioning society. It's the reality of self-determination; more real than all the theorizing that happens in this place."

Billy moves forward, intrigued. "How have you done that?" he asks.

"By civilising; by looking out for each other; by protecting and caring for our own humanity. By pooling our resources and communicating and allowing no one to become isolated; from my baby boy Marley, through to our old neighbour Ivy who's eighty-something. Isolation and loneliness are the scourge of modern society and there's an unspoken pact to defeat it. So when you talk about feeling lonely, I know exactly where you're coming from."

"That sounds fascinating," Billy says. "I admire your equanimity in the face of your hardships."

"Thank you," Elsa grins, "But I wouldn't say calmness and composure are my strong suits. My mother and sisters certainly wouldn't."

"Mother, daughter, sister... *partner*?"

Elsa, chain-smoking, reaches for the tobacco almost as soon as she puts out the lit stub. "That's you fishing," she says.

"Just asking."

"Partner gone, like yours. Unlike yours he left me holding a baby."

"Ah, sorry to hear that."

"Don't be," Elsa says. "If the relationship isn't working... Besides, he gave me the gift of Marley and Marley is the love of my life. His father: bittersweet. The Estate's falling to pieces and full of lunatics but it's where my heart is, *my love*. All the people I care for are around me, my family and neighbours."

"Your light and liberty," Billy says.

"Yes," Elsa says. "There's freedom and light in love. We don't need to wander the country, I just want to get off the Estate, get out of Hulme. It's hardly a perfect personal world but the love I have there I cherish."

Drums begin to beat from somewhere in the house, a surround sound arising simultaneously from several sources and Elsa gets to her feet turning towards their source. Billy feels an unexpected touch of emptiness with her movement, the change, a draft of cold air from somewhere.

It's Belzaire, big and brash who bounds into the room towards them, laughing and clapping his hands, his eyes ablaze with enthusiasm, embers burning brightly in his coal-dark Gallic face. He's accompanied by others for who the place seems a gateway to fill up the rooms, who throw up percussion in many guises; hand drums, tom-toms, bongos and maracas produced like illicit contraband to be beaten to death. The drumbeats call people to the house, people who arrive and bring in the cold night air and more drink and laughter. They'll be there for hours during the night, spontaneously in different rooms; long, smoky, candlelit hours that become ceremonial in their shamanic qualities; persistent drumbeats in the fire lit rooms of the house with no electricity.

"Come, join us to the party," Belzaire shouts, beckoning and leaving them in quick succession.

"The other thing," Elsa says calmly turning to Billy as she goes; "Is to get my sister away from *him*."

*

Later, closer to dawn emerging from the darkness, and the house quietens. With the calm the remnants of revellers disperse to darker corners. Max returns sometime after Sam, Billy unsure of his whereabouts in that time. He, Max, strikes a brief, flashing rapport with Belzaire but quickly tires. He drinks an offering of cognac then crashes and departs again. Billy watches his friend disappear alone and notices his distance; perhaps the recent mention of his brother still lingers. Others soon retire too, leaving Billy and Belzaire, Sam and Elsa alone at the kitchen table. The stock of candles has not been replenished since their initial appearance and only a couple remain, shrouding the room in flickering gloom once more, seemingly deeper after the earlier light show.

"We're the last," Billy says.

There is no reply.

It's late and tiredness prevails with accompanying silence and foggy distance. Belzaire picks through beer cans on the table to see if any are unopened or half full. Binge detritus. A fridge used for storage has been emptied, its contents turfed on to the table; a cathartic session into which others have added and dipped, then disappeared.

"Any more?" Billy asks.

Belzaire says nothing but shows a flicker of pleasure when he comes across one remaining can of McEwan's.

"There is always this point of the evening."

Sam brushes the empty cans aside with the back of her hand; hollow, metal timpani. "Heavy," she says. Her round face is pale and her eyes bloodshot and watery.

"It's all there is," Belzaire says at last pouring a small glass for her and pushing it across the table between the drinking debris. Billy accepts, Elsa declines when offered too; Belziare ever generous in the final throes of the evening.

"Here's to the candles," Sam says taking the glass and drinking two small sips in quick succession.

"And not many of those left."

"The extravagance of electricity," Billy says.

"The suffering of the working class will be the fuel of the revolution!" says Belzaire.

Sam rolls her eyes, puts the glass to her lips again and peers into the liquid. "I have candles in my room," she says, lifting her gaze to Belzaire over the rim of the beaker.

Elsa closes her eyes.

"Bakunin? Proudhon?" Billy asks.

"Belzaire!" says Belzaire.

Sam drains her glass and returns it delicately between thumb and forefinger swinging like a tombola before resting it. She keeps the last of the liquid in her mouth before swallowing loudly.

"Shall we get them?" she asks.

Belzaire grimaces, an acknowledgement of sorts.

"Well?" she prompts.

Nostrils flaring Belzaire takes a deep breath. "You both look tired my dears," he says of the sisters. "Get some rest."

"Leave the boys to it." She smiles thinly, arches her neck and takes to her feet and stretches her arms above her head with fingers folded. The movement reveals her bare torso and the tattoos of pistol handles on her hip bones that rise from beneath the waistline of her pants. Billy notices Belzaire's overt lascivious regard and Sam's returned gaze, lifting his head so his priapic beard protrudes. He clears his throat seemingly about to speak but says nothing.

"I'll be there in a minute," Elsa says, rolling a last cigarette. She's seen it too.

Belzaire drinks, his leg bouncing repeatedly beneath the table, the ball of his foot pressed down, the heel lifted so the movement is reflexive, continual. Elsa watches him through the return of dim flickering candlelight, the darkness like tedium burgeoning.

"Why don't you paint anymore?" Sam asks as she leaves.

"No reason," he says and stares at the drink in his hand.

"You've lost your muse," Elsa says. It's a statement, not a question.

An unconvincing smile, but even its feebleness extinguishes the dark solemnity his features, the late look of night and alcohol. Billy has seen this sudden transformation earlier in the evening, quick and unexpected with a rapidly emollient effect. It's an endearing quality and by Sam's reaction to it Billy sees she buys it too.

"I've lost nothing," he says quietly and takes a long draft from the beer can that gurgles on the edge of his mouth.

She pads out of the kitchen, her bare feet gently slapping against the naked tiles. Belzaire does not disguise his leer as first his eyes then his head follow her, leaning back in his chair, head falling backwards over his shoulder. The door behind his chair closes with a gentle click and footfalls grumble against the shifting floorboards behind it.

Belzaire gives a little grunt; "She's crazy," he says softly to himself.

"She's crazy about you," Elsa says.

Belzaire makes a face that suggests her observation is simultaneously undeniable and expected, a devilish smile that borders on conceit.

"She has good taste," he says smirking.

"What about Bernie?" Elsa asks. She's been biding her time waiting for the moment and now is as good a time as any, maybe to catch him off guard late at night or early in the morning alone around the kitchen table with alcohol at hand; Belzaire's court.

He grunts again, his sunshine smile clouding.

"How does that work with her?" she continues.

Billy watches them both, anticipating the duel.

"We understand one another," he says after a while.

Elsa sits upright to observe him more closely. "Do you really?" she asks.

"I take lovers; Bernie takes lovers, Sam takes lovers, we all take lovers. In the end we will go back and forth to each other."

"And Bernie?"

"We are like boomerangs; like yoyo's we swing and bounce back to each other." Belzaire twists a mirthless smile, more of a grimace at the probing.

Billy, siding: "That's some special relationship you have with her."

"Yes, it is," Belzaire agrees.

"Do you ever feel any jealousy; or guilt?"

Belzaire laughs, inhales and breathes out as part of it, deeply and loudly. "These are pointless, Bourgeois emotions," he says. "There is no place in my life for them."

"Maybe," Elsa muses sceptically, curious at the politicisation of his feelings. "But even pointless emotions are feelings, nonetheless. All emotions are valid emotions. Sometimes we have no control over our feelings, don't you think?"

"This is true," Belzaire says, the thick black hair of his head and face moving as one. "But it is what you do with your emotions that count. Bernie and I have a deep connection and understanding. We knew it as soon as we met many years ago when we travelled with each other and stayed together when we returned to Europe. We have an *affinity*. It is not necessary to require the fidelity of the flesh. In this sense it is not perhaps conventional, but what is convention?"

"You're saying your head can rule your heart?" Billy asks.

Elsa acknowledges his supporting intervention with a wave of her hand.

"Yes, that is what I'm saying."

"And which is it that's talking now Belzaire; your head or your heart?"

Belzaire's head jerks upwards; disdain or lassitude behind the whiskers, no smile to annul them, and not for the first time, impatience and weariness.

"In youth that may seem impossible," he says. "But with

maturity comes understanding and with it familiarity of emotions. The first time you ever fall in love is like no other; full of richness and wonder. You may chase that feeling again but you will never rediscover it. That emotion will always be tainted by pragmatism. Realism and practical matters will start to sharpen your soft focus. Cynicism appears. And after a while you begin to realise that this is a virtue and not simple dilution of the sensation, or that you're getting older and more difficult to please, which of course you are. This is the beginning of your understanding of yourself; this is being self-aware."

Elsa's irked by Belzaire's didactics. "Do you love Sam?" she asks reining back the subject.

"Baah, what a question!" Belzaire says unflinchingly. "But of course. And love has a multitude of forms, for which physical urges count for only one of many. Does that sound too cold and distant for you my dear?"

Billy thinks it does, identifying himself what Belziare has detected in Elsa's expression, her body language that's exposed it; her disdain at the notion equalled by her sister's involvement.

"And Bernie?"

"Love grows and diminishes and always, always it changes," Belzaire continues. "People constantly change so if the love does not alter also it will die. With age comes appreciation of one's own emotions. I know I am a juvenile man at heart. I love the mischief and the jokes. I love to live in this house with the raw youth. I am a big kid, but where my understanding of love is concerned, I am mature; I know myself. I understand my feelings and as important I understand Bernie's and she mine. I am big and she likes lean, and so do I; why be resentful of that? Is it that I should diet or run a tread mill like a hamster and *boeuf* up my body? No, no, that will never happen I can assure you of that! So, take a younger lover for the beauty of naked youth but take my mind for what I know and who I am. Both have lust; both have the zest of life. And because of this appetite we will sleep with others because this is our urge we have no wish to deny. And in this way, Bernie and I, we have the best of both worlds. We can love one another and take other lovers as we wish too. *Comprenez-vous ce que*? Do you understand that?"

Belzaire leans back in his chair and drinks down the rest of the McEwan's then dents the can between his thumb and forefinger and places it on the table. With its bottom curved it rocks gently, and he searches for another one to drink, then in turn to Elsa and Billy.

"Why don't people crush the cans when they finish them?"

Billy sees the spread of Belzaire's broad black haired back beneath his shirt riding up as he reaches across the table. He pictures his hirsute flesh enveloping Sam's protruding hips with their pistol tattoos digging into his white softness, like the impress of a mould, a cast that remains long after the first press. He bestows his gifts on those around him, his opinions, experience, his flesh, his largesse; all on his terms.

"What about the others?" Elsa asks.

"The others?"

"Those who you and Bernie leave behind in your wake? What about them?"

"I've never denied the way things are; we are all adults and we all make our own decisions in life. I have never been covert or secretive. When two people get together, at first they only have the time for one another. But after a while the lustre begins to dull and even though the love can remain it is only realistic to recognise this otherwise you are fooling yourself. So why is a relationship exclusive in this way? When two people are together and are in love with each other why exist in a bubble that excludes others when carnal desires are sated but the love remains between them? What you see is what I am. I have never harmed anyone with how I am."

"Do you ever think they might not know themselves as you and Bernie do?"

Belaire raps his fingers on the table. "Who knows? You are looking to protect your sister Sam *mon cher*, and I don't blame you for this. We all have to work ourselves out at some point in our lives, huh?"

It's a pompous reply and at Belzaire's first acknowledgment of the sisters, at the mention of her name Elsa rises to challenge it, to defy him, to jolt him out of his self-assured pomp. "And you're ok with banging them both." Again, it's not a question.

"Of course," he says and smiles; that is, his mouth twists into the upturned curve of brilliant white teeth, the beam of his grin like the game show host who turns it on and off when the need arises. His eyes however are clouded and dark and the smile remains in his mouth but not the eyes for there is no light there, only a silvery sheen of indifference or arrogance. "And others too."

"Do you know what I think? Elsa asks, leaning closer. "I think deep down you do mind; that your intellectualising rationale remains intact so long as you are the one doing the screwing. You have it all worked out so you and Bernie can have and eat your cake together. You and this house in Denbeigh Street are made for each other and you both need it for those who satisfy your needs."

Billy listens to Elsa's heartfelt tirade and sees that Belzaire doesn't really care at all.

"You consume drifting, momentary relationships and you and Bernie play with them complicit in your self-deception that you are like two suns in the same sky around which all the planets revolve."

Belzaire smiles at this analogy but says nothing.

Elsa rises from the table and stubs the last of her cigarette in a beer can. "Know what else I think? That you're a selfish fucking pig!"

The pubs and bars of Glasgow; Summer 1989

Max leaves the house early gently closing the door behind him. In the quiet of early morning his footsteps have a dead heavy sound the hour muffles like snowfall. Everyone asleep. He inhales the chill June deeply and feels it in his head, stinging the nape of his neck; a cleansing numbness that makes him want to snap at the air. There are no people or cars and all the metal shutters on the ranks of shops are closed, some perhaps permanently. He walks briskly down the incline towards the City Centre. It feels good to be out of the house and into bright daylight, to be in motion again, smooth paced, even and swift, the brief elation of being out of the shadows and into the morning behind his lightness of step.

With his hand looped through a carrier bag of possessions he feels money in his pocket between his fingers, a levelling of sorts for this disappearing without word or traceability, forgetting the trauma of Sam's advances and the enigma of the alleged killer Bernie Frichs in his rush to leave the house. The thought quickens his pace, past the brown stone of the old buildings sprouting vegetation, brickwork that's pink in the early morning light and a chronic dusting of industrial air. In the distance a bus glides over crossroads, the first signs of life, the gradual groggy reawakening city with whisky on its breath. The house like the city will soon awaken too and with it the cursing and spitting of its people, and Billy who will discover the note left in his tobacco pouch for his first smoke of the day.

Further life here; a newsagent with bundles of papers on its step, a hot bakery, street sweepers flicking detritus from the gutters and a queue of two smoking at a bus stop; weekend workers going into the city, this being a Saturday, a half day for overtime to burn in the bookies on the *fitba* then the pubs. Two shuttered shops further on from scrubland plots and a red and white twist above an open doorway, Max peers in then enters and takes a seat.

"Can I get a shave as well?" he asks.

The barber smiles. There are gaps aside his teeth like those around his shop, his cheeks red veined and bloated.

"You can buy razors yersel nowadays you know?" he says with a chuckle. His tongue blisters through the gaps as he talks. Two old boys waiting join in the laughter.

"Can I?" Max persists.

"Aye, nae problem, pal," says the barber, and indicating with scissors: "Take a seat, son."

"Used to be standard, pal," says the man in the chair, the barber clipping his nose hair; "Trim and a shave and something for the weekend, eh son?"

"Aye; thick as a fuckin' Macintosh," says the other, "but no for the Tim's, eh?"

Max unfolds a newspaper and waits.

There is therapy then, the haircut and shave, the barber
dipping his yellow fingers in water to smooth down his hair
and the grate of the razor crackling over his neck and chin.
The absence of hair elicits clarity; he can see plainly now.
Cold, sharp, he is clean and unencumbered, his skin exposed
to the world. He leaves the barbers in this spirit and feels the
fading chill on the morning air around his scalp and ears,
the wind burning his face. Even the sounds of the city seem
louder, shrill, more immediate. He buys a newspaper and in
a charity shop next to it some clothes; jeans, T-shirt, a large
coat. In his suit jacket he feels his dead brother's presence,
that of his arms wrapping around him pulled closer with
every tug of the lapels. Removing it, he smooths down its
mis-formed shape, stained and torn in places and hangs it on
the back of the door. Then in a nearby laundrette he throws
it all into a washing machine, shoes included and sits alone
in his new clothes on a bench marked with almond cigarette
burns like bugs waiting to jump. The shoes knock against the
glass with dull thuds as do the clothes, the arms of Daniel's
jacket waving as they circle and with eyes glistening, he forces
his gaze to the form page near the back of the paper and in a
casual way chooses a runner at Leopardstown, a horse called
Fond Farewell which seems appropriate.

Then to *Tam's Cafe*, half a mile from the barbers, a
smoke hole with mirrored walls and a set of optics behind the
counter and passes on the fry up and orders toast and frothy
white coffee and a whisky instead. He wants to stay hungry
after the food. He's folded his brother's suit and carefully
slides it into a carrier bag, the smell of it, Daniel's scent finally

extinguished, smothered by Daz. Replenished, he checks himself in the mirrors and continues into town where there's a betting office with the old-fashioned *TURF ACCOUNTANT* above the doorway, smiling as he enters at a missing "*R*". There are punters already, old boys with cigarettes clamped into their teeth, rheumy eyes oblivious to the rising smoke as they check the form for their wagers. Max takes out a £20 note. It's one of the last and gives it to the manager and the slip with the words *Fond Farewell to win*. The manager stares at Max and takes them from the counter, scans the note under the UV and hands the carbon back with 25/1 circled in the corner.

"Good luck wi' that!"

Max turns to leave unable to say if the sentiments are genuine or spiced with sarcasm.

"Lay that one off Michael?" asks the assistant sitting at the counter next to him, her large fingers punching the fat calculator buttons.

Michael, the manager shakes his head and watches Max leave his shop. "No need for that, Hen," he says quietly. "No need for that."

*

The tobacco-stained note informs Billy that he's has gone and won't be returning. The details of The Horseshoe Bar in the centre of Glasgow is the rendezvous, the note unequivocal, terminal in its clarity.

Billy grabs his few things then searches the house, its many rooms and retreats for the likely location of the person he wants to see before leaving: Elsa.

But Elsa's gone already and it's Sam he finds in a mid-morning sunlight charcoal grey room.

"You're no different," she says. "People come, pass through and leave. Some return, some stay, others you never seen again."

"I can't say which category we'll belong to," he replies.

"I think we both know," she says, smiling warmly. "You want Elsa's address, don't you?"

"How did you know?" He feels the heat rising in his neck.

Sam's smile is canny, playful. "Come on now," she says.

"If that's ok?" Billy says and Sam's glow intensifies.

"Sure," she says, although it's then without certainty. "It's just, I thought..."

"What did you think?"

She reaches for a pen and finds an envelope to write the details.

"The two of you, together. It doesn't matter; we all sort of got on well," she says validating his enquiry. He watches eagerly as she writes, her tongue protruding, the pen held awkwardly, ink revealed beneath inky fingers.

"What about you?" he asks as she writes.

She stops scribing and glances up at him. "What do you mean?" she asks.

"What are you plans?"

Placing the pen down carefully she folds the envelope and hands it to him as though its passing is somehow illicit.

"I live here," she says smiling briefly before lowering her shining moon eyes.

"Your sister; you know she's concerned for you?"

"What do you expect? She's my sister."

"Ok then," Billy says. "Thanks for this."

"Give my regards to her when you see her. Say goodbye to Max and make sure you look after him."

"I sure will," he replies.

It's early afternoon when Billy locates Max in the Horseshoe Bar on Drury Street in the City centre. The place is busy with lively lunch time drinkers, clutching drinks with elbows braced around the U-shaped bar, one being Max who has his back to the taps watching the high TV at the far end of the room.

"Wow!" Billy says. "You got your haircut."

"Like it?"

"It works as a disguise; and the change of clothes too; I hardly recognised you."

Max twists on the stool and leans into the bar to get the barman's attention, ordering more drinks for both of them.

"What's happened?" he asks.

"I walked," Max says.

"Why?"

Max's dark eyes glisten in light revealed by his haircut. His cheeks are gaunt in the absence of his dark hair, face paler, lips redder. Billy notices a number of scars on his head visible now with his hair cut so short, like cue tip chalk marks on a snooker ball.

"Sam, you know..."

"I don't."

"A bit cosy Billy; you and me and the two sisters. I'm not looking for that. We're on the road, aren't we?"

"Sure, we are but we only just got here."

"And that Frichs woman."

"What of her?"

"She gave me the creeps; all the paramilitary stuff."

Billy sips at his lager in quick pulls and studies his friend, his dark, troubled cowl. He guesses the absence of his brother's suit is a sign of his issue with Bernie, its resonance.

"Too close to home, right?"

Max says nothing but the hard pull on his drink suggests as much.

"We are on the road together," Billy says. "And we can go anywhere we want to."

Max stares at the TV screen. "I had a plan," he says after a while. "It seemed like the right thing to do, to put it all in the hands of destiny again. So, I put a score on a horse."

Billy stops drinking, swallows hard and puts his glass back down on the bar. "What horse?"

"*Fond Farewell*," Max says. "I thought we could have a decent bender for a few days."

"If it came in."

"If it had come in."

"You're speaking in past tense," Billy says.

"Just watched it, up there." He points to the TV screen behind Billy's head and purses his lips. "Not to be."

"No Kalamazoo," he says, closing his eyes, no need to turn to the screen.

"No Kalamazoo," Max repeats.

"So, what," Billy says. "We've enough money for a session

now. Let's sit and have a few drinks here. Let's drink and think!"

They remain in the Horseshoe Bar until around six that evening, drinking and talking over the details of the last few days; the Bowman gig, their escape, Billy's cousins, the house in Denbeigh Street, Samantha and sister Elsa and the various random characters there, Bernie's suspected dark past, Belzaire's imperiousness. By the evening they've determined to move on and be out of Glasgow in the morning. The bar quickly fills with football supporters, Bhoys, boyish, boisterous and stimulating, a surge of a green crowd pouring in with the game over and the swell is a sea-change, rowdy and sweating, deliberate pushing and lurching, jostling for drinks at the bar for the attention of the meagre staff. Money waving in the air and the noise levels rise. This sudden influx of crowding men is a welcome change as they gather around Max and Billy vying for service and the effect is invigorating by necessity for the volume of their own voices and the engulfing dynamism of the crowd prevents them from declining any further into maudlin drunkenness.

No longer daunted, more excited by their options they consider their destinations with growing outlandish ebullience, the thought of moving on being thrilling and not problematic. Drinks are spilled and refreshed by the surrounding mob by way of contrition. Ignoring the obligatory *Sassenach* jibes Max and Billy are sucked into rounds with groups of men and the raillery becomes fluent and easy and with it the laughter, the *Craic* a life of its own. They wear the close and humid swell of male company like a blanket, wrapped in its earthy warmth with the odour of smoky breath bursting from laughter, the whiskery scratch of connection and the stain of spilt pints. It's a time to be drinking in the pubs again, in the working class domain of machismo and bravado, like they had in Liverpool, the other great working class city. Now Glasgow, in a bar long enough to accommodate all the singing and swaying and elbows and pissing and spitting in grandest Victorian toilets of shining brass and fluted ceramics, revelling in base masculine emotions of lads in a football crowd; pride, bravery, loyalty and love, virility, of winning and losing and of nothing in between, the ironic cheers, the banter, piss take and laughter.

Later, the crowds begin to thin and Max and Billy hang on to a small band of men, all Rabs and Tams and Wullys, moving from bar to bar where the music is loud and the slurring talk challenging. Gradually they too disperse but not before local opinion of the places to visit in the city have been garnered and with recommendations Billy and Max take to the busy streets. Drunk and assaulted by the cold air the nagging fact of having nowhere to stay seems insignificant and they continue to see where the vagaries of the night will take them.

A handful of bars down, an hour or so in each until they're sat in The Three Blackbirds; all amber frosted panes in a double bay window over which hangs the sign of the eponymous creatures perched in a tree. It's an effort to enter with the doorway busy and a loud dispute involving several people spilling at the entrance, men and women, young and old, some entering, others trying to leave, among them a man and a woman who are at the centre of the argument. Gone midnight the bar is beginning to fill out and the drizzle begin to swirl outside. At the busy bar, the service is quick and careless, spilt pints slammed on to towels. Billy is side on to the bar when he feels a hand on his shoulder and turns to see the gaunt features of someone he vaguely recognises whose pale and watery eyes drill into his own, his face too close, for anything other than a startled reaction. He's wired, teeth and gums working overtime, his denim jacket hanging off his narrow frame and the cuff of his wrist tugging at Billy's shoulder like a hastily dressed mannequin.

"*You!*" he shouts over the clamour of the bar; an odd salutation.

Billy looks at Max for enlightenment and sees his friend doesn't recognise him either.

"Ah seen yous at Denbeigh Street, the night aye?"

Billy's eyes narrow gathering recollection. Over his shoulder, in the murky depths of the bar's long room he sees more pale faces staring at them from a table beyond; one other face he thinks he recognises, a friend of someone from the squat perhaps, he can't be sure.

He says nothing. The non-committal response triggers a momentary furrow of confusion across the man's face that makes him look stupid and ugly, then disappears as quickly as it has surfaced. He presses on regardless.

"Mah name's Jet. What you doing out here?" he asks.

"Having a couple of beers," Billy says.

Jet's head jerks backwards then back into Billy's face, staccato movements like a bird pecking a worm in the open field.

"Okay mate, just asking," he says alighting upon Billy's reticence, his tongue thick in his mouth as he talks. "Just *making enquiries.*"

Billy doesn't like him; the encroachment into his personal space, his emphasis on detective work, natural for him, obligatory, it only adds to his aversion of this man. He doesn't remember his from the squat. He glances at Max and sees he is studying Jet intently, narrowed eyes moving quickly trying to work him out.

"This your pal?" Jet says, picking up on Billy's own eye contact with Max.

He reproaches himself for this ocular slip but Max, quickly seizes the initiative and reaches out to grab Jet's hand, shaking it from behind at shoulder height due to the bar crush so the hand gesture is more a light grasp of the fingers, his wrist angled to the ceiling. "Hello," he says. "Who are you?"

Jet smiles. His teeth are chipped and stained like old teacups. "John," he says. "People call me Jet; you can call me Jet an'all."

"Jet," Max repeats.

"Aye," says Jet.

"Why Jet?" Max asks.

Jet smiles conspiratorially and narrows his eyes, suggesting the reason for this is obvious. His shoulders rise and fall repeatedly as though moving to music. He flicks a glance at Billy then back again to Max, his eyes accompanied by head movements without independent motion within the sockets adding to his avian-like qualities; wiry, faltering, nervous; dipping in an appropriately named bar.

"Always jetting around from place to place," he says moving from one foot to the next and back again, upsetting those pressed against him, excited, agitated.

"Right," says Max.

Jet's smile remains though contained within his mouth tinged with an edginess his upper lip reveals as a twitch like a demented Elvis impersonator. His head is in perpetual motion, moving around above his neck draped in the loose-fitting collar.

"I'm having a few drinks with my pals over there," Jet says. "Come and join us."

His breath is sour, and Billy moves his glass up to his mouth to cup his nose against the miasma, taking a small step backwards, out of range. The request feels more an instruction than invitation.

"Come on," Jet says and turning back towards his table, presses something into Billy's hand as he does. He looks over his shoulder as he walks away, raises his eyebrows and winks at Billy. "Come on."

"A wrap," Billy says to Max as Jet sits at the table with his two friends, all of them by now watching him at the bar, peering through the throng, tracking the delivery of the package, a little white hook to bring them in.

"Recognise him?"

Max shakes his head.

"What do you reckon?"

"Do you want to end up all night drinking with these goons?"

Max thinks for a moment. "No; but the gear might come in handy if we don't find a place to crash."

"I'll pass," Billy says.

Max looks at the three characters talking at the table, glancing at them at the bar. "Who is that?" he asks.

"He must have come to the squat last night and recognised me. Motorhead."

"Hence the name."

Billy nods. Max sees his teeth work his bottom lip.

"Trustworthy?"

Billy raises his eyebrows and puffs out his cheeks, the lip released. "Does he look it?" he says.

Max looks at the three again. Jet catches his eye and wobbles his head and beckons them over again as he takes his seat.

"We should leave," he says.

"What about this?" Billy says pushing his upturned fist towards Max's abdomen.

"Give it to me," he says, taking the wrap from Billy's hand at hip height.

A man in a Crombie tries to work his way to the bar. "Are you's two getting served or just wanking each other off there?" he says and dips his shoulder and drives forward between them.

Max moves aside and leans into Billy's ear. "We'll go over and give it back; have a quick drink then make our excuses."

He hoists his drink above his head and walks over to the table and Billy follows. With a quick hand he presses the wrap back into the cold dough of Jet's palm, a fumbled movement the receiver doesn't expect. "Thanks for the offer," he says; "but we'll pass."

Jet eyes him with suspicion and confusion, the now familiar bird face returning then slowly puts the wrap in the coin pocket of his jeans. "Alright," he says; "Whatever. Pull up a pew. This here's my brother Stuart and ma pal Joseph."

Joseph, wire-framed and weak-looking grins but says nothing. That he looks more like Jet than Stuart throws Billy who thinks he might have confused the introduction.

"How do?" says Stuart; a large man pale in an ill-fitting nylon T shirt that looks like it could ignite with a stray cigarette, an inadequate covering for his distended belly. His voice is high-pitched, the excess skin around his neck constricting it to a falsetto utterance. There are tattoos around his navel, indecipherable, a few of the letters exposed but blurred.

He turns to his brother. "These two guys from the hoose on Denbeigh Street you were talking aboot just noo?" he asks.

Max remains standing before them with the distance of the table between. His appearance is composed, and Billy is more at ease because of this. He sees that Stuart is wedged between the table and the back wall and looks anything but relaxed. Joseph quietly watches, his dark eyes set wide across his face and thick lips constantly whispering to himself.

"Aye," Jet jerks his head, then to Billy. "Sit yersels doon."

A stool slides from beneath the table propelled by Stuart's foot. His thick legs fill out grey tracksuit bottoms where there should be slack; the flesh between the drawstrings and white socks dappled dark and purple. "Take the weight of your pegs and make yersels at hame. You's two are at the house wi' all the heppies and the like aye?"

Despite their pact of swift exit and to Billy's disappointment Max takes the stool. He's fluent, sitting quickly but without hesitancy that might betray vulnerability of sorts. Billy follows his lead so he's not the only one standing.

"Correct," says Max.

"Ne'er trust a heppie, eh?" Stuart growls leaning forward and winking at Max. The flesh beneath his eyes and jowls are such that there seems to be an invisible force above his head pulling the skin against gravity, puffiness with its own elasticity.

"Ah didnae recognise *you*," Jet says, "only you friend here."

Max observes him but says nothing to this; there is nothing to say.

"Ma brother here tells me of all sorts of stuff that goes on it that hoose," Stuart says.

"Really?" Max says nonchalantly.

"It's good for business," Jet says.

"A right fucking mad hoose of free love; orgies and all sorts," Stuart continues. "Birds who dip their tetties in paint; blokes who drink their own pesh. Is that what really goes on there eh?"

"Jet's a vivid imagination," Joseph says, his first words thin and watery, he looks to Jet whose inane smirk suggests he is not affronted, more proud of his observation.

"I wouldn't know," says Max.

"Tell me then, Big Man," Stuart says, the edge of hostility juxtaposing his jovial face. "What would you know?"

Joseph shrinks from the table and pulls his pint with him, holds it before his face and peers over the rim of the glass. Jet's eyes widen and flick from one person to the next, excitement of anticipation across his face. Max, at odds with Billy's expectations leans forward, puts his elbows on the table on either side of his drink and rests his chin on his hands. "Well, your brother here, the nodding dog, he missed the bit about the child sacrifices," he says staring Stuart squarely in the face. "Every full moon, up on the roof."

Stuart says nothing, a momentary hiatus of halted breathing and silence before he begins to chuckle at this and cast a glance at his brother then back to Max. "You're a funny guy!" he says. "Ahm sorry if I offended ye about your pals being heppies an' all just noo but see, ma brother isnae a dog either ken? I know he talks a load of shite," he takes a sip of beer, savours it over lip and tongue then continues; "but that's just poetic licence. And ah know about the retail too, that shite ma wee brother takes roond there to shove up people's hooters and that's fine if that's the way you want tae live your lives. It disnae bother me at aw. Just dinnae muscle the patch, ken?"

Billy interjects quickly. "We're moving out, tonight," he says, his voice emerges shrill and the conversation halts abruptly for a second time. He senses the heat rising in his neck and burning in his ears and draws hard on a hastily rolled cigarette to conceal it.

"Ah don't blame you's, says Jet. "It's a shaytehaw!" And turning to his brother; "You know there's no leccy in the hoose,"

Stuart beams as far as his spongy face will allow. "No

leccy?" he says excitedly, his eyes glistening with disbelief. "How can you fuckin live wi'out electricity?"

"Imagine living wi'out the leccy," Joseph joins in.

"The Corpy cut it off," says Jet.

"Even ma council hoose has leccy" says Joseph. "And that's goat tae be the biggest shet pet in Glasgow."

"How can ye live in the fuckin' dark for Chrissake," Stuart says, shaking his head.

"At least in the dark you cannae see the shite," Joseph says, and they all laugh merrily and forcibly.

Billy leans into Max's ear. "We need to go," he says quietly.

"Where you's off tae then?" Stuart asks. "Back tae Londin or wherever it is you's came from."

"Somewhere with electricity?" Billy says.

Laughter: this time with more warmth and a grip of tension is released enough to create a gap to fill with goodbyes. Max leans backwards and Billy sees a mouthful maybe two remains in his glass, enough to be able to toss back and return it to the table with an emphatic thump to indicate a full stop, a halt to the proceedings from which they can depart and bid their farewells.

Stuart watches him as though reading his thought. "Some advice for yous two, if you're staying in the city the night; you'll need tae be careful drinking in the wrong parts of town with those accents, ken?" he says.

"Thanks for the advice," he says. "We will."

"What about this place?" Max asks. "Is this the wrong part of town or the right part?"

Stuart gives a furtive glance to his friend Joseph sitting to his left and forces a laugh that causes his sizable frame to move with the effort, his head wobbling on his shoulders. Joseph, withdrawing again, sensing something, says nothing.

"He's just saying best stay focussed," says Jet. "That's friendly advice. And mah friendly advice is tae always heed friendly advice. You never can tell."

"The divided city, eh?" Billy says quietly and begins gathering his things; tobacco, cigarette papers, lighter, the conversation terminated, off and away with the advice, good, bad or indifferent.

Stuart shuffles in his seat and leans forward. "You never can tell when there might be some big ugly Feenyin standing in a dark corner somewhere ready to put his big size ten up your fat jacksie," he says and winks at Billy.

"Are we safe in here?" asks Max. He looks over his shoulders left and right and Billy knows this is a mock gesture and hopes the others won't see it that way.

"We need to go, Max," he says again, louder this time.

Stuart laughs once more, his shoulders rolling and cheeks squeezing his eyes shut with the mirthless glee. He takes his pint glass in his hand, the drink small in his thick white fingers and drinks and the others are quiet awaiting a cue from his response. "They might be around the next corner," he says after a couple of mouthfuls.

"Let me know when you see one," says Max.

Again, the chuckles, the Oriental eyes. "How do you know you're no looking at one right noo?"

Jet waves his hand in the air. "Get tae fuck man," he says.

This time it's Max who smiles. "I couldn't give a fuck if I am or not," he whispers.

"Well, mibbee ye should."

To Billy's dismay he sees Max bristling. "All that Proddy and Tim shit means fuck all to me, mate."

Stuart's eyes widen, his eyebrows raised in thin, perfect arcs like dirty fingernails. "Mibbee not to you," he replies, "it willnea matter what you think when your heids all stoved intae a barrel."

Max finishes his drink at last and gets to his feet. "The same shit my brother had to put up with!"

The filial comment seems to throw him briefly. "I'm no saying it's right or wrong," Stuart replies adjusting, floating his upturned palms to shoulder height and waving them around him. "I'm just telling like it is."

Max sneers; "Proddy; Catholic; Rangers and Celtic; the Blues and the Greens; it doesn't mean shit to me!"

Stuart chuckles again. "Aye, Queen and Country; Pope and Vatican! We're never happy wi'out two camps to prop oorsels up. But it's no a game of noughts and fuckin' crosses pal! So mibbees you and your sweetheart here would be well to mind that, ken?"

Mock laughter and Jet's eyes are dancing with delight while Joseph recoils further into his seat. "Dinnae shoot the messenger here!" he says.

Billy grabs his friend, but Max pushes him away. "I think you fuckers actually need each other; you'd be lost with no one to hate?"

Stuart stands up quickly now and the movement and the

girth of the man pushes the table outwards, knocking over the glasses and the ashtray from its centre. "You think what you like pal. I'm just offering you some friendly fucking advice here," he says.

"Aye; friendly advice," Jet repeats.

Max takes a step back, the spilt liquids spreading, glasses rolling around the table and continues; "Fuck your advice! And fuck you; fuck all of you!"

Billy grabs Max's arm again, more firmly this time and yanks him sideways. "Max, we need to go now."

"That's right," Stuart says. "Listen to your boyfriend here. Do yoursels a favour and get the fuck out!"

Max leans down and fumbles for his carrier bag from under the stool, the one containing his brother's suit and shouts, "You can kiss the Pope's ring, kiss the Queen's arse; and kiss my fucking ring!" and turns to leave.

The men who emerge from the shadows, prophetically as Stuart has predicted are small but powerful; one tattooed with the four suits of a card deck on the knuckles of each hand. Max turns from the table and walks straight into them. The swinging boot is too accurate to be coincidental smashing Max fully on his coccyx but the second takes his standing leg and already off-balance with Billy's imploring manhandling sweeps him like a scythe. On the floor he's suddenly game. Others emerge too. He hits the deck, wrist first, then elbow, the floor sticky to the touch and littered with cigarette ends. Light refracts through the arcing lager spilling before his eyes, an strip of gold brightness in the bar light. It splashes along the dark floor and with it more colour; a tartan beer mat, the blue and black tiles of the floor. The space beneath the table is dark and grey and then speckled red, brighter now with the blood erupting from his busted mouth. It's these colours that Max observes, clearer than they should be, flashing and whirling before him.

Then everything goes dark.

Part Two – Some Rare Delight in Manchester Town

The Hulme Estate, Manchester; Summer 1989

Always the footsteps and voices; the heartbeats of the landings. Whispers and footfalls glide past the bolted door towards the stairwells where strangers go about their business. Mostly they go up because they all rise from the pits of Hell, higher and higher, never to come down again. But where do they go, these strangers? It must be to Heaven to be with the angels where they all talk in hushed voices, undecipherable utterances of the messengers of an unfathomable deity. It's God's work they're doing. It's better not to enquire, too dangerous to find out. For your own safety, just in case. They're on the outside and you're wrapped up in here.

Manchester; Madchester; *Gunchester*!

Building blocks of hope and despair shoe-horned into square boxes with traces of human life, rounded and uneven in a world of straight lines, upright chessboard, white façades and black windows, glazed and glassless, an entire world of vertical and horizontal planes. Here concrete pillars uphold level balconies, the doors, panels and windows so perfectly spaced over and again; door, panel, glass, door, panel glass and stretching out into the great parallel space beyond. Such an angular and unnatural cubic world of clean concrete angles should allow for no deviance from its cemented rigidity. The perpendicular rules. The strip lights visible beneath the balconies disappear like tracer rounds, their target the boxes and blocks of shadows and light and repeated between concrete colonnades, downpipes, drainpipes, squares of paving laid evenly before all. It helps to batten down shutters from top to bottom but the walls have ears and the ceilings collapse and the floors may rise up still. They frequently do, and in pours the dreadful noise of the outside.

The Hulme Estate.

But people? The soft residues and retinues of cats, dogs, rubbish, posters on the walls pasted and repasted, cars used and abandoned, pavements cracked and stained, bollards broken, a nonconformity brought to the cubist world, resisting the realm of angles. Banks and banks of graffiti bring colour to the grey and sweeping swirls to the linear, like giant screens broadcasting their messages countering the objectives of notional models of living. Spreading out spiderlike, the mark of the youth; ink and spray-paint ivy that creeps across the walls like capillaries coursing throughout the Estate, no space spared: *Fuck Work; House of fun? Pigs Out; The Second Coming; GET DRUGS HERE.*

Far below a name; Otterburn Close, a sign of things long gone, a wistful relic of what was once before when anything so rustic now seems inconceivable. Above and beyond where they all end up, looming into shape through the peephole, the infamous crescents ominously rise and stretch out of the black soil. These massive cathedrals recline into formidable giant arcs of slapping wetness, the brown crescents curving around, a hug in a tower block; simultaneously hospitable and threatening. Bright lights and deep obscurities, intimacy and exclusion, the thinking behind them and the bittersweet it is, lawless and free.

"I heard someone, here."

Shadows flicker on the walkways, hooded and faceless, murmuring coded language and passing unknown secrets. One comes by as the other leaves. The talk is encrypted, deliberately arcane for minimum exposure, maximum distress.

"Who's that then Tammy?" Elsa stealthily slides her toe into the just open door for her neighbour's own security, though she knows she won't see it that way.

There's no answer and the face barely illuminated by the fizzing strip light recedes further, the door knocking Elsa's foot as she knew it would.

"I heard a knock on the wall Tammy; are you sure everything's ok?"

"Is Sam here?"

A dusty breeze kicks up from the courtyard below, a timpani of beer cans.

Elsa sighs. "She sends her love to you Tammy."

A strange cry drifts from somewhere, takes off on the wind.

"Did you see her?"

"In Glasgow, yes."

"Not here?"

"No, not here Tammy."

There's a pause. She's processing the information but her demeanour reveals that something's not right.

"Is she alright Elsa?"

Elsa withdraws her foot. "I'll let you know as soon as she comes back. Just as long as you're ok; ok?"

"Someone mentioned her name," Tammy says quickly with just enough time before she closes the door, her self-maintained isolation involuntary. Elsa steps away from it towards the balcony edge, almost dismisses the parting comment, then begins to consider its significance before something wholly physical jolts her from her contemplation.

The something is a man.

It's his uncertainty that makes the difference, his indecision. Turning towards Tammy's flat he walks straight into her standing in the darkness of the access deck from the top of the stairs. He falls sideways and with him another who slides down the wall. They must be off their heads but then there's a cry of pain, a dog's yelp and a chasing whimper. Another step back, Elsa reels from the impact of the collision, startled by the sound; both his and her own. Winded and gasping for air a flash of her mother's condition comes to her and the panic the want of breath brings. She braces for a strike or a verbal threat at least, instinctively cowering, arms raised to face. Instead, the man vacillates, unsure of who to go to first; his moaning companion doubled and sliding to the floor or Elsa wide-eyed and ready, sliding away herself, hands trembling before her in a gesture set for defence, not submission. Caught between the two he babbles, and she knows then she will not be harmed.

"Jesus; are you alright?" he asks.

"You frightened me," she says.

"I'm sorry. It's me!" He indicates to the missing light above them.

Elsa is parallel to Mrs Smith's front door and hears the awkward and familiar footstep of Martin padding down the hallway inside, moving towards the door with more urgency than usual. He fiddles with the locks, alerted by the commotion. She glances pointedly over her shoulder at the door to bring attention to the sounds of the unlocking latches.

"What's the matter with him," she asks, turning back, pointing to the man on the ground.

Then Billy steps out of the shadow and into the light of recognition and with his face comes Elsa's own enlightenment of the person standing before her. With excessive contrition, Billy straightens and extends his hands towards her. "It's me," he says again. "It's me; Billy." And to add clarification, "From Denbeigh Street."

"You," she says, slowly not without caution. Ignoring the salutation, she turns instead as the door opens behind her and Martin Smith stands wide in the doorway, vague and uncertain, a fuzzy silhouette of linty clothes, hair and whiskers. She wishes he appears somehow more imposing but knows he never will. He peers at them on the walkway, his face dark in dim light behind him she knows will be slack-jawed and gawping, white spittle about the corner of his lips, her certainty verified by his question.

"Whass goin'on?" he asks. His head moves from side to side, a caterpillar on a leaf, his eyes adjusting to the darkness, unable to fathom with requisite speed. "Elsa, that you? You alright Elsa?"

The sound of her name reassures her, certifies her connectivity, a concern, doubly so as Martin repeats it. She turns back to Billy and Max and waits for their answer, reasoning it's for them to answer the question.

Billy almost obliges. "Sam," he says. "She gave me your address."

Momentary silence and bar her neighbour's sustained head weaving they remains still, weighing things up on the narrow decking, the damp concrete encasing it all.

"Why did you come here?" Elsa asks eventually, not unreasonably Billy thinks. The way they'd left things in Glasgow, it isn't how he imagined. She seems disappointed.

Martin breaks the silence with typical brusqueness. "Who are you?" he asks, blunt and direct.

From behind Billy, Max pushes himself off the balcony wall, a move that requires him to dip his shoulders forward to gain sufficient momentum. He flicks Billy's arm with the back of his hand. "Give me a hand...," he says.

Elsa stands to one side and sees Max's grimacing features.

"My God it's you, I didn't recognise him... you're hurt," she says. "What happened?"

"Elsa, it's a long story," Billy says.

Martin repeats; "Is everything ok Elsa?"

"I think so," she replies without turning to answer him.

"Are you sure?"

"She's fine," Max says loudly, wincing with effort.

"Why *did* you come here?" Elsa asks again, this time more assertively.

Billy straightens too once his friend is more upright. "Because we need help."

*

"They're trouble."

Elsa's mother Kathy has her hands thrust hard into shallow pockets so the cardigan is stretched into a hard lines. It's the same shape as her mouth and she knows it. It's a grimace, a stance that shows her daughter just how unhappy about the situation she is.

"Why do you say that?"

"I've been round the block a few times to know it. I smell it, and those two are on the nose, alright. They jumped you out there. They're trouble."

Elsa smiles at her mother's typical distortion of her version of events. "They didn't jump me," she says. It would have riled her once; now she has her measure, shows more composure. "If anything, it's the other way around; I spooked them. Besides, I know them, at least one of them." But not really, Elsa thinks, not at all.

Kathy Kelly pulls at the sleeves, looks at her wristwatch then lowers the cuffs over her palms one after the other. It's an instinctual habit Elsa knows only too well when her mother is challenged.

"What do they want, at this time of night?" she asks, her narrow chin sliding forward. It's turned midnight.

"They're looking for a place to stay," Elsa replies.

"Here?"

"Uh-huh."

"What are we now, a hotel? Send them over to John Nash with all the other wasters."

Elsa drags a chair from beneath the kitchen table and steps up on it. There was a time when the noise of chairs scraping over the kitchen floor would have elicited broom handle raps on the ceiling from below, Sheila McEllin and her overweight husband Tom, rehoused some months before, a benefit of sorts. She reaches up above the kitchen cupboard where there are a number of tins gummy with grease and dust and checks each one by shaking them. "I think these guys are different," she says. "I met them at Sam's house in Glasgow a few days ago. Billy and Max. One of them is hurt."

Kathy looks up at her. "Hurt how?" The chin remains in position.

"He thinks he might have broken his ribs."

"How so? He's a fighter."

Not conjecture, fact.

"I don't know Mam," she says. "They say they got jumped in Glasgow the night before, so they baled and ended up here instead."

Kathy rises slowly. Moving unsteadily across the kitchen she turns to face her daughter, her hands resting on the crumbed surface, wrists outwards, white with the pressure. A tiny pulse is emitting a shadow below her cardigan sleeves. Even this minor manoeuvre across the small room causes her to wheeze, the struggle for air narrowing her thin face further. With it, Elsa's unease for her mother's health grows proportionally each day.

"Glasgow, you, say?" she says seeking spaces for breath. "That's a long way, to be coming from." Kathy Kelly's Irish always flowers with scepticism. "What makes you so, sure they're not bullshitters, just like the other waifs and strays, around the Estate?"

Elsa shrugs. "I don't," she says, offering no other reason. "Billy seems honest enough. His friend needs a place to stay."

"Oh, sure," Kathy concedes. "And what about Baby?"

Elsa wants to correct her; *Marley*, she should insist but this isn't the right time to be addressing her mother's intransigence. "I wasn't thinking they could stay here, Mam. I was thinking Mr Henry's old place. I still have the key; somewhere. They could stay there a day or two and be no trouble to us."

Kathy leans forward and returns to the other side of the kitchen, pulling the second of the two chairs from beneath the table again and returning to where she'd been sitting moments before.

"How do you know; they won't cause trouble?" she says. "Mr Henry's is mighty close. They're encroaching."

"We can't stop them *encroaching*," she says. She doesn't like her mother's use of this word, meaning trespassing, a kind of violation. "Besides, these two are not the same as the others. Like I say, they're different."

The "others" Elsa refers to are the new arrivals on the Estate, a far more problematic influx of late than usual. The place has always had plenty of issues; troubled families, drugs, poverty, mental health worries, accompanying crime and violence. She, her family and friends have grown up with it all, gone to school with it, hung out with it, pushed boundaries and got into trouble together. Drugs have been a part of her life in one guise or another; mostly dope, occasionally Class A's if she was able to afford them, but nothing too serious. They're always around. Most of them but not all have steered clear of the *heavies*, like heroin and crack. Even Nelson who is trading plenty, weed and now E's, wouldn't get involved with that; it adds a different dimension he said, the punters more desperate, further at the edge, anything for a fix. Nothing is safe with heroin and crack addicts around. Didn't she know it, what with Mark Tulip roaming the landings? And the new arrivals are like this, only more so; wreckers, smackheads, crackheads, selfish, attracted to the lawlessness; they don't give a shit. It's all she can do to keep them at arm's length until her family is relocated, off the Estate and away from it all. The noise, the raves, the madness, these things don't bother her at all. If anything, they help by adding some humour to their dreadful situation. What does trouble her is the robbing, the threats of violence, not the gangs, they've always been there and fight their own battles. But the addicts, the loners glazed and wired and out of control who smash the place up and start fires. Now Marley's in the world and it adds far more weight to her anxiety. The fear of fire worries her the most with all the surrounding empty flats for anyone to break into.

Elsa considers this thought then voices it to give it credence. "You know Mam, I think I'd rather know who are in the flats around us; it feels safer. Anybody can move in at any time; they boot the doors in, and they move the junk in and set light to things. At least these two have introduced themselves. They asked if I knew where there's a place to stay. They came here specifically to see me; they didn't just smash their way in."

Kathy nods and gets to her feet again. Her restlessness is born of a combination of pain and the doctor's advice about mobility but more so her natural energy facing effrontery. The brief walks around the access decks and her movements between rooms in the flat are her sole forms of exercise. Her arrival is precipitated by reedy breathing, a spectral glide formed by the shape of her mouth, opened wider with heavier gasping, though the blockage is deeper in her lungs, rendering the wide mouth ineffective, a whizz-topper stuck in her craw. She's always suspected the asbestos on the Estate and that has firmed into a genuine cause now, after years of denial.

"Your man," she says, "the one who's hurt. Why doesn't he go to hospital?"

"I don't know," she says. "Maybe he will tomorrow."

"Well, I don't like it; it doesn't seem right with Baby here as he is." She wants to look Elsa in the eyes, to challenge her face to face and is frustrated by her searching up high for the key to the John Henry's old place. Thumb and forefinger at the hem, she pinches Elsa's jeans around her thigh and pulls at it a few times to get her attention.

Elsa gasps. "Here it is," she says, holding a silver front door key aloft with a broken leather fob hanging by a thread, at last turning to face her mother, knowing fully the reason of her irritation, a little guilty pleasure. Elsa marks her mother's irked expression and also her fatigue, the same fire of the old matriarch still burning within now with less intensity, no longer with the heat it once had. Her powers have waned as the people have left her fold, rehoused or died. Now her health contributes to her diminishing authority. Elsa wants to feel sad for her and faced with that familiar squat stance and hard eyes now worn and diluted does so to a point, the spirit still there but not the means to deliver.

Kathy Kelly is an aging pugilist unable to keep up with the young ones, no longer ruling the roost because there's no more roost to rule. Her hegemony is gone; this is the end of an era. When the ranks of terraced streets were cleared to make way for the new build late in the 1960's Kathy embraced the new and welcomed the change. The new Hulme Estate was the way forward. Unlike many of her neighbours she harboured no reluctance, no nostalgia for those bricked up, bricked in, back to back hovels the air raids spared, even if you could talk to your neighbours in the ginnels. The housing was damp, mouldy, draughty, broken, unfit for any community, even one with an indomitable spirit like theirs. It attracted vermin and was ingrained with deprivation. Change was coming and it would be a new age that left the dreary post war decline behind. Kathy championed the Corporation's vision, the thinking that lay behind it, its reasoning. Working for change was a good thing; it brought out the inherent socialist from within.

She watches Elsa carefully stepping down from the chair and sliding it back under the table, everything rickety and rocking. It's not just the furniture, it's all around them, the walls, the ceiling, the entire block is creaking and crumbling within and outside. It all went wrong so quickly. After only a few months it was clear the new buildings were not fit for purpose, that the designs were wrong, the materials substandard. The ground was poor, the falls settled and cracks appeared. The universal heating harboured cockroaches, and those spared infestations suffered damp and mould instead; the very things they were supposed to leave behind. Within a few years families began to move away but the poverty endured, along with the ills of association; theft, muggings, drugs, isolation, health problems, mental and physical. Misguided or deluded at best, misled and cheated for many. Kathy's pride exposed, not culpability just intransigence. She fought for them, tirelessly, endlessly, despite the distrust. Now, decades later, they're the remnants on the deck of a ship long sunk to the bottom.

"I'm not asking your permission Mam," Elsa says more harshly than she'd intended, then reaches out with both hands and rubs her mother's shoulders to soften the words.

Kathy shrugs the gesture and turns away and Elsa, unwilling to give further succour leaves the kitchen and heads down the hallway with the key firmly held in her grip. As she opens the front door Billy and Max are stood on the balcony, smoking in silence where she's left them some ten minutes before. Together they look up at her, expectantly.

"Here," she says handing them the key and two spare blankets gathered in a bundle. "It's three doors down that way. There's some graffiti, *Kenny* scrawled on the door, no number, just *Kenny*. Just don't wreck the place. And lose the key and you die."

Max smiles wide enough to reveal the gap where a tooth

is missing at the side of his mouth. "Course not," he says and reaches for the blankets, taking them gingerly under his arm.

Billy takes the key, holds it up, smiles in acknowledgment and follows his friend to the vacant flat where she watches them enter and hears the sound of the bolt slide behind them.

Elsa's sleep is broken that night. Her mother has been colder towards her and retired to bed before she returned to the kitchen from delivering the key and blankets. Elsa calculates as much. She harboured some vague thoughts of discussing things further with her, but Kathy's absence has settled that.

She checks on Marley regularly. On occasions she prods him at night when he sleeps, gently disturbing him, just to stir him, to marvel at him, his movements, his stretching and yawning, to hear him breathe; the simple things she is so moved by. She tucks his blanket beneath his hands and finds him awake, not crying but restless, lying on his back in motion, limbs moving in his jerky, fitful manner. She lifts him out of the cot, settles him in the crook of her arm with his head close to hers and walks around the small room, back and forth, jogging and rocking, singing soothing words and gentle rhymes of nonsense. He looks about him, arching his back and peering over her shoulder, active and observant at the new world about him. She inhales his smell and listens closely to his voice, his taking in air and the clacking saliva from his mouth and the back of his throat, the tiny passageways of his nose. He has creamy dark skin with tiny white spots about his nose and cheeks, shiny black hair, clean and new in tiny, downy curls. He is her preoccupation, the look and touch and smell of him that fixates her for hours. Like all new mothers she supposes the delights she must have given to her own mother during the first months of her own life, perhaps Sam more so and Freya less; the recurring patterns of thoughts a new-born life throws to the fore.

Exhausted, she returns his little form to the cot, but he begins to cry as soon as he's down; a learning curve, she shouldn't have disturbed him in the first place. Unable and unwilling to leave him unsettled she spends the following hours rocking and soothing him back to sleep. Eventually when she feels able to return him to his cot she retires to her own room. Beyond tired herself now she lies awake and listens to the sounds coming from the Estate; shouts, distant loud music, a car's revving engine. Disordered thoughts run through her mind; Marley, the changes he's brought about in her outlook and in the day to day practicalities of her life; her mother, Freya, Tammy and the others and now Billy and his friend, their decision to head to Manchester, Max injured, both at Mr Henry's flat; then Nelson, his whereabouts, Mark Tulip, dangerous, she thought it was him at first that evening when she'd collided with Billy; her work at the hospital, maternity, motherhood, Marley, her mam Kathy. Round and round it goes and snaps her back to consciousness as she tires.

She rises at six, wired, goes back to check Marley and seeing him awake again, or still, scoops him up once more with a heavy sigh and holds him firmly to her while she makes herself tea in the kitchen. The flat is silent and still. She reaches for the cigarettes from the cupboard above the sink and slips them into the pocket of her anorak, wraps it around her, places Marley in the pram in the hallway and unlocks the front door.

The cool air hits her nostrils briefly stinging a spot between her eyes that causes them to water. Instinctually now she pulls the cover higher under Marley's chin; vicarious insurances against cold, hunger, comfort and other basics; an innate product of child rearing. Thin tears film both their eyes. She blinks away the moisture to bring into sharper focus above the hood of the pram and the outline of Billy up ahead leaning over the balcony outside Mr Henry's flat further down the crescent, smoking a cigarette and looking out across the green.

He turns to her as she steps out on to the balcony.

"Hi," he says. "I couldn't sleep." Then, "not because of the flat, I just woke up. I needed a smoke."

With the cool morning air around her throat Elsa pulls at the lapels of her anorak, squeezing them closer. Billy watches her manoeuvre the baby's pram, bucking the front and back wheels into a position against the balcony wall. He can see the baby's hands reaching for the plastic shapes strung across the width, hitting them irregularly but with intent.

"I couldn't sleep either," she says.

"So, this must be...?" Billy asks clutching for the baby's name, kicking himself for being so slow.

Elsa reaches for the handle. "Marley," she says rocking the pram, staring into its white and linty depths, disappointment again framing her words.

"Yes," Billy says. "I remember now. After Bob?"

Elsa laughs but neither confirms nor contradicts. She takes

out the cigarettes from within the coat and offers one to Billy who holds up his own by way of declining.

"How do little one. How old is he?"

"Nearly twelve months, now." She lights the cigarette and steps away from the pram, the smoke taken away quickly on the air and over the balcony like a discarded towel. "How's your friend?" she asks plunging the packet in to the pocket of the jacket Billy sees is two sizes too big for her.

"Asleep. I'll leave him be."

"I think he needs to go to hospital," she says.

Her accent thoroughly Mancunian, nasally, *hospital* hollow, like the building itself. "I think you're right; see what kind of state he's in when he wakes."

"He looked in a bad way last night."

"We needed to get our heads down. We've been on the road for ages, knackered. Thanks for putting us up. I don't know what we'd have done."

Elsa nods, her hair the colour and consistency of wet straw falling into her face. She pushes it back behind her ears and the repositioning changes the shape of her face, at least reveals the true outline; full, high cheek bones and a long nose. An honest face. "Why did you come here Billy?" she asks.

"I—," he begins then falters, grasping for something succinct to say, something meaningful but the real reason is complex; more layered than just that he likes her or that they need a roof over their heads. It's more of something she'd said to him about place and freedom in Glasgow some days earlier. He can't describe it in a few words and a longer explanation seems inappropriate here.

Elsa, perhaps sensing him floundering intervenes. "From Glasgow, you said last night you got mugged."

"Max was set on, in a bar and kicked all around the place. Wrong accents in the wrong part of town I guess."

She purses her lips, the thought of the place, or imagining the event evoking her own pain. "You have to be careful wherever you are."

"Sure," Billy says.

"It's no different here."

They smoke in silence for some time, then Billy asks: "How long have you lived here Elsa?"

"For all time," she replies.

"You're pretty street wise."

The pursed lips again and Billy sees how Elsa's face dints below her cheek bones, small lines and shallow creases diagonally from the corner of her mouth until they fade. "Pretty," she says staring out across the balcony and over the buildings.

Beyond her, the Estate panning out around them is an ugly broken mouth, her home, the place of her upbringing, anything but pretty. But the love she spoke of what she cherished here; *her* light and freedom; Billy remembers that.

"And you?" she asks.

"Streetwise?"

Elsa turns to face him and he sees her eyes moving about his face, a swiftly executed scrutiny, a quick analysis and summary made. "Not especially, if you keep getting yourselves caught in the wrong part of town." She looks back over the balcony, downwards this time, a boy on a bicycle riding by below them.

"No; I guess not," Billy says, resignation tinged with humour, the contempt of her observation, or its levity.

"You're no fighters."

"I'm a lover not a fighter," Billy says, trying to recover some ground to move her or at least discourage indifference.

Elsa smiles. "My mother thinks you might be. She thinks you'll attract trouble."

"We aren't and we won't."

"Remember Billy, she lives here, and my sister Freya too."

"And your baby."

"Yes, and Marley."

She continues. "Is my mother right to be wary of you?"

Billy turns to face her, drops his hands to his sides and pushes his palms outwards towards her. "Do I look like trouble?" he asks. "And with my mate Max all duffed up, is that how we appear to you." He casts his thoughts back to the details of the Kellet Bowman incident Max had romanticised around the big kitchen table in Glasgow, wrenched from the condemnation of his cousin's wife Becca before that. Now fortunes have changed once more.

"What does trouble look like? There's so much of it around here it all seems to blur into one and the same. Your friend's biffed face is enough to alarm my mother."

Billy feels suddenly unsure of his ground or where this exchange is heading. He sees the curtains move behind one of the flat windows and a face appears, more a face-shaped white blur that quickly disappears again.

"As soon as Max wakes I'll drop the key back around to your place," he says. What was he expecting to find here?

The front door opens and a girl, Freya, dressed in grey school uniform appears, unkempt hair and bleary, sleep-filled eyes. She scratches her head behind her ears with both hands, sending up minor explosions of hair from behind her head, quick waves crashing on rocks. Her face is plump, puffy beneath the eyes and pouting lips, the facial muscles yet to respond to the rest of her body. She bears little resemblance to her sister, Billy thinks, more perhaps Sam.

"Who's this," she asks, a scratchy voice.

"This is Billy," Elsa says. "Billy this is Freya, my little sister."

"Are you the one with the beat-up friend? Is he staying at Mr Henry's?"

Elsa turns to Billy. "There's nothing she doesn't miss," she says.

"Can you get me some breakfast, Els?" Freya asks.

"I'll be there. Give me a moment."

Freya turns and walks back into the flat. "Nice to meet you Billy," she says with her back to him, holding a hand up, waving as she leaves.

Elsa turns to Billy. "I think she slept in her school clothes. She's thinking ahead; saves time in the morning. What are your plans now?"

Plans, intentions; the quick exit from Glasgow was essential but it had happened with Billy's knowledge of Elsa's address in his breast pocket. *What had been his intentions?* Only, he knew, to see Elsa again, and beyond that to see what happened. "We haven't got one. We don't seem to make plans," he says.

Elsa raises her eyebrows briefly. "Maybe you should," she

says. "Now would be a good time to start. You need to get your friend to the MRI; he needs to be looked at. If he hasn't broken his ribs, they'll be badly bruised. They'll X-ray his chest to check there's no problem with his lungs. Either way the treatment's the same for ribs busted or bruised; they have to knit back together so he'll need plenty of rest."

Billy watches her as she pushes the dead cigarette end into the soil of a plant pot by the door of her flat. "Ok," he says, compliantly. "You are a nurse."

"Yes," she says. "I am. Get your friend to hospital but drop the key back first. Then come back here and I'll give it back to you when you return."

*

That evening, Kathy Kelly agitated and restless calls for a meeting. She used to call them tenants' meetings, even *councils*, when more of their neighbours lived on the Estate, before they moved by choice or fortune. That terms seems grandiose now. Back in the day she'd call for an assembly of residents and if there were too many to fit in the flat the meeting moved to The Iron Duke instead, an insalubrious venue where the drink would fuel discontent already felt. They came in large numbers to argue the issues of the day; the poor quality of the housing, the crime, the lack of facilities, the absence of welfare. Kathy witnessed the brave new world of the modern estate born in the Seventies as it crumbled and died around them over the next decade. She observed but refused to accept it, not without a fight. When Elsa and Sam were young, they'd seen their mother stand on chairs and speak passionately before meetings of thirty or more people while baby Freya lay in the pram next to her swaddled in smoke. Her delivery was clear, words measured in a language the residents understood; the common tongue. She likened the squalor to the slums of the Victorian era, that which ironically the Estate was meant to replace by the terraces cleared before it. She railed against the standards of the new housing, the cockroach outbreaks, the lack of services and amenities. The whole living experience was akin to pre-war Britain, before the creation of the welfare state when people had to band together to form the mutual associations and friendly societies for their own protection. She urged them to do the same, not just bemoan the deficiencies. Throughout the decade of Thatcher administrations Kathy denounced the government's onslaught and denial of the notion of society as the very real concept of welfare became increasingly eroded. On this issue she became a thorn in the side of what she considered to be the toothless authorities that did little to help those on the Estate.

As time went by Hulme fell further into dysfunction and disrepair. Families moved out. Children discouraged. It was clear that the magnitude of the problems was too much for any one person to tackle, not even a loud, cigar-smoking Irish woman with too much to say for herself, who spoke articulately then cursed more with every drink inside her. Her championing waned as people tired of the degradation around them. After years of campaigning and berating there was no point in trying anymore. They were defeated.

The exodus began and grew. Then later the rehousing started but Kathy continued to stand for those who remained. The venue for her meetings moved from the Iron Duke to her flat and the number of those attending diminished until only a handful remained. "I'm like the captain of a ship slipping beneath the waves," she said, refusing to leave the Estate behind until the others around her had been rehoused, despite being offered immediate relocation when the rehousing scheme started by the City Council in an attempt at quick appeasement. Kathy vowed to stand by her neighbours until every last one had been rehoused.

Some thought that decision rash. Samantha couldn't see the sense in taking this stance and soon departed for new horizons herself. Those remaining under her protectorate as she considered it consisted of herself, Elsa and Freya, Ivy Smith and her son Martin from next door and Tamsin, the agoraphobic woman who lived next to them. This is now the quorate of the meeting along with Verity, Elsa's friend who does not live on the Estate but often stays at the flat. And Baby Marley.

Kathy pulls out a tin full of biscuits and hands them to Freya to pass around. She knows her powers of speech-making have waned significantly with her failing health but that won't stop her telling them what she needs to say. The biscuits are an aid; the hungry attendees are unlikely to talk over her with their mouths full, particularly Martin who is prone to uttering constant mumbling but also has a penchant for a Wagon Wheel.

"It's been a long time since we've had one of Kathy's Councils," Ivy Smith says leaning into to Freya. Her voice is cracked and well-worn with warmth, lips creased by a life-time of cigarettes. Freya smiles and waves the tin under her nose like smelling salts. "Marley's taking the minutes," she whispers, quelling a laugh, knowing from previous meetings her Mam likes to keep things serious.

Rheumy eyed Ivy looks at her nonplussed and Freya thinks it's because of the mention of the baby's name she doesn't yet acknowledge.

"Where's Elsa?" asks Martin appearing at her side, his eyes on the prize.

His mother looks around the room and shakes her head without concern.

Concealing her frustrations, Elsa is outside having a stuttering conversation with Tammy through a face-wide gap between the front door of her flat and its jamb, a portal into her private world restricted by a door chain. There's the familiar solidified odour of hot food gone cold and Tammy with it, avoiding eye contact and Elsa demonstrating the requisite patience that few can muster, carefully choosing her words and delivery.

"Kathy would really like to see you Tammy."

"I'm not so sure," she whispers.

"There's only us and the Smiths. Verity's here too but she'll be going again soon."

Elsa knows the phrases to avoid, the words which result in withdrawal or even total shutdown; *you need to get out more*; *you'll feel the benefit*; *you have to try Tammy, try a little harder.* All are red-flag phrases that can spark fear and panic and Tammy's belief however timorous that no one else understands how she feels. This could be true. Elsa has tried this approach before and had to back-peddle quickly and clumsily.

Futile. Far better, she has learned to describe the situation so Tammy can visualise the circumstances, contextualise and grasp the arena in which she will imminently be entering; or not.

"We've got a tin of Fox's Assorted and there's a pot of tea on the go. We can walk together, me and you if you like. Ivy and Martin will be listening to Kathy talking and Freya will be reading a book or doodling in a sketch pad, you know what a book worm she is."

A giggle from within is enough for Elsa to gently press home.

"You can sit in the chair by the window and listen to Freya's stories if Mam goes on too much." It's difficult not to sound overtly condescending with Tammy and at times Elsa wants to reach out and grab her shoulders and shake the timidity out of her.

Tammy says something Elsa doesn't quite hear. She leans forward and puts her ear against the gap in the door. "What's that you say Tam?"

"What's Verity doing?" she asks.

"Verity's making the tea. She'll stay a while before going to the pub." Verity works behind the bar in The Spinners.

The door gently closes. Tammy fumbles the latch and unlocks the chain inside and at last steps out. "Don't forget your key, love," Elsa says, as nonchalantly as she can muster, and sighs relief as Tammy at last tiptoes along the walkway.

Kathy has commenced her address when Elsa and Tammy enter the flat. Elsa knows the reason she's called them together and passes a furtive look between her mother and Tammy, a sign indicating Kathy must take care with the impact of what she's about to say in Tammy's presence. The look is excessive; her mother knows to be gentle where Tamsin is concerned and how to choose her words wisely. Her pursed lipped expression says as much.

Elsa takes a seat.

"We were talking about the money, ladies," Kathy says, speaking to Elsa who indicates the chair by the window to Tammy as previously intended. Verity sits next to her on a chair pulled through from the kitchen. Gently squeezing her knee and rubbing her arm they exchange smiles.

Kathy continues. "We would like to know if, it's something you want Elsa to carry on doing for you? We don't mind shopping for everyone, but we don't want you to feel pressured, in to giving us your money. That was never the idea. It's your money, and you need to tell us, if you prefer to opt out, or if not whether you think it's the right amount."

Ivy Smith chimes in; "If it's not too much trouble for you, love." She says it to Elsa, her words heartfelt, imploring even. "It can't be easy with Baby and all."

Rising, Elsa positions herself against the arm of the sofa. "It's no trouble for me Ivy. It gets me out of the flat to be honest and Mam looks after Marley when I'm gone." She stresses the child's name. "It's good exercise climbing up and down these stairs and the midwife says I need to lose a bit of weight anyhow."

Ivy waves her hand with a limp wrist. "Nonsense; you're lovely and slim," she replies, then; "isn't she?" counsels the room and the others quickly agree; Verity warmly, grinning at the spectacle; Tammy barely able to lift her eyes to the rest of the room; Martin with the customary unease he displays when the talk is of Elsa, unable to conceal the unease of his private thoughts for her.

"Whatever;" Elsa, dismissive. "I don't mind doing the errands."

Kathy continues; "And the extra money means we can buy in bulk for the discount prices; the meat and cheese, the washing powder, the bogofs. We get more for our money, when we club it together, than if we each pay for our own shopping separately, so it does make sense."

"More bang for your buck!" Martin says.

"Yes, but as I say, I'm not forcing any of you to continue with this, it's only my suggestion we do, so if you want to change, then you need to tell us about it."

Heads together, Ivy Smith and her son utter the strange tongue that's hardly ever spoken these days, more a brogue than a language now in a unique exchange between them. Although brief, the meaning is demonstrably understood as a unanimous decision between the two follows. They both turn to Kathy, affirmative in unison. Elsa warms at Verity's look of incomprehension of this exchange.

"We want to carry on, if you don't mind," Ivy says.

"We don't mind at all," says Kathy. "It must be your decision and not our influence."

"No, we want to carry on."

"The same amount?" asks Elsa.

"Fifty pounds a fortnight from the Giro," Ivy says, "and twenty a week from my pension."

Kathy smiles warmly. "Ok," she says.

"I need some of my Giro for—" Martin begins but Kathy stops him saying anything more with two hands swiftly held up and waved.

"There's no need for justifications Martin. What you do with your money is down to you. Is that ok? Now, Tamsin, what about you my dear?"

Tamsin visibly tenses at the mention of her name. They've seen this before and a collective coping strategy comes at once to fruition. Verity strokes her leg again and feels her bony knee beneath the light blue of her jeans, the lack of muscle in her thighs, her constant trembling. Elsa begins a separate conversation with Ivy, a hasty distraction of alternative noise around the room to smother the silence of expectation and shift the focus of Tammy's response and with it her anguish. She talks quickly and loudly to Ivy about the first thing that comes to the fore, Marley always her prominent focus; his feeding, his increasing weight, the stinky nappies, *remember them Ivy*?

"Do you ever hear him crying in the night Ivy," she says. "I sometimes think he must wake up the whole crescent with his wailing when he's hungry..." and presses on forcefully giving Ivy no chance of reply to disrupt her monologue. Ivy Smith locks in to this aside, but Elsa sees Martin sitting next to her is simply staring at Tammy's protracted awkwardness, his mouth hanging oval with incomprehension and concern. It's a reflected image guaranteed to cause Tammy a major wobble if she notices him.

Elsa changes tack. "*Martin*!" She almost shouts it. "Did you see any more of those two guys today; The ones who came last night? My friends?" she asks, pleased by the rapidity, knowing he will have no interest in Marley and baby world. What surprises her is the go-to subject of her quick thinking.

Martin closes his mouth and turns to her, incomprehension still about him, the physical indicator of his recall being the exact same as his concern for Tamsin's discomfort. Slowly he shakes his head. A tiny pool of saliva has risen to the brim of his bottom lip, it glints in the electric light of the naked bulb.

"No, I haven't seen them," he replies and with it a quick suction of breath.

"Not at all?"

Martin shakes his head, his features darkening. He's the spitting image of his mother and looks to her for some sort of interpretation of Elsa's questioning. Oblivious, Ivy gives no clarification and Martin withdraws unsettled and sufficiently unsure of himself to prevent re-engagement in meaningful conversation. He slumps into the sofa, his knees and shoulders at equal height, hands resting on his thighs.

"You let me know if you see them," she says then quickly turning to Tamsin, "you can talk about this later if you like Tammy."

Verity checks her watch. "I need to go soon," she says.

"You still working in the pub?" Ivy asks her.

Verity rolls her eyes as confirmation.

"That's what you need to do; get yourself a job, young man," she says to her son.

"I've tried," Martin complains, his voice a monotone, unconvincing, constricted by his posture.

"If Verity can manage to find a job, I'm sure you can."

Verity grabs her jacket and stands, ignoring the clumsy comment she might have interpreted as derogative but doesn't for the effort. Elsa stops her.

"Hang on Vee," she says. "Mam needs to mention the *other* thing."

"Agenda item number two," she says and sits again. Tamsin relaxes once more, the room's status quo returning.

"The other reason, I've asked us all here tonight is less savoury, unfortunately," Kathy begins. "It's a warning about this Mark Tulip fella. He's the one who's been snooping around the decks recently and we think he's a proper danger."

"Who is Mark Tulip," Tamsin asks, a simple question gently asked, an exceptional contribution that briefly silences the room.

Elsa interjects. "A man from the Estate. I've known him for years, sort of a friend of Nelson's."

"I know him," Verity affirms.

Kathy Kelly continues. "He is a crack addict. He's been in and out of rehab and prison for years. He's a drifter, comes and goes; nothing to do with the gangs but he's PV as we used to call them; *Potentially Violent*."

Verity, quietly to herself: "Nothing potential; the blokes a fucking psycho!"

"A bit strong Vee," Elsa says with a hand gesture indicating delicacy in Tamsin's presence, furtive signals commonplace for her and Elsa wonders if they simply feed her affliction and whether it would be better just to say things how they really are.

"Like all addicts there's only one thing on his mind, which is his fix. He's not usually a problem but lately he's been hanging around these decks. He's after money or anything he can sell to get it."

"You can't be too careful when the drug addicts are around," Ivy says sagely. "They'll nick anything to feed their habits; your shirt off your back, the slippers off your feet."

Kathy resumes: "That's right Ivy love but your man Tulip is going further; hiding on the balconies and jumping people. Day or night time there seems no pattern to it. So, I'm just saying we should be careful and look out for one another, just until he goes away again, which I'm sure he will, okay?"

Ivy asks; "What does he look like?"

"Tallish, dark hair; non-descript really," Kathy says. "You just need to be mindful of anybody hanging around the decks or the stairwells looking a bit shady."

"Half the fucking Estate," Verity says quietly.

"Where was he last seen?" Martin asks.

"Far end of this deck," Elsa says, "beyond Mr Henry's place towards the far stairs."

At the mention of Mr Henry's place Elsa instinctively touches the key to the flat tight against her hip in the pocket of her jeans. She's curious to know now what's happened to Billy and his beat-up friend. It's Billy more so, of course. Her interest pinches her like the key in the fold of her pocket. It's something about his honesty and her desire lies in part to there being a close proximity to honest people, for the truth is that Elsa is afraid. She will never reveal her fear to anyone, an almost atavistic trait moulded by life on the Estate. She's beginning to feel encased in vulnerability because things are different now Marley's around and not only her son but the others too, for Ivy and Tammy here in this room, and useless Martin.

But it's for her mother she has the greatest concern, her declining health, her increasing frailty and susceptibility. For what Kathy has not revealed to those gathered is that while Elsa was in Glasgow visiting Sam some days before it was she, Kathy who was the victim of Mark Tulip. Walking to the shops with their communal money, struggling for breath and reaching out at the balcony walls he'd seen his opportunity, offered a helping hand then waved a blade under her face with the other. Calculating her compliance he calmly took the purse from her bag and the money within it. The purse lay on the stained floor of the access deck and with no care to hide his identity he walked away, flicking the hood of his top over his head, no need to check behind him, stuffing the money into his hip pockets, the length of the blade flat to his side.

Kathy told Elsa what had happened. They agreed to release few details and only to those who needed to know or wouldn't panic or go to ground: Freya and Verity of course, her close friend with who she has no secrets, who Kathy would expect her to tell. And Sam; Elsa informed her by letter. The money for the communal shopping was replaced by her savings she could ill afford but hid reality. Elsa sees Verity's mouth shape sympathetically as she listens to her mother, her lips thinning, disappearing into her mouth.

"So please remain vigilant and keep an ear to the ground,"

Kathy continues. "It could be a one-off thing. He might have moved on but it's best to forewarn you."

Verity stands and grabs her jacket. "Thanks for that Kathy," she says reaching out and rubbing Kathy's arm. "We'll all look out for each other. Now, I need to get to work."

"Take a torch," Kathy says.

"Don't worry, I've a screecher," Verity. "Always carry it."

The news has caused a haunted sallowness to bleach Tammy's features already devoid of colour and Elsa moves to her on the arm of the chair, stroking her flare-white, blond hair that's coarse between her fingers. "Don't be fretting about this, Tammy," she says. "Forewarned is forearmed, that's all Mam's saying."

Tammy smiles weakly, soothed but unconvinced, a short-lived, fragile peace that's quickly broken by her shock at seeing Verity's face reappear around the door into the room, an expression that's matched by Elsa's leaping heart as she says with a bemused, questioning smile; "There's two blokes out here Els, and they're asking for you."

*

In the morning Elsa takes them tea and a plate piled with toast. Billy rubs the sleep from his eyes and watches as she breezily brushes past him into the flat and places the tray on the floor, her long arms short of muscle definition, thin and white.

"Why are you doing this for us?" Max asks sitting upright on the bed, pulling at the legs of his jeans under him to sit cross legged.

"Because you came here asking for help; because I'm nice," Elsa replies. "Take your shirt off, let me see the bruising."

Gingerly Max pulls his shirt up and over his head. Elsa undertakes a careful inspection, scrutinising his bare torso with narrowed eyes and tilting head.

"What did they say at the hospital?" she asks.

Max places two fingers against the left side of his body where his skin is heavily discoloured. "These two are the most painful," he says. "The bruises look worse on this side but there's no broken bones here."

"Painful," she says emphatically.

"As fuck," Max says. "They advised me to quit smoking, but I advised them I won't be; I'd be hacking for England if I did. It hurts most when I cough."

"It usually does. You need good pain killers," Elsa says.

"What do you have in mind?"

"Nothing like you've in mind," she says. "If I was at work, I might be able to get you something stronger, but you'll have to settle for bog standard non-steroid anti-inflams. All I have is Arnica."

"You work in the hospital?" Max asks.

"I'm on maternity leave."

"Where's the nipper?" Billy asks.

"Marley."

"Where's Marley?"

"Mam's feeding him breakfast, trying to."

"And you're feeding us," Billy says intending levity; "the other kids."

"You'll need rest," she says to Max. "At least your face seems to be healing. Your lip's lost its swelling."

Elsa reaches her hand out to touch his face and Max recoils. She stops then tries again, slower the second time, taking his chin on either side with two hands and tilting his head; first left, then right. "I am a nurse," she says gently.

Max closes his eyes and Elsa rubs the Arnica cream into her two fingers and reaches down to his body, lightly dabbing against his bruising. "Lean back," she says and once more gently rolls her fingers this time down over his ribs.

"They did a good job," Max says.

"And some. I can see the imprint of a boot on your side here; they stamped on you?"

Max looks across at Billy who's grimacing, vicarious sensitivity. "Probably, while I was down. *I don't know I was really drunk at the time*," he says; then more solemnly. "It's all a blur from the moment I hit the ground."

"Who were they?" she asks.

Her slow-moving hands spread over Max's battered body gently and dextrously pressing inch by inch, her thin fingers delicate and white against his dark skin dappled purple. Billy watches with a mixture of compassion and unexpected covetousness. He winces with his friend where the contrast in colours is at its greatest.

"Not sure," Max says. "Local boot boys up for a Saturday night on the swedge at a pair of out-of-towners."

"They could have been Catholics or Proddies," Billy says. "In the interests of parity Max went about slating both."

"So, you provoked it?" Elsa says. "My mother's right.

Don't go bringing religious differences around here or you'll have her to deal with. She's the loud Irish woman roaming these balconies. You can't miss her. You think you're in pain now—"

"It wasn't like that," Max says sullenly.

"We got out of the bar where they'd jumped him again," Billy continues. "I thought it was just a little local difficulty with people we'd met in the squat; I hadn't realised there was a bunch of them taking note of proceedings. By then it was too late, they took it into the street."

"You boys..."

Max's features tighten, his jaw clamping, facial muscles skipping. "They had the scent of blood in their nostrils, bloody bead-jigglers, Jaffas, who knows."

Elsa sighs. "Don't use terms like that," she says, sternly. Teeth gritted she promptly increases the pressure on the bruising under Max's arm.

Yelping Max recoils. "Hey, take it easy."

"We used to get called things that all the time; Chuckies, Fenians," Elsa says. "Mam had a world of anti-Irish shit thrown at her and we don't want to hear it again."

Max shakes his head. "I don't care one way or another. Religious bigotry's the same whichever side you're on."

Elsa scowls, picks up the tube of cream and throws it at him, striking him on the shoulder. "You should care," she says. "It's easy to see how you got into your local difficulty."

She stands quickly and Billy does the same, facing her the breakfast tray between them. "He has his reasons," he says weakly.

"Sure," she says. "Doesn't everyone? I need to see to Marley now. You'll need to help your friend apply the Arnica cream; it will be too painful for him to reach around and do it for himself. Bring the breakfast tray around when you've finished."

"Elsa—".

She turns and walks out of the flat and pulls the door behind her with a gentle click that has a peculiarly greater impact than the slamming Billy had expected.

He looks down at Max who has a mouthful of food.

"Well done," he says.

Max swallows a mouthful of tea to clear his mouth of food.

"What does she know?"

"She's helping us out; she's looking after you."

"I didn't know she'd spit the dummy."

"Yeah," Billy replies sitting down cross-legged opposite him. He looks at the toast on the plate but no longer has the appetite for it. "Make a mental note about what not to say."

"I'll go around and apologise to her," Max says. "After breakfast."

Billy frowns, grabs the mug of tea and takes and a mouthful. It's lukewarm and strong, the tannin chalky in his mouth. Elsa's tea remains untouched on the tray.

"Remember, Max," Billy says. "Don't bite the hand that's feeding us."

Later that day the sun is hot and high in a summer sky and casts short shadows. There's a grass bank where the black soil is held back by a brick wall split at the bottom. The flowers, daisies and dandelions grow in clumps and cracks, tough and wiry. A few trees with damaged branches where children have climbed or hoofed footballs stud the edge of the grass bank and behind them, through the black bark and fluttering leaves the high hulking shape of The Crescent. People sit on the grass and the children play, running, shouting, roughing and tumbling, feral kids, parents with an infrequent eye on them. A few others sit or stand around, talking, fanning themselves in the heat, the occasional hiss and crack of a beer can opening, amongst them Billy and Elsa.

"It's a way of saying sorry," Billy says to her, clipping the top off a beer bottle with the bottom end of his lighter. He offers it, the frothy top spilling out over his fingers, the colour and consistency the same as a volcano set he'd had as a kid; vinegar and baking soda. He remembers it now, surrounded by children playing, infant cries.

"Thanks," she says tipping the neck of the bottle towards him, "apologies are not necessary."

Marley lies in a dark blue carriage cot next to them with a parasol attached to the side shading his body. His limbs are in perpetual motion like the dying seconds of a fly. Elsa checks him. "He'll be crawling soon," she says. "Then there'll be trouble."

"Where's his dad?"

"Nelson." She waves her hand, regally. "He's around," she says breezily: "Somewhere."

"*Somewhere*?"

Elsa does not elaborate and Billy has a sudden sense of being watched from the layers of balconies that arc around them.

"Does he get involved, with the nipper? With Marley?"

Quick learner. "Take a wild guess," Elsa says.

Billy looks at her and sees how her skin is translucent with the sun shining on her face, a small scattering of freckles around her forehead and the end of her nose. Her eyes have an occasional intensity that makes him uncomfortable; she's checking him out, seeking the real reason why he's come to Manchester, looking right into him, and seeking what? Truth; depth; affectation; affection. The sunlight around her irises adds a laser penetration to their gaze.

"How is he?" she asks. "Max?"

Billy takes a drink. "In some pain," he says, the bottle popping off his lips. "Sleeping. I took him the paper, a couple of beers and some fresh tobacco. That'll make him feel better."

Elsa chuckles, the sound at the back of her throat; a stick against railings. "He's going to be in pain for a few weeks," she says. "I've dealt with ribs before. There's no quick fix. How long do you want to stay here for?"

She asks this question and follows it with a movement of her head to one side, from left to right, turning her ear towards an immediate response. Her eyebrows lift higher. Billy regards one side of her face as hard and aloof, but it's the whole of her features that reveal more: warmth with prudence. She's offering up a place for them to stay, sorting them out until Max gets to his feet again. This is what it is.

"I really don't know," he says honestly, giving way to her lead, for her to say, not him.

"That's right," she says. "You don't do plans do you?"

"Until Max gets better?" More a proposal than a statement.

"And then?"

"Then we'll see what happens. I guess."

They both drink at the same time. Marley gurgles and a scruffy black dog scuds across the path at the bottom of the grass bank.

"What did you do in Glasgow after I left, aside from getting beaten up?"

"We left soon after too."

"Sam told me she thought Max was troubled."

"His brother got shot up by the IRA. He's still grieving. Glasgow's probably not the best for someone with such religious sensitivities."

"For sure. I didn't know."

"Why did you leave so soon?"

Elsa looks up, her mouth opens a little showing slightly crooked teeth. "I just needed to. Marley, Mam; I had a feeling I needed to get back here, back home again."

"Your home. What's it like living here?" Billy asks.

Elsa takes another mouthful of beer. "I've lived here all my life Billy. I've had a great life, running around, going to parties, hanging out with the nutters, the crazy freaks. It looks like a bombsite and it is, but there's plenty of inspiration here too. There's never a dull moment. It's life at the edge."

"I can see," Billy says. "Like giant Bohemian statement against modernism."

"*The possibility of change born of the occupation and emancipation of a twentieth century living space.*"

Billy laughs and Elsa's kitten eyes return, the first since he'd seen them in Glasgow. "It's alright here," she says, "until you have children; then it's not so. We've had to look after ourselves; self-govern if you like. Having a young baby makes that so much more difficult. Everything changes. Having Marley has altered my view of it all; it's the one single event that's changed me the most. I guess you don't know unless you have children, and if you don't you hate those that do saying it. You have no children Billy, do you?"

"No, I don't."

"Did that lead to one of the differences between you and your ex-wife?"

Billy thinks for a while before answering; her question's accompanied by the same intensive scrutiny, her head turned to one side again while looking into him, within him almost. He accepts the challenge and considers his answer carefully.

"It wasn't a subject as such, but I suppose it was heading that way. We'd been together for years; I was looking for something different, nothing like the things she wanted. You could call it drift. There was no one else involved for either of us. My marriage just became rudderless. Maybe a child was something we needed, a focus, a distraction."

"All the wrong reasons," Elsa says. "And is she out of your system?"

Billy looks at Elsa; her penetrative probing.

"*Jackie,*" he says. "It takes a while, but yes. What about...?"

"Nelson."

"Yes, Nelson," Billy says, recalling the name. "The guy who left you holding the baby."

Elsa smiles. "You've been paying attention."

"Has he ever seen Marley?"

"He has no interest."

"Oh." Billy shifts his position on the grass, a slight dampness rising from the soil and into his thighs.

"It's a big thing isn't it, having a child? We didn't plan for it but when we found out I was pregnant I knew I wanted to keep him. Nelson didn't seem to mind either way and the pregnancy continued. Too late after a certain time. It wasn't his thing and he walked away. I don't hate him or blame him. I worry what Marley will think when he grows older; hope it doesn't cause him sadness. He will want to know about his dad and things might have changed by then. We'll deal with that when we come to it. It's better to have two parents but it's not essential."

"That's very positive," Billy says.

"Is there a point in being anything else?"

He has no response to this question; it's not only rhetorical but the way it's put with overwhelming confidence and equanimity there's an irresistible quality of certainty about her in some ways the same as the Estate around; down but not defeated and with a resilience about it, ingrained with a sense of chance in the face of overwhelming adversity. Elsa's a product of the Hulme Estate, and it's a product of her. From these connections between the people and their places Billy reflects the differences in communities are born.

Marley, his wriggling more staccato begins to cry a stiff, stuttering noise akin his movements.

"Come on," Elsa says. "I need to get back to feed him and you'd better see how your mate is."

"Both our babies," Billy says, dusting the moisture and the grass from his backside.

They walk back to the access deck, past the murals and the running children and animals. A bearded drunk in military fatigues lies motionless like a dead soldier on the grass in the shade afforded by the crescent block above him, empty cans around him like spent cartridges. At the foot of the stairwell the concrete is damp and loose and broken in places that abruptly halt the wheels of the pram and silence Marley's crying with the jolts. Billy takes the front end at the foot of the stairs, bending his back and lengthening his arms to make it easier for Elsa behind him. They climb three flights of stairs then the fourth, past the first deck access, the lower balcony, the sunlight briefly lighting up the grim cracking concrete and the corners of the stairwells otherwise dark and dank.

They turn off the stairwell and on to the second balcony, the skywalk stretching round in a perfect half circle, the sunlight brightening the walkway in square blocks between the massive vertical struts that lurch from the ground and the banks of grass from where they'd been sitting.

Billy stops, short of breath. "You do this every day?" he asks.

"Oh yeah," she says, the wheels turning here. "Saves on the gym fee."

She opens the door to her flat and pushes the pram through, levering the front wheels then those at the rear over the dented threshold. As her mother's voice from within calls out her name, Billy turns to leave and as he does Elsa turns herself, abruptly and holds his arm firmly above the elbow.

"Take me out," she says; "tonight!"

He stops. Everything is in sunshine.

"Where?" he asks and sees her mouth that frowns and smiles simultaneously, her bright eyes widen with the expectancy of her demands.

"Take me anywhere! I don't care; just, take me away."

"Tonight?"

"*Tonight!*"

The pubs and bars of
Manchester, Summer 1989

Billy's seen plenty of wild parties full of people pushing the boundaries but not so many where the people haven't a clue where their limits are. In this sense there are none. As the Estate belongs to nobody and is effectively an authority no-go area the sense of property and ownership is completely absent and the drug consumption overt. The parties are not events as such with invites and venues and start times; they're more a greater concentration of people and chemicals at certain times in one place with people who drift in and out of other flats. Music plays, drink and drugs consumed, and mayhem happens in higher levels of intensity. Life on the Estate for many is one big party, only at times more extreme than others. You can tell it in their faces, in their smoke-filled grainy voices, their fatigued eyes and unfathomable expressions. The two parties Elsa and Billy go to that night have been going for days. They seem to be fading out at one point as people disappear or collapse with sleep deprivation or hunger only to start up again at some point with the arrival of different people or the injection of a fresh chemicals. They're like house fires reigniting where glowing embers linger in the brickwork. The whole gamut of drug culture is present in an unconscious manner, manifestly relaxed and casual in a way born of a freedom *to* do it, rather than a freedom *from* being stopped.

The flats are open houses, some smashed up, others done up with spray paint and murals. At the first party one of the rooms has a floor that drops into the flat below, tilting into a corner where the joists have given way beneath, lights beaming up through a huge gap in the corner. Like a scene from *The Italian Job* someone has thrown a four pack of Special Brew that's wedged on the edge of the abyss and a group of people are edging towards it then back again, sliding, laughing as the floor bends and cracks with their weight. Nobody cares for their own safety if the floor collapses and no one seems to care if there's anyone below.

Elsa and Billy leave hastily and wander. Peals of laughter and shouting are heard from every room, barking, raucous, an explicit mission to get as high as possible, to have a good time with no regard for anything else; personal safety, personal sanity, the next day, the next week. At the next party, the music is loud and funky, high rigged rooms packed with full on wide-eyed dancing, people away with the music they're hearing or with anyone who's happy to share a drink, grab hold of and fall over with.

Billy and Elsa are not two who are.

"We're coming in on a different level," she says scanning the room. "Some of these people have been going for days."

Billy feels her unease. He doesn't know if it's because of the state of the party people or that she might recognise someone she doesn't want to see, Nelson perhaps.

"Where do you want to go?" he asks her.

"You're taking me out remember," she says.

"Let's get off the Estate," he says, and Elsa's eyes swell and seem to change colour as she moves towards him, places her hands against his shoulders and grips him there lightly. She pulls his chest against her face stares with her searing blue grey eyes searching his own and kisses him full on the lips.

"Oh, I'm with you," she says.

They skip off the Estate to a pub called the Junction Hotel, a wedge-shaped old building at odds with its surroundings and step through the doors, Elsa's arm linked through Billy's, his hand in his pocket to make the loop. It feels peculiar to him because it's unnatural and yet not, the approach a couple might take, as with Jackie months ago. Then he'd held his arm in the same position, stiff and tense, worrying his thumb over the rough side of their house key in his pocket, stepping out into a wet evening street. He'd had the weight of his pre-occupations about him, pressing down on him. She'd noticed and told him he needed to relax, though didn't trouble to find out why; appearances more important than the cause of it. He could not unwind. And now a new acquaintance, a different woman, new to the touch, her weight and feel dissimilar, a different shape, unique scent. Holding someone different feels odd to him, a misfit that brings back forgotten sensations of closeness. But this someone new has just kissed him unexpectedly in a kitchen party full of animals, kissed him deeply, intensely, something Jackie never did. He doesn't like to compare but does anyway and feels the excitement and there too lies the difference. He feels it in his stomach, in his loins and limbs filling with a chilled heat that moves around him, that makes him shake as she unlinks her arm, and he eases her before him to the door with the flat of his hand against her lower back. He feels the curve at the base of her spine, the dints on either side against his palm rippling with her movement. Every touch matters now and every action too. A prickling heat spreads up his back, into his arms and surges through his chest. Hesitating, he allows her to go before him, gentlemanly though in truth it feels better this way; her terrain, for him to hold back, for her to lead on.

Smoke, light, noise; a soft wall mounted juke box competing with a fruit machine pumping money into the plastic tray with machine gun precision. The barman seems to know Elsa, though no words are exchanged. He smiles at her then stares at Billy vigilantly as he hands over his money. A gin and tonic and a pint, they take their drinks like a married couple to the corner of the brightly lit room, avoiding the elbows of serious pool players at the table piled high with coins. Old men, three of them in browns, blacks and beiges, socks and sandals, are lined up at the next table, softly crooning to each other in streams of cigarette smoke burning between fingers, rising columns in uniformed angles like smoke from Lowry stacks.

"Cheers," Elsa says, raising her glass as she pulls up a stool. "Sometimes the Estate is just too much. It's good to get out; you have to." In the white light flooding out from beneath tasselled lightshades Billy notices she has powdered her face, uneven and patchy in places as though she's not practised; she's made the effort and it's for him.

He touches her glass with his. Lager spills.

"So," she says licking her lips and resting her elbows on the table and her chin on her folded hands.

"So," says Billy.

"So, impress me!" Elsa says.

"Impress you?" he says back.

"Yes. Do you have any talents? Do you have any *things*? You don't have a car! Have you got any money? Do you have *prospects*?"

She smiles, it's more of a twitch, a broad upward movement that lifts her cradled face still higher in her hands but maintains its symmetry. Her eyes are the colour of a cold ocean. Like the sea they change often.

Billy hesitates, then recovers his composure. "Well," he says, "I can juggle with four oranges at a time, and I play a mean game of pool." With apposite timing a coloured stripe disappears like a bolting fox down a pocket on the pool table and with it a sudden doubt comes to his throat, his own smooth, hard sphere.

"At the same time?" Elsa says. "Do you hustle?"

He belches silently through his teeth and into his fist. "After a few drinks, with some Dutch courage," he says. "How about you?"

"Talents?"

"Qualities."

"Are they different?"

Questions.

"Depends," he says sensing his inability to grasp these subtleties.

"Well...," she takes another sip of her drink leaving a half moon against the glass. "I have strong white teeth, good child-bearing hips. I can hold my breath for a minute. And I make a mean chicken curry."

"That's not from your mother, is it?" he says. "I would have thought a traditional Irish stew."

"Not mine; Nelson's mother."

"Ah." Billy, unsuspecting again looks around the room and in the brief ensuing silence, stumbles at the mention of his predecessor and the hips, but more the former. It's illogical, he knows, irrational, but he feels it nonetheless. To ease the awkwardness a little too jauntily he says; "Tell me about Nelson."

The look of scrutiny returns, the same he's seen in the afternoon sunshine, hard and direct, drilling into him and clawing at layers, motive-seeking. Emotions shift, her eyes adjust again.

"What's more to tell?" she asks.

He feels the hot tingle of his own incursion, though she has said his name; Nelson her previous lover, not that Billy is incumbent. An hour before she had kissed him hard on the lips and made a mark, laid a claim. With the mention of Nelson for some reason he questions the certainty he'd felt with the kiss back there; was it a prelude to something more or was it merely an itch for her to scratch? He feels infantile for raising the question and dismisses misinterpretation but still senses he's no longer so assured as before about many things. Where once certitude, he now treads more carefully. With Elsa, he's hesitant, he doesn't want to make the same mistakes again.

Caution makes him clumsy, uncertain of direction. Her

flirtation with longevity, prospects, childbearing and the like, it's premature and unsettles him, whether she's serious or not or if her intention is to toy with him.

"Were you together long?" he asks. He wants to say, *for example*, his tone more serious now.

"Oh, I knew him from college," she says. "I always liked him. We had a thing going on when we left. It was nothing serious. Then a few years later we met again at a party on the Estate; talked, reminisced. My dad had just passed away. I was raw and Nelson was kind and gentle with me. It sort of grew from there."

"Do you miss him?"

She lifts her gin and tonic to her lips but pauses to drink, the question direct and unexpected. "Yes, in a way. But if you're asking if I want him back?"

"He is the father of your child."

"He won't be coming back. I know this."

There's the certainty again; something in her manner, in her *knowing* that some things are guaranteed and unassailable. He can't help wondering if she had the same conviction at first with Nelson.

"Good," he says. He has an urge to reach across and kiss her, make his own mark but it's all too clumsy, the stretch across the table, a lurch from his seat. He thinks better of it. "Good," he says again.

As though reading his thoughts she withdraws her legs from beneath the table and crosses them. Her jeans are tight across her thighs and knees. "Well," she says, "don't let this date get too serious."

"Sorry," he says.

"Don't apologise. I like you. You're nice."

"*Nice*?" Billy's back straightens, a physical reflex.

"Okay," she says reaching for her cigarettes. "Maybe not *nice*, perhaps that's the wrong word. Handsome? Courteous, amusing? How would you describe yourself?"

Billy rolls his eyes.

"Come on, indulge me; I want to know, what makes you tick. Ten questions, I know it's silly, just go with it. Describe yourself in three words." She lights her cigarette.

"Three words..."

"Uptight," she says, and smiles. There's a gap in her front two teeth, a small one he hasn't noticed before. The accumulation of intimacies

"Is that what you think?" he asks.

"Virtuous? *Thoughtful*!"

"Really?

"You know those three words you would use to describe yourself won't describe you at all," she says, "at least not how you really are to other people. You'll choose words that describe how you *want* to appear to others but not how you actually are."

"Classic amateur psychology."

"Don't be cruel," she says releasing a thick fold of smoke drawn from the cigarette.

"I haven't picked any words yet," he says. "And you've chosen two."

"So go on."

"I can't," he says, lamely. "Think of another question."

Elsa rolls her eyes. "What a dull boy," she says.

Billy leans across the table. "I'll ask this time." He said. "What makes *you* happy?"

"Marley," she says emphatically. "He is my life. It's a powerful and personal thing. It's spiritual really. That sounds terrible, doesn't it?"

Billy shakes his head. "I guess it's only natural," he says.

"Of course you wouldn't know," she says, "and, God that sounds terribly patronising doesn't it and I don't want to bore you."

"I can empathise," Billy says.

"I would say he's made my life complete, but that's too glib. Actually, he's bridged a gap between me and my own mother, a generational span."

She stops and studies him, then says; "I don't want to go on with baby talk Billy; you'll run away and I'll never see you again."

Billy laughs. "You're close to your mother."

"I am now. I used to hate her for calling me Elsa, after the lion in *Born Free*, because that was what she said I was, *born free*!"

"An unfettered lioness; why hold that against her?"

"So cheesy; that's the kind of thing matters when you're young. Now I think the name was just her playfulness. She fought for us with joie *de vivre*, even after Dad died. Always this sense of right and wrong and injustice and fairness. Then I found I was pregnant, and Nelson disappeared and that's when things really improved between us. I figured out she was so much better in these situations, where there was adversity.

She promised to support me, single mother, and she did. She made it ok for us all, despite her illness."

"What's the matter with her?" Billy asks.

"Emphysema caused by smoking, smoky pubs, living in damp houses; recently diagnosed though her breathing's been like it for years. Now there's legal cases about the presence of asbestos. She's still strong, tough and brave and since Marley's been with us, she's been amazing. She's a survivor."

"Like you."

"Yeah..."

She turns away.

"Don't let this date get too serious now," Billy says.

"You're right," she says, wide eyed. The lashes gathered into little black spikes. "I think we probably best drink more alcohol."

"Always a good idea."

Elsa smiles, stands and kisses him again. He tastes the bitterness of the tonic on her lips, the zest of lemon on her tongue brushing against his teeth. She squeezes him hard, the inside of his thigh.

"You know I don't come alone," she says; "if you take me on."

"I know," he says. "And you're right, it's probably best we drink more alcohol."

She goes to the bar to order more drinks. Billy feels the pain in his leg and watches her swagger as she crosses the dusty room to the bar. She sees him looking at her behind as she walks, and he doesn't avert his eyes because he wants her to notice him admiring her. She returns with halves of lager and two Tequilas they knock back quickly, closely, shivering faces of lemon and salt.

"There's a place I want to show you," she says. "It's a secret place; somewhere I go to when I need to get away from everything."

"Where is it?" Bill asks, smacking the tang from his mouth.

"You'll see." A change of colour in her eyes again, darker spokes of blue in the blue wheeling outwards. "It's my secret." She moves her face closer to his and lowers her voice to a whisper. "I'll take you there if you want me to."

They leave the bar and into the balmy night, Billy turning the meaning of his invitation to this hidden place in his mind, the phrase characteristically unexplained, euphemistic carnality, a tryst at Lover's Leap, Sunset View or a smoky Blues Club. Two arms in his one once more she clutches him to her, their joint gait awkward, pitching left and right as with the unsteadiness the drink brings, her desire to hold him close as they walk and talk. Along Stretford Road and into the University quarters to Oxford Road they avoid the shouting bands of students moving crablike along the pavements and move through back streets, unlit in places around the hospital where Elsa works and knows well and to another pub, The Gamecock, an unfashionable and obdurate watering hole that reminds Billy of a wedge of cheese where they try to order more tequila but are met with derision and a limited, unfriendly bar. From here, giggling through a park, a children's rusty and glass-littered playground and on through tight terraces of houses, red brick, rutted cobbles and ordered if ragged through time. Eventually they're at a large building that looks like an old Victorian warehouse where Elsa pulls him closer, kisses him once again and says to him; "*This is it!*"

With no wish to curb her enthusiasm Billy allows himself to be led towards this tumbledown building through a gate loosely chained and squeezes sideways though it into a small patch of open ground, an empty space for cars to park within the walls. To his left a large chimney, black and fluted rises high above them into the darkness shrouded with an orange glow. Below this a smaller building beneath the walls of the main structure, a club sandwich construction of red and yellow layers regimented with high gable end windows and a glass roof top partly obscured by the parapets.

"Follow me," Elsa whispers disappearing into the shadows at the foot of the building.

"Where are you taking me?" Billy's laughing, giddy with the sensation of being led away somewhere, excited by surprise, a child again. He's in character and looks around furtively, though their movements are easily hidden by the perimeter wall.

"Watch your step," she warns.

"What is this place?"

"You'll see," she says. "Come!"

Holding his fingers in her hand she leads him to a small outbuilding and pulls back a wooden door badly rotted at the bottom. From the wiper-blade arc on the ground and her sure feet Billy guesses she's done this many times before. The door twists, opening wider at the top than below where it scrapes the ground and Elsa disappears inside briefly then re-emerges with a small length of metal, flat at one end, like a crowbar.

"We're breaking in?" Billy asks, instinctively lowering his voice.

"Sort of," says Elsa. "Stay close to me."

She moves to the wall, and carefully slides the metal bar into the edge of a flat steel door covering an opening which gives easily, then pulls it wider but just enough for them to ease through. Inside there is no light barring the sliver from the aperture they've just come through, which Elsa quickly extinguishes by closing the door behind her with a soft clang, leaving the metal bar beside it.

Darkness, moist warmth, a carbon smell and a vague hum like tinnitus. Billy senses an enclosed space by the proximity of their breathing, the deadening restriction of sound.

"Hold my hand," Elsa says. "Don't let go and take your time going forward. I don't want you to hurt yourself."

They ease forward in the darkness on to a smoother floor beneath their feet, edging on into the blackness, Elsa's hand gripping tightly around Billy's, the ring on her little finger digging into the base of his thumb. Stairs abruptly halt their forward glide, risers and steps carefully mounted, a dusty metal handrail to their left aiding their ascent then a door at the top. Billy hears Elsa grappling with the handle. She pushes and a rush of cooler air and a hint of dim light comes upon them as they step into a short corridor, still in darkness, easing forward and to another door at the end of it.

"You'll love this," she says, opening the door and guiding him into a high tiled hallway, the surfaces dark and shining as fragments of light picked up from the streets outside filter through high stained-glass panels and into the room. Billy touches the walls, smooth and cool beneath his fingertips and turns to Elsa whose features he can see in the half light. Within this space of glossy ceramic, a distinct smell.

"A swimming pool!" he says.

"Follow me," she says, and skips quickly down the corridor, her footfalls smacking against the tiled floor, the light and her knowledge of the layout allowing swifter movement. Adjusting Billy can see the tiled walls around him are dark and green, the colour of beer bottles offset by lighter-coloured tiles above his head. The light is better here, and his fingers detect ornate undulations on their glazed surfaces. Beneath an archway he turns to follow Elsa but suddenly loses her in the gloom, the sound of her steps diminishing to his left while to his right a wide, liquid dark staircase rises into the blackness of the floor above, thick balustrades like fat calves propping wide bannisters tiled the same and glinting light. He peers into the darkness of the other direction and follows the sound of the footsteps, long gone now bar their sonic ripples about the corridor. Through another archway he can smell the water and feels the moist air around his eyes and face, the taste of chlorine on his tongue. Then out through another archway he's at the side of the swimming baths, an old Victorian pool that stretches out before him with a high glass roof bathing light over the languid dark water rippling lattices of light off its surface. Blue changing cubicles run regimented down the length of the pool on either side, each door closed and above them a balcony and a viewing gallery with bench seats to watch.

Billy cannot see Elsa.

He whispers her name, his voice a brittle hiss echoing around the room, the *S* of her name reporting against the hard tiles like breaking glass and captured high in the vaulted glass roof.

"*Elsa,*" he says again, fearful of the noise and the attraction it might create, her name called the second time overlapping the remnants of the first.

At the far end of the pool, the deep end, she emerges dancing at the side of the baths from the shadows beneath the balcony in the corner of the hall. Billy narrows his eyes and stares at her through the half-lit space across the water and after a moment of adjustment sees she has stripped. A surge of anticipation flows from within. He wants her. Naked she steps with pointed toes to the edge of the pool, her arms out wide and turns a full circle with straight and outstretched legs. Repeating her move she tiptoes from one side of the pool to the other and Billy watches her dancing enthralled by her pale, lithe body spinning and moving around the edge of the pool like a water nymph. In the half-light he sees her smiling and hears her laughter as she turns and with a final graceful stretch of her arms upwards, stands as a Y shape at the edge of the pool, the teardrop shape of her breasts swelling over her ribcage sand-ripple shadowed. She is pale and motionless, and Billy is aroused, his desire of her newness, the novelty and appeal of her shape, her inclinations and appetites.

He watches her close her eyes and with a deep breath leaps high in the air from her standing position and into the water, an entry of grace, the surface parted with the softest of sounds.

Beneath the surface she swims towards him, a shimmering white Exocet, the outline of her form buckling and reshaping in the undulant water until she surfaces in a bubble, the liquid meniscus breaking over her face as she stands shoulder high in the water, wiping her hair to the back of her neck with both hands clasped against her skull. Billy sees her two dark eyes, peering from her white face in the dead centre of the pool and he feels the excitement surge again.

"Welcome to my secret world," she says softly, the sound floating across the water. "Come and join me."

He begins to undress, and turning away to conceal his arousal, backs into the water. "You are crazy, Elsa Kelly," he says, laughing.

"I used to come here before I was pregnant. I'd swim in the daytime and come back again at night when the place was dark and empty. No one would dream you could get into this place; no one would ever guess. It's so wonderfully free, the whole pool to yourself. You can shed your clothes and leave all your troubles outside, with this whole beautiful building to yourself, to indulge yourself in the water."

Billy slips naked into the water, the cool surface rising up his body like ribbons of a cold silk veil being drawn over him, chilling him and tightening his flesh. He pushes a bow wave out before him towards her, the water in his mouth, eddying through his toes and fingers until at last he's with her and she's upon him, her arms around his neck and shoulders, her legs wrapped around his waist, her liquid mouth smothering his. And with the lightness of flying, buoyant and defiant of any earthly pull or gravitas they float, twisting and turning in the fluid ambience and dusky light with no distractions or thoughts of anything but themselves in the swaying body of water, the centre of the universe, unencumbered by clothes, unconcerned by cares; free.

Back again to Manchester's Hulme Estate, Late Summer 1989

She gets picked up because they think she's a man. The lorry drivers' have an unwritten code by which they won't go for a single woman hitch hiking just in case. *Just in case what?* In case she cries rape? This, she is told once she's in the cab of a truck heading South, the white-vested driver offering to break the golden rule just for her, just this once. Such largesse! There's male fantasy in there somewhere beneath she knows, it reveals itself flirtatiously in his conversation and the way he adjusts himself in his seat on the journey but with the ride safely secured she doesn't care. *Give me your money or I'll tell the cops I was sexually assaulted!* Fat chance they'd believe you could prize that gut from under the steering wheel in time! She gets to Manchester in record time; quicker than the train and at no cost other than the suggestive intimations she can just about tolerate for a few hours, but no more.

Elsa's so pleased to see her and she's missed those gorgeous grey eyes, the feel and smell of her and holds her wide shoulders tight and breathes deeply into her neck.

"It kills me to say it—"

"I'm not gloating—"

"Just don't gloat!"

"I'm not, I'm not!"

"You were right."

"It's so good to have you back Sam."

She showcases Marley, holds him up to his Aunty and the baby's all cute beams and chuckles. He swims in the air and drools from a frothy wide smile, and she appreciates his happy mood can be erratic but is well timed for her arrival; it bodes well.

Freya leans against the wall and waits her turn until the baby cooing and tickling is done then silently hugs her big sister and doesn't let go for a long time; there's more in that longevity than words can ever say.

Kathy is less agreeable, but indifference has always been her way with Sam, more thick skin than hard heart. "So, you've come back," she says evenly but Sam is in no mood for combat and embraces her mother regardless. The absence of commentary on ink and metal suggests a thawing. She hears the struggle of her breath in her ear in quick, inefficient draughts and winces at the sound.

"How are you Mam?" she asks.

Kathy fusses the question away with handholds and side steps. "As well as can be expected."

"You look well."

Eye contact returns. "What brings you home?"

Sam doesn't probe for the details of the mugging; Elsa's letter was descriptive enough and there'll be plenty of opportunity over the few weeks she plans to stay. A reason too, perhaps salient is the end of the affair with Belziare who has another lover with tattoos and piercings and an artistic flair. A notch on his easel; a woman too far, this one called Ana from Belgium like he's collecting passport stamps. Sam lost her temper, threw a half bottle of wine at him, then a full one. He laughed, the wine dripping from the walls behind him then complained of the waste of a good drink. Ana shrank behind him, wine-spattered and afraid. She was right to be, but Sam made the call that night and left the following morning, happy if she never saw either of them again.

"I want to see how you are," she says to her mother, then more expansively; "how you all are. Tell me about this Billy who's come to see you," she says to Elsa. Another reason. She smiles at Elsa's change of colour.

Freya moves from side to side, restraint impossible. "They're staying next door," she says. "And Billy took her dancing."

Elsa shoots a look, but her pleasure dilutes its effect.

"How quaint. And are you *courting*?"

"The other's got broken ribs. Mam doesn't like him; says he's trouble." Freya's good for the headlines; always quick to say it like it is.

"Tell me all," Sam says.

"I'll share mine if you share yours," Elsa says.

Sam is ambivalent about returning. The Estate sings to her, she dreams about it often but there's something defeatist in her coming back. In her mind she plans to stay for just a couple of weeks, three at a stretch but somewhere lurking is the prospect of longer. She's light of foot with few possessions bar her jewellery and the tools to make it and not much else. That works both ways where Manchester is concerned; easy to leave and to return. The friendships in Glasgow are meaningful but can be remembered and left there, like the books on her shelves. She wishes there were more depth but there isn't.

The short stay span involves reconnecting with family and friends, Elsa mainly. She harbours nagging concerns about her own lack of empathy for her mother's health but thinks this will change as they spend more time together. The prospect dismays her; it's not supposed to be a chore. She knows there will be conversations where she'll have to hold her tongue to avoid fall out but hopes recent events, baby Marley, the terrible mugging might have blunted her notorious edge. According to Elsa, it has. There's a room made up for her which is one thing but even that she finds faintly dispiriting.

She mentally details a schedule pieced together over the past few days to prevent the next ones slipping into weeks and then more. She spends time on the decks with Elsa, with Verity and Tammy who has an inherent connection of security with her that no other can elicit. Her departure was a further cause of Tammy's withdrawal from the world and her return injects renewed succour, a rediscovered comfort blanket. It's not enough to coax her further from the access deck to put distance from her flat as bolt hole but there's an hour or so in the sunlight that Sam observes she's in desperate need of to prevent her evaporation into anaemic oblivion. She's happy that Sam has returned, and Sam does not divulge its intended brevity. She wonders how she will cope when the little clique is disbanded when they're all rehoused. Broken it may be but there's community here. It's a paradox to Sam she acknowledges that the security she herself seeks following the travails of Glasgow is an alternative place so wholly unsafe.

Sam's time with Elsa is compromised by Elsa's with Billy. He's good to her and *with* her and their feelings for each other are clear, the candour prominent and selfish. More than once, fleetingly she feels intrusive. There's no intention, it's just how it is for new lovers and she's enamoured by her sister's happiness and the thought of her own failed liaisons chokes off her pique. She's not in that space at the moment anyway. One of the recent times of course has been with Max, the injured one laid up in a John Henry's old flat and that brief and awkward exchange in the draughty room at the top of her old place has left her with feelings she struggles to interpret; beyond rejection and into curiosity, disclosure even. It's one part of that evening she'd like to forget but can't. He's another on the list of her diary dates.

On a diet of sweet black tea, white bread, tobacco and fitful sleep, Max begins to make a recovery. He spends his time in the flat, too painful to leave, propped up with pillows and blankets to keep his torso in such a position that will lessen the aching in his ribs. The pain naturally subsides by small degrees as the bruising fades from black to an odd, jaundiced colour that reminds him of a foreign sunset. He presses his fingers into his side to see what pain he can endure, his tolerance rising daily, the pressure increasing before it's too much. During this convalescence he reads newspapers

Billy brings from the newsagents and writes a couple of long-distance calling cards with the flat's return address to people he knows around and about and a rambling letter to a friend in Marbella, unsure whether there's a postal service operating on the Estate for return correspondence.

"There is," Sam says, returning the sports section of a newspaper to him. The names of horses have been ringed in a number of races. "Looking for the next big winner?"

"Chance would be…"

"How are you?" she asks.

He waves a hand down his bruised flanks. "What brings you back to Manchester?"

"Everyone's asking that."

"And…?"

She looks around the room and can't tell if the corners are dark with shadows or mould. "Came to see what's happening in my old stomping ground."

"Not much working around here," Max says.

She sees the letter on the floor. "You can get mail sent to Post Restante at the nearest Post Office."

"I never thought," Max says. "I should have put them on the envelopes."

"What are you writing?" she asks. He looks different to her now he's lost the ill-fitting suit and with short hair, more gaunt but healthier than she imagined. She remembers with fondness the animation in his dark eyes that remain despite his predicament.

"About what happened to me and Billy, our adventures;

where we've been and the people we've met along the way, where we are now, where we might be going to next."

"You had a bad run when you left the squat."

"I've had better days I can't deny; I'm not dwelling on that part."

"That's admirable," she says.

"*Admirable?* I don't see it that way."

She smiles, trying to evoke something similar. "And what is next?"

Max shrugs and winces with the movement. "I don't know," he says. "Wherever the road may take us."

"*Us?*"

The plural hangs in the air like a tasteless joke. "Maybe me."

"Gooseberries together—; again."

"Yeah; about that..." He shifts his posture to ease the pain and leaves the statement unfinished as though this might suffice.

"What about that?"

He grimaces, a sign of the painful repositioning or irritation at her pressing him, perhaps both, she can't say. "There's a lot to it," he says.

"Tell me. I've broad shoulders you know. I'm not looking for apologies."

"What are you looking for?"

Here he is before her once again, all surly appearance and the stories of derring-do behind him, but fragile and vulnerable, just as before. It's a transparent shield of armour.

"The truth."

"About?"

"About you. About you and Billy, your friend who's pulling out all the stops for my sister."

"Does that bother you?"

"Does that bother *you*?"

Light glints on his fat lip and the bruising about his face changes colour; the intensity of her query, its impact. It reminds her of a purple slug pulsing across his mouth. "You have feelings for him," she says. It's an observation not an inquiry.

"Sure, I have feelings for him." He reaches for the blanket around his waist, curls it in his fist and pulls it in. "He's my friend and we're on the road together aren't we?"

"You know, in Glasgow I felt a connection between us that night. What happened is that after we talked and you followed me upstairs, I understood the connection I wanted was never going to be, was it?"

Max looks at her, his attention fluttering over her face. "You're so smart," he says.

"You're good at appearances; at hiding it."

"Hiding what exactly?"

She moves further into the room, getting to the heart of it. "Does Billy know how you feel for him?"

He pauses. "We're on the road together, looking for redemption."

"*Does he*?"

"He's not my type."

Sam smiles. "Who is?"

"Where I was brought up if you talk about things like that you're setting yourself up for a good kicking."

She laughs, more of a loud exhaling. "Seems to be your thing."

He doesn't respond.

"How *were* you brought up?" she asks.

He pats the blanket for cigarettes and chokes out disappointment on finding only an empty packet. "Stepfathers, real fathers gone; different ones for me and my brother. Crazy mother who tied one of them to a bed in a sex game then beat the living shit out of him."

"Class. Who was he?"

"Tommo his name; beat the shit out of me when I untied him then left to put my mother in hospital. My brother couldn't hack it, so he joined up and finished up at the wrong end of an Armalite. Not a great atmosphere to talk about... well, you know."

"The real you?"

"To admit to anything that would get you a good kicking. Do you have any cigarettes?"

"I'm all out; sorry. Is that why you left?"

"Sort of."

"*Sort of*?"

"Why do you want to know all this?"

There's an old chest of draws with a large, cracked mirror pushed into a corner of the room, a remnant of furniture from the relocation and Sam tests its strength before sitting on it. "My mother always warned me of people who answer questions with questions."

Her manner is less adversarial than her mother's maxim; she's not as pugnacious as her, her love not as unsympathetic.

"*My* mother always warned me about my father, and my brother Daniel about his. My brother's father was a tyre fitter called Daniel too who fixed her car one day then fixed her the next. When he found out she was pregnant he took off, but she didn't have that option. She stuck with the name Daniel, maybe she thought it might bring him back. It didn't."

"What about *your* father?" Sam asks.

"Little Daniel needed a father in its life and made a beeline for a local Italian; Lou Lucciani, son and heir of the Lucciani Ice Cream business and a fleet of ice cream vans. Their paths crossed because she craved Double Whip and he had a fondness for milky mothers. Lou stuck around for a while when Danny was a baby, long enough to get her pregnant again. And that was me! The son of an Italian ice-cream man."

"You have the Mediterranean look about you Max; brown eyes, dark hair – before you had it all chopped," Sam says.

"For sure, and my mother had the temperament. Lou was already a father, and the old man couldn't make the sums add up for two mothers, so something had to give. Our mother the fall girl again so she made sure their rocking sessions in his ice cream van went public. The fall out was long and loud and stretched all the way back to Napoli."

"Two boys, one mother, no father."

"Your maths is good. *Step*fathers a plenty. They came in and out of our lives and never stayed too long. Lots of domestics, rozzers in the night and Daniel and me had to hide to keep away from the trouble. When the novelty wore off the big scenes followed, shouting and scrapping, doors slamming, and Daniel always made sure we stayed together and kept out of their way. Don't be seen, he said. He made us invisible.

Then there was Tommo; crazy eyes, tattooed neck, Borstal Dots. We knew the type, the feral, glazed look like a beaten dog wary of humans. We developed an instinct; avoid eye-contact, always sat next to a door when he was around. I came home one night and found him shackled to the bed, naked and beaten; UNTIE ME you cunt, untie me! She'd had him for all the shit he gave her; for being a violent, thieving bastard; for head-butting her; for nicking the rent; for the cig-arette burns he gave her; for stoving in the front door. When he'd asked for pain, he hadn't counted on quite so much my mother had inside her. She was just biding her time, waiting for the chance to get her reckoning on *man*kind, and there he was at her mercy. So I untied him, and got a beating, then he left to find her and put her in hospital when he did; one for the money, two for the show.

After that Daniel went and joined the army and I was on my own."

"You left home?"

"Sort of. Daniel was my protector; always one step ahead of the game for me to walk behind. He made it safer for us. Where he'd been I'd always followed but not the military; that was a step too far. He was seduced by the army and returned from the Recruiting Office full of talk about career opportunities and the benefits of army life; skiing, scuba-diving, mechanics. I told him exactly what I thought of it. He didn't want to know. His mind was made up. When you've got nothing the opportunity to get out of a shit life is a good alternative, like we're doing now me and Billy. It's a chance to see the world, ski down mountains and chop through jungles and mess about with shit you wouldn't get a chance to in Civy Street. Then he ended up in Northern Ireland in that dirty nasty little war of shit smearing hunger strikers, informants and betrayals, infiltrators, kidnaps and torture. And that's where it ended for him. And I left and went back, left again and back again, trying to get away from it all."

"But you can't run and hide from it."

"I don't see it as running and hiding," he says evenly. "I call it moving on. I've been moving on from stuff all my life."

"Then Billy turns up and the real you shines through."

Confronted by naked truths Sam notices him genuflect, his physical subjugation to its probity, like he's been guilty of trying to outwit things but is now resigned, a fair cop. "Yeah," he says equivocally but his posture says too much. "Can you get me some cigarettes?" he says forlornly throwing a decoy.

The breeze and noise sliding in through an open window reminds Sam of the world outside the old flat. "We can get some from the pub if you're feeling up to it."

"Ok," he says, brighter.

"Does Billy know?"

"Which bit?"

"About your brother?"

"I never like to talk about it," he says.

"What about the other thing; the real you? Does he know that?"

"No, he doesn't, and he doesn't need to know, so don't tell."

"OK," she says. "Why not?"

"It would change things and besides there is no point is there? He's a proper happy bunny now he's with Elsa."

"Perhaps she's his redemption."

Max stares and but says nothing.

"Let's get you some cigarettes," she says. "And a pint, you look like you could do with one."

The Spinners is a building that was already in bad shape when she left and has not improved since. It's more like a brown bricked detached house from the outside but has a bar in one room and a separate room for a pool table. It's so dilapidated Max wonders if there is any beer to be tapped, but the pipes are one of the few things that work and in the late afternoon there are a few punters drinking and Verity serves them drinks at the bar. Max manages to walk upright into the room, part dignity, part advice from the rehabilitation leaflet. He's carefully positioned on a bar stool when Billy arrives some moments later.

"I thought you'd ran out again when I saw the flat was empty."

"How d'you guess I was here?"

"I didn't; Freya told me."

"The all-seeing one."

"Nothing gets past her," Sam says.

"It's good to see you up and about."

"Fill him with enough of this stuff and he won't feel a thing," says Verity. She's a short-limbed woman with a wide, friendly face shaped like a pear-drop and an abruptly pointed chin. She drops a packet of cigarettes on the bar. "On the house," she says. "If you're still here later when the place is busier, I'll refill your pints too; *on the house*."

"You're an angel Vee," says Sam.

"It's good to see you back home again. And how are your injuries, soldier?" Verity asks Max. She has a short tongue to match her limbs.

"A thousand times better," he replies. "I must be a quick healer."

"Or the palliative care is proper," Sam says.

"Why'd you take a beating?"

"We didn't run quickly enough," says Billy.

"Too much to say for myself," Max says. "As usual; me and my big mouth!"

"I bet you're a sweet guy really," Verity says, her words wrapped in the lisp.

"He is," says Billy.

Max smiles and drinks deeply from the first pint in a while that leaves a tide mark on his lip. "Where's Elsa?" he asks.

"She's with the baby; she'll be here later."

"Know what you're doing?" Max asks, guiding Billy to the stool next to him.

"Meaning?"

"The kid and all."

A low sunlight is down across his face and eyes, giving them a hardened edge, picking out the auburn buried in his whiskers, copper in soil.

"It's only been a short time," Billy says. "We're not making plans."

"Are *we*?"

Sam reaches for the unopened carton of cigarettes. She's thinking she ought to leave them alone for a while and seeks out Verity who's serving another punter on the other side of the bar. She sees beyond her shoulder a familiar face that looks like Elsa pushing at the door from the weakening evening light and into the smoky electric glare of the bar.

Verity sees her too. "Sam," she says. "It's your sister Freya."

"What does she want in here?"

Freya, smooth faced and pale, dressed as usual in school uniform inappropriate for the surroundings has been running. Hair strafing her face there's a look of urgency in her eyes, a silent siren as she struggles for breath, coughing with the smoke-filled air of the bar room.

Sam's at once resolute and serious; "Freya! Breathe! What's the matter? Talk to me!"

"Elsa," she says, hands to knees then quickly back up gasping for breath. "Elsa..." she says again, the word floundering in the shallows.

Billy blanches. "What's happened?"

"Elsa want's you back quickly." The dam of Freya's message bursts. "It's Martin; he's been attacked on the skywalk."

Sam takes her sister's hands in her own and pulls them towards her and Freya's head snaps back, a shock movement that gets her immediate focus.

"How bad? Does he need an ambulance?"

"I don't know," Freya says pulling her hands loose again. "You've got to come, quickly."

"*Tulip*," says Verity.

Red eyes and tear streaked faces greet them. Elsa's there,

a serious pallor about her, as has Kathy. Ivy Smith whose lips are quivering paces the room, stopping intermittently to place her shaking hands on her son's shoulders; a disruption of her anxiety. Martin is in a chair wrapped and shivering in a yellow blanket with a silk hem that shines in the electric light, a blood-stained tea-towel pressed against his head. The blood is dark and black in places between his fingers and down his cheeks and neck. Time has elapsed since the assault. Fresher, wetter blood mixes with tears. A dark bulbous drip congeals to a point of his chin, quivering in the whiskers preventing its fall. He whimpers and shakes, and his mother is behind him, touching his shoulders and patting his arms, his form unpalatable to her like this.

"Did you call an ambulance?" Sam asks.

Elsa's at the patient and confirms. Billy and Max are stood in the doorway behind Sam who's assured by her proficiency in a crisis.

"I did," Kathy says, "they take so long."

"How long ago?"

"Fifteen, twenty minutes."

"Which was it Mam; fifteen or twenty?"

"*Twenty.*"

Elsa's head is at Martin's knee. He's grey faced and sobbing rhythmically, a trance-like condition, in shock. White spittle clots in the corners of his mouth, fresh deposits forming over his trembling lips.

"Maaartiiiin." She's whispering his name as though waking him. "Listen to me Martin. You're going to be alright. I just need to look at the wound again."

Martin recoils but soon settles.

"I am a nurse remember," Elsa continues, "so I want just another peek under this tea towel. Let's see. This is like being back at the hospital for me Martin, before I had Marley."

The platitudes are effective. "This is Mam's best she brought from Rhyl. You must be a very special person for her to give you *this* tea towel. Ok that's right. Ok, now here we are. I see the wound."

The wound has a big egg bulging around it. "It looks ok. There's swelling there which is a good thing; it means the pressure's coming outwards and not against your brain. But we're going to have to get you to the hospital just to be sure everything's ok; everyone goes to the hospital if they've banged their heads. You'll get to see where I work at last Martin, you've always wanted that haven't you. I can make sure you're looked after properly. So just stay here and keep very still and nice and warm. You'll get the best treatment when you get there and we'll be away shortly."

She stands and turns away from Martin and Billy sees her face contort, her mouth severe, and facing her mother behind her with a silent snarl through clenched teeth says: "*Where's this fucking ambulance?*"

*

Warm English summer rain falls lightly for hours then increases in intensity. The cloud is grey in lumps smeared over the blue sky like a child's painting and the low flat disc of a darker band moves into the skyline behind. Billy sees it as a huge portent rolling in. He puts a cigarette together that picks up the moisture from the rain spattering against the balcony wall. It makes the paper wrinkle between his fingers and he moves back with the damp offering to his lips. The greyness clings above Manchester hanging in swollen boulders and he listens to the white noise of the rain on so much concrete. With his eyes closed it's the sound of a waterfall, white water on rocks out there on the moors someplace.

The sound fades. Billy opens his eyes and the downfall has briefly cleansed the Estate of its inhabitants. Above the vast crescent building opposite him and past the shimmering rain the blue returns and with it the warmth of the sun. Pavements glisten, steam rises. Billy squints at the light on the slick surfaces and crushes out the already wet cigarette in a puddle, returning to the flat where Sam is in the kitchen making strong tea for all and handing them to Max to distribute.

"Want one?"

Billy shakes his head and moves into the front room where Elsa's talking to Ivy, both sat on the edge of the sofa, Elsa with her hands between her knees.

"The CT scan picked up a contusion. It's one of the most common type of injuries following a bang on the head because it's a basically a bruise; blood vessel damage just like you'd get if you're bashed anywhere else. He was lucky Ivy."

It's the third time she's explained it, a deliberate, slow drip-feed of information and the reassurances of minor memory loss and a bad headache for a while, steering a light and palat-able path through the gravity of it all. Elsa makes the time to repeat without tiring or betraying her frustration at Ivy's grasp of it.

"It might have knocked some sense into him at last."

Ivy pulls an unconvincing smile, a laboured grin brought on by the nervous energy burned at the hospital. And at her age. She's been close to the family for years, in the days of the terraces, house to house hairdressing for young mothers, to the demolitions, her husband's demise, the upheaval of their relocation, then skyline decades in the crumbling Crescents. Frying pan to fire. She's been through it all. And now this. They'd spent hours pacing the ward corridors, waiting for news. The delay felt interminable but when it finally came Ivy heard nothing but an alien lexicon of medical terms spoken by the staff; *cerebral contusion; intracranial pressure; reduced motor functioning*. Elsa was on hand to translate but for Ivy only the term *brain injury* properly registered and this conclusion resulted in a sudden ebbing of her strength and a clutch of hands easing her into a nearby chair.

Patiently, thoroughly, Elsa explains again. Ivy's understanding is sluggish, her thoughts preoccupied only by the date of his release. Her world has been turned on its head and no matter what Elsa offers, her soul is lost to deep anxiety. Alone in her flat for the first time ever she has not slept since leaving her son in hospital for observation. The strain is evident.

"Does she want sugar?" Max asks Elsa pushing the mug before her.

"Why don't you ask her?" she replies.

Ivy shakes her head. "As it is," she says. She just wants her big, lolloping son home again so *he* can bring her tea instead of this loud stranger with his own bruises on his brooding, unshaven face, shuffling around the flat, wincing as he bends and slamming the cup down next to her like he doesn't care.

Max turns away and places a second cup down for Kathy who's sat at the table working the buttonhole of her cardigan in her fingers. She doesn't notice the offering.

"Do you want sugar?" Max asks.

There's no response.

"Do you want sugar?" he repeats, louder.

"I need to call another meeting," she says.

Later in the day an argument brews and it's over Tammy. Kathy insists on all the neighbours attending the gathering she's called. Sam counters; Tammy's already had to listen to it and has heeded the warning about Mark Tulip previously, she won't want to surface again. If Sam can't coax her out who can? Besides, she maintains, Tammy's condition makes her the safest of all of them because she so seldom seen outside her flat. But Kathy is adamant and Sam feels the needle of old. "She needs to understand what happened, to Martin," she insists. "Tulip's a danger alright, a threat to us all. He'll stop at nothing. This man's no hesitation at attacking innocent people. With Martin he used the cosh, with me the knife. He's violent and unstable, who knows how far he'll take it." She's certain of this; it's partly the personal involvement of having been on the receiving end and also a marker laid out for her wayfaring daughter, for the gall of her trying to override her on her return. There's a tactful intervention from Elsa who's vigilant to the dynamics of it. In the end it's their Mam who has her way.

Standing watchful in the doorway of the hall, Billy levers himself off the frame and into the room. "How do you know it's the same person?" he asks.

"We do," Kathy says with distant hostility, the question somehow impertinent to her; she's had enough disrespect from her own.

"He might not return."

"The guy's an opportunist," Max says. "He'll be back."

"He never even demanded the money; just bashed Martin then rifled his pockets," Elsa says.

"Shoots first; asks questions later."

"A desperado," Max says.

"It's not a Western," Kathy shoots. "I found Martin later, out there on the balcony. He had twenty quid on him, that was all."

"He didn't try to break into the flat."

"There's nothing in there to steal," Ivy says.

"So what? The last thing we need is a psychopathic crackhead running around the place looking for stuff to hawk to for a fix."

"Maybe he knows there's nothing to take," Kathy says. "He's familiar with the people up here so he knows where to go hunting."

"Does he know you?" Billy asks.

"Sort of," Elsa says. "He comes and goes from time to time. He's always been a drug user, a petty thief but not always so violent. He used to be a runner for Nelson."

"Nelson?" Billy's surprised to hear this name.

Elsa spears him a look; *what of it?* "This is new for him," she says. "Something must have happened to turn him from running for Nelson to mugging people." This past is a cause of friction between Elsa and her Mam and she's eager to keep it there.

"There's nothing left to steal on the estate anymore," Sam says. "Nobody owns anything worth lifting. There are more empty flats now than when I was last here and those occupied have nothing worth taking."

"She's right," Kathy says. "Except for us. We're probably the last ones living around here with anything of any value. Maybe he knows that. He knows us and realises he'll find pickings here."

"And he'll have an easy time without much retaliation, women living alone up here," Billy says.

"Mere women?" Kathy's quick on her reply.

"And Martin," Ivy says meekly, oblivious to the meaning of her neighbour's remark.

Max fixes his look upon them both, briefly hesitating with a cigarette paper horizontal against his lips before zipping it across his tongue. Elsa next to Ivy observes his stillness, perhaps it's apathy; not one for showing contrived consoling gestures.

"There's not much you can do if someone jumps you with a baseball bat," he says. "Even if you're six foot and built like a bull."

"And he's going to do it again," Kathy says. "He'll go out and score, then he'll come back again to score again. We're ducks in a pond and I'm not one for taking things lying down. We need to do something about this situation and quickly before we pick up another casualty like Martin."

"What about the law?"

"What law?" asks Sam.

"Not a chance," says Elsa. "They're leaving the Estate to eat itself; they don't even bother with enquiries."

A knock, the sound of the door to the flat slamming, the familiar jump of the letter box flap makes them all start. Freya walks into the room, returning from school, throwing her bag into the corner of the hallway. Behind her Verity, shorter, busier, more urgent of step.

"What's everyone doing here?" Freya asks with all her teenage insouciance despite the recent events.

"I thought I'd walk her home," Verity says. "From school; because of, you know, the problem."

"Thanks, Verity," Kathy says. "That's kind of you love."

"I can look after myself."

"How's Martin?" Verity asks.

"We're expecting him back home tomorrow," says Ivy. Her optimism is plaintive.

"They're keeping him in for another night of observation," Elsa adds. "Perhaps longer."

"Vinegar and brown paper," says Max quietly to himself, only Verity hears it and stares at him wide-eyed, biting hard on her bottom lip to thwart her smile spreading.

"What's been decided?" she asks.

"Nothing; yet."

Billy asks; "Where does Mark Tulip live?"

"Why?" asks Freya returning to the front room with a half packet of biscuits. "Are you gonna go round and sort him out?"

The silence in the room falls around Billy like a dark cape

pulled over his head, around his shoulders, shrouding his body. He slows his thoughts in the understanding of it and looks to Max for some sort of steer; what can they do to help here? What's the expectation? To his surprise, Max smiles a full beam that exposes the gap in the teeth, his tongue in it. He gives Billy no enlightenment to its meaning. Billy wants his own counsel, a private one for him and his friend alone, away from this arena of hope.

"The caped crusader," Max says eventually.

"I'm not a damsel in distress," Elsa says. "And that's a bad idea, Freya. No one's going to get sorted out. We don't want escalation for some crack-crazed nutters poking around looking for revenge. We're all vulnerable and there's Marley too, don't forget!"

"He's hardly in a fit state anyway this one," says Verity, reaching around Max's shoulder for a spare mug of tea. She references him with a flick of her head.

"In a fit state for what exactly?" He raises his eyebrows, the humour still in his eyes.

"A fight!" shouts Freya. A burst of biscuit crumbs explode from her lips. Her words cling to the space in the room as the fragments fall on the carpet and a conspicuous silence descends that's not one born of the need for a plate.

"No," Billy says quickly, "God knows we've had enough of that. But some sort of warning; a shot across his bows. Something that will scare him off or make him think twice about coming back this way again."

"*High Plains Drifter*," says Max. "We could paint everything red."

"Oh, that's brilliant," Verity says. Her brown eyes widen. "That would really freak the fucker right out."

"I wasn't serious," Max says quietly, dryly, ignoring her hanging smile that lingers despite his censure. "What kind of deterrence did you have in mind, Billy?" He asks, freezing the others out by the emphasis of his friend's name.

"I don't know; I was just suggesting something. We could talk to him, make him aware we're here; let him know we'll be ready for him if he comes this way again."

Max emits an unconvincing grunt. "You and your plans," he says. "Do you think he'd listen to us?"

"Probably not." Wings clipped, Billy sits down but his agitation is manifest and jittery.

"Besides," Max continues, tapping the end of his unlit cigarette on the table; "we don't know where he lives."

Elsa sighs. "He moves around; NFA. He could be any-where."

"Think this through," Billy says and stands again, as though to aid its process. "He's taken money; that's not going to last him long, so he's likely to return."

"He might be whacking people all over the Estate," says Max.

"But if he isn't, it won't be long before he's back here again."

"You need to set a trap," Max says. "What about the blonde next door; tie her to the balcony outside as bait."

Elsa withholds her reproach but not the others.

"Take this seriously," Kathy says. "Ivy's son's in hospital with head injuries and you're making wisecracks."

Her rebuke brings silence, a gap which gives Billy tries to hang on to. To Billy, Elsa's regard for him is as serious as her mother's tone. Kicking his foot against the hollow door that oscillates in its frame he recalls the failure of the last situation, his own nebulous and botched thinking in the Travel Hotel, the plan that hardly materialised until Max stepped in, the start of their recent run of things. Max's flippant remark adds to his recollection; the same now as it was then, it won't happen like that again, he's certain of that. "He'll resurface," he says. "He'll come this way again and when he does we can be ready; give him a warning so he's not so sure next time."

"Good luck with that partner," Max says, putting the cigarette to his lips and reaching for his lighter.

Billy watches his downturned mouth, his eyes rolling, a slow and almost imperceptible shake of his head. "Don't smoke that in here," he says.

Triangulation comes days later when Martin Smith returns from hospital with his head tightly bound in a clean white bandage and a bemused expression in his eyes. His comedy look and the relief felt by all on his return to his mother has them giggling and coddling him affectionately, the tension of the previous days released and bubbling, a gurgling stream of relief undammed. Martin, shy and uncommunicative is uncomfortable with their collective welcome but happy to let them fuss him. He stands motionless with his straight arms pinned to his side and head bowed as the others surround and hug him, stroking and squeezing his thick, weak arms. Their smiles are contagious, and he grins with the flurry of his extended welcome; the additional female attention, home once more, warm and safe again, if a little discomfited after the hot noisy wards and strangers in the hospital beds next to him.

But Billy is keen to question him and can see his own presence makes him nervous. Like they'd done in the hospital he asks difficult questions; who his attacker was, if he knows him, whether he can describe him or if he could identify him again. Martin backs away as though his probing is too forceful and invasive and just wants to forget about the incident now he's out of hospital and the medical staff have finished their own interrogations. He just wants to be left alone with his Mam and wishes everyone else would disappear.

"I don't want to go through it all again," he says, but Billy's insistent; what did he see, what hit his head, how hard was the blow? Does he remember anything else at all, did he get a look at the guy?

"Leave the poor mutt alone," Max says to Billy. "He can't remember anything; and what he does he wants to forget."

"I need to find out," Billy says.

"Of course it was the Tulip guy; twice in the same place and look how tall Lurch is." Billy watches Martin, a big-boned ungainly man of well over six foot, his bulk and inelegance accentuated by bandages around his throbbing head almost brushing the low ceiling of the flat where the stringy webs of dust hang.

"So?" Billy says.

"Tulip's the same height they say, tall. He's the one you want."

"*I* want?" Billy says. "Are you with me on this?"

"On what exactly?" Max asks.

"On stopping it happening again."

"So you can show to Elsa you're her Great Protector?"

"Max," Billy says slowly, exhaling his name. "This Tulip's a nut."

"Look where your last crazy-assed plans got us back in Lancaster."

"Us!" Billy smiles. "That's right. Not you or me, but us; together."

"Two bums on the road."

"On the road together, right?"

Max turns away and looks down at the floor. "Sure" he says. "You only want me in because you think I'm half handy in a fight. Well look at me Billy; do you think I'm up for that now with these busted ribs? And if this guy's carrying weapons, what are you going to carry to defend yourself? Have you even considered what you'll do if he pulls a knife on you? No, no you haven't, I can tell by your face you haven't thought of that. I know how much you want to show to Elsa that you're her shining knight, but you have to think it through properly."

"I want to help her Max. I don't want her to get hurt."

Max stares into Billy's imploring face, looks but says nothing, just holding his contemplation. "Yeah," he says after a while, "well I don't want you getting yourself busted up either."

In the days that follow Max and Billy remain close to the flats, casually walking the balcony, alert to the people they see passing by. The surrounding flats are a mixture; a few are inhabited or occasionally occupied by people arriving with nothing, then leaving with the same. Most are just deserted. Encounters on the walkways are with passers-by using the skywalks to get from one side of the crescents to the next. Most of the flats further on towards the far stairwells are empty or locked up with boarded doors and windows and no signs of tenancy. Some are fire damaged. Graffiti adorns nearly every surface, thicker and more pervasive and colourful where the flats are empty and showing no other signs of life, a gaudy indicator of their abandonment. One place has had its guts dragged out on to the balcony, a pile of old clothes, rugs, cardboard boxes and broken furniture damp and fire damaged, the remnants of an emergency evacuation. There's a pushchair too, blackened and smoke stained; and Billy is reminded of Elsa's professed greatest fear.

They move on further and over the days familiarise themselves with the balconies and the decks above and below them; the alcoves and recesses, the damp corners, the carbuncles and warts. Maintaining vigilance during the daytime and at night they casually linger on the balcony looking out across the green space below, smoking cigarettes in the balmy summer's air, watching for signs and waiting. One evening they're accompanied by Elsa and Sam and Verity too when she's finished her shift at the pub. They haul a two-seat sofa from the flat and wedge it in the balcony with enough room for walkers to pass by and sit talking, loud and conspicuous to remove any suspicion of their lying in waiting, surreptitiously attentive to anyone who might show themselves furtively or otherwise on the balcony. Plenty do. Occasionally one or two who know Elsa join for a smoke and sit down to talk on their way along the walkway. Others who've not seen Sam for ages catch up on her news. But nobody can identify the person they're looking for. Mostly Billy and Max sit alone, chewing fat.

"There was a time," Billy says, "when they imagined these walkways as the future blueprint for all architecture in British cities." His angle of vision on the sofa is just enough to see through the slats in the balcony walls and out to the greater expanse and the silvery darkness beyond.

"Who did?" Max asks.

"The architects, the planners."

"Jesus; what kind of future did they see?"

Billy sits back and slings his feet over the arm of the sofa. "Well, not this kind that's for sure," he says.

"They got it wrong."

"Maybe," Billy says, "but you can see what they were getting at, what they were trying to achieve."

"You can?"

"Yes, I think so. They were looking to create a better way of life or build an environment that would support a better living space. It was a way to improve on the endless rows of terraces that were all slum housing by the fifties and sixties."

"How do you know this?"

"Kathy told me."

"The mother in law?"

Billy smiles. "She explained the thinking, back then when they were rehoused. The sky walks were built to elevate the residents from the slum terraces and up into the air and light. Like flowers lifting their heads from the undergrowth. Instead of just tower blocks they wanted to combine the best bits of what went before; that's what the access decks and sky walks are all about, literally to raise people out of the cobbled gutters, to lift them high above streets, away from all the cars and traffic and up into the light and the air above the noise and pollution. These crescents are based on old Georgian housing like the ones in Bath and the planners recognised that people wanted green spaces as part of where they lived so they created that down there." Billy sweeps his hand out before him to indicate the large green area below that's enclosed in a vast horseshoe shape monolith that is the crescent.

"They got what they wanted."

"In a way they did."

"It must have been convincing on paper, so where did the reality all go wrong?"

"Who knows," Billy says. "Misguided architecture, bad housing construction, the wrong type of concrete, the wrong type of residents."

"But they're just regular people; I mean before all the nutters got hold of the place."

"I guess so. This sounds crazy but I sort of like it. It's like a Utopian ideal gone awry. It's a hard existence but it's a liberated one."

"You're insane. The place is a fucking dive."

"Yeah; but there's something here. It could have been so much better but for a few tweaks. It could really have worked."

"You think? Do you really like it for what it is, or do you like it because of Elsa and your newly adopted family?"

"Well," Billy sighs, the truth of it stated so bluntly has a solid feel. "Of course Elsa has something to do with it. I like her values and those of these people stuck up here in the midst of it all; the way they help each other and look out for one another. It's real Socialism Max, they're living it. And the Estate is like a vast and lawless breeding ground for edgy creativity and alternative people and lifestyles."

"Very romantic. They're on a waiting list and can't wait to get the fuck out of this place."

"Yes they are," Billy says. "And I suppose Socialism always works best in the face of adversity."

"It does? If there's no hardship there'll be no need for it."

"Maybe it's a means to an end instead of the end itself," Billy says pondering the idea. "Or it's a blueprint for an end and the final product and the ways to get to it are one and the same; live as you're destined to go on."

"Like a religion."

"Perhaps, or a doctrine." He rests his head against the soft cushion behind him and feels it cool against his neck. "Like travel; they say the travelling is part of the experience, it's not just a means to get you to a place. Unless you feel differently when you've found what you're looking for."

"When I land at the place I've been heading for I want to leave and head out all over again," Max says.

"That's because you've never found what you're looking for."

"Have you?" Max asks. "Have you *arrived*? Is this what you want; Elsa with someone else's kid in tow with an over-bearing mother and an estate with a maniac crackhead on the loose."

"Well," Billy says pulling his legs back off the arm of the sofa; "When you put it that way... Part of me doesn't really know and another thinks it's quite possible that I do."

"Yes," Max says getting to his feet, "there couldn't be a straighter way of saying it, Billy. Undress it and that's what it is."

"You're not wrong," Billy says, strangely unable or unwilling to offer any more; silent on his thinking behind what it is Elsa is beginning to mean to him, of the sensation within him that he feels expanding in his chest, nudging its way out from inside of him.

Max stretches out his arms, up into the air and wriggles his fingers at the roof of the balcony and the small calcium growths hanging in the seams of the concrete slabs.

"Your ribs are much better," Billy says.

Max nods, slowly. "Yes; but I've had enough," he says and puts his hand on Billy's shoulder. "I'm tired now."

Max softly closes the door to the flat behind him and Billy sits alone on the sofa listening to the faint plop of water dripping from somewhere, a runnel or ginnel. In the dark the estate takes on an atmosphere of degeneracy, of night time activities deeply ingrained with a sense of intrinsic danger carried by shouts, the slap of running feet over the walkways and the quick buzz of bicycle chains whirring over oil-less cogs out there in the darkness below. Bright fizzing lights cut deep shadows around the crescents, a nocturnal concrete forest; wolves, foxes, snakes, insects, hunting, hiding, dying, all creatures of the night. From the high balcony vantage Billy ponders how long it will all last and what will signal its ultimate death; the bulldozers; a sweeping inferno of self-destruction; a plague born of fleas on rats, or a rogue batch of chemicals cut way too pure or mixed with something meant for industrial use that will wipe out the inhabitants and users within the space of days. Beyond the castellated skyline lies the rest of Manchester glowing electric orange and sodium white with a sleeping commuter belt and suburbs and safe and predictable living like any other city, like every other one. Patterns of time are roughly divided into convenient parcels; children and the old folk tucked up in bed, night workers clock-watching, kebab vans and chippies, last trains and buses, bar towels thrown over beer taps and the last bells tolling. Chains latch front doors, curtains billow, cats are put out, films start, lights turn off and back on, then turn off again. The gentle ticking of a car's cooling engine parked at the kerbside out front, the fast, passing traffic on Princess Way, home-taped music, games of chess. Babies crying and the lights turn on again, soothing words and tender care of flourishing love, threading generations together in the hearts, in the flesh and in the bricks of homes. A door is opened against the wall with a familiar hollow knocking, the handle and the dent in the wall spooning each other like the husband and wife asleep in the room above it. The face of Jesus, or possibly Che in a pattern in the wood grain. There's pee on the toilet seat, an unfinished book with a broken spine, the corner of a page still turned over after all this time and marked forever. Flowers in a vase, just on the turn, milk left out of the fridge, ditto. The flapping of trousers swishing to a steady walk against quickening feet. Amongst the furniture and pictures on the wall, the cards and carefully chosen colours of walls and fabrics a woman lies in a deep bath surrounded by Conches and Cantharus and scented candles that cast a myriad of flickering lights over the water's surface where her long hair floats in a delta on the surface like black seaweed. Relaxed and lonely, unfulfilled and content; lives of people unbeknownst to anyone but themselves. Secrets and unspoken words. Intimacies and personal pleasures and all over disappointments, private and hidden from view, known to a few but to so many; comfort eating, night driving, late night radio, pills to help sleep, a dark and silent swimming pool in which another woman, pale and naked swims, her shoulders cutting the water's surface in a silent wave that spreads effortlessly before her. The swishing sound of the arms of a jacket against its pockets and the sound of wet rubber tyres against tarmac roads outside, onward motion like the inexorable march of time, of progress, of development and redevelopment like waves beating against the pebbles of the beach with a swishing sound, the sound of water, of shingle, of erosion, of change and flux.

For Billy the swishing noise, the constant, the rustle of the jacket arms, the jeans legs, its diminishing more prevalent than with a motion towards him and Billy watches the man walk away from him, tall and rangy, a volte-face at the top of the stairway he might have let go if he hadn't seen him looking back over his shoulder from behind a hood and a marginally hastened stride. Billy watches him, intuition tingling, an instinct born of beating heart, shaking hands and a shot of adrenalin that quickly courses through him better than any of the chemical he can get from the Estate. He slides off the sofa and eases the door of the flat open and quickly finds Max.

"It's him," he says. "Get your shoes on."

Max pulls his feet from the chair and is immediately alert, far quicker than Billy had expected. He goes back to the balcony to make sure of his track, locking on to the figure moving off behind the uprights of the terrace along the angle of the crescent.

"Let's go," Max says. "Walk quickly but *don't run*."

They stride out, Max ahead and Billy is alert to the sounds of their pursuit, his breathing, their footfalls. At the curved angle of the balcony they pick up speed, the noise of the air moving against his ears lifts him for more. In the sullen concrete of this walkway their footsteps are heavy and he guesses Tulip must realise it's him they're following. At that Billy sees him turn quickly left and drop abruptly into a stairwell. Ahead, some moments later Max peers into the same staircase, quickly glancing back at Billy then disappears into it too. As he gets to the stairwell Billy's sees Tulip's white hand slide down the handrail and disappear at the end to their left. Then the hand of Max above and behind it. He turns and jumps down the stairs gulping in the stale air of the enclosed stairwell with its dampness and dank smell of mildew and piss in the concrete. He jumps steps in twos and threes then halts as the turning left along the balcony affords another view of the figure.

Closer now, Tulip has his hands deep in his pocket and moves quickly and easily. If he believes he's being followed he's not showing any distress by it. Perhaps, Billy thinks that's a front for his concern; perhaps it's genuine. He wants to run but Max hesitates then turns to him and holds him to the doorway of an empty flat.

"Wait here," he whispers. "Don't follow until I tell you." Then turning back along the walkway, calls out; "Hey! Wait up!"

Leaning out from the shadows Billy watches for a reaction to his calling. At last Tulip looks back and squints into darkness but is not minded to hang around to see who wants him and continues on again, with more urgency now.

Max calls out again. "Wait! Wait there!" He quickens his pace and is lighter of foot than their quarry. Now Billy steps out and elects to follow, in and out of the upright pillars as they go. Tulip is in the shadows and shouts something but doesn't look back and Max eases into a run at last. From behind the buttress Billy quickly follows, walking at speed then quicker again. Tulip wavers a moment and at last breaks into a run himself. But he's no athlete for sure. With his back straight and head back he pumps his arms, elbows and fists high in the air. There's no speed of movement and Max catches him within seconds and clasps a hand on his shoulder where he quickly stops and turns to face him.

Seconds later Billy's there too.

Stepping backwards, he switches his attention back and forth between the two of them, sizing them up, square shoulders flat against the wall. He's neither gaunt nor broken-tooth ugly the way Billy had imagined. Instead, he's compact and slender, a neat build, short hair and a clean shaven, symmetrical face with soft brown eyes, tender even with distress, his cornered expression a mixture of fear and confusion.

Billy feels a sensation in the pit of his gut that's a surge of excitement and trepidation that both weakens and fortifies him at landing their man.

"Hey," Max begins, his voice calm and measured, no hint of tremor or tremble.

"What do you want?"

Billy's reassured by the contrast of distress and composure.

"To talk." Max's words unfold evenly, naturally. "We want to talk."

"What do you mean?"

Billy sees the fear in his eyes and hears the tremor in his words. His own heart is smashing against his chest and the adrenalin pumps through him, constricting his throat, denying him the power of speech. He tries to swallow to release it but can't and gulps in more air instead, his mouth gagging until he feels like retching. He clears his throat with force but it's Max who speaks again.

"We want to talk to you," he says, the effectiveness of the words repeated adding to the slower delivery, keeping him guessing, preventing his offense.

Max is a foot off, square on to him but not in his face. Billy marks his posture. It's easy and relaxed with his hands still in his pockets. His words are more a supplication than a threat and yet he observes this absence of intimidation as a menace in itself, the danger latent, a fast-flowing current beneath still, dark waters, strength from poise. This posturing, the behaviour is unnatural to Billy. Ignorant of any rules of engagement he's unsure if Max has composed his approach beforehand or whether it just comes easy to him. He has a talent for it; grace under pressure and Billy's fascinated by it; the confidence and certainty his friend exudes and the effect it produces. It's as though he's suddenly a different person. It's all at odds with the bruised ribs and broken skin that lie beneath his jacket.

Tulip lowers his shoulders and his head drops further forward and Billy sees him physically relax as though somehow comforted and exonerated. He notices too the fear receding from his eyes leaving a dewy residue of insolence. It sickens and dismays him that he's loosened his guard against them, that he's taken stock of the situation and something has given him belief of his chances against the two of them. Maybe it's his hand on a blade in his pocket. Billy's alert and sees the boldness returning to his face in muscular spasms, his lip curling and cheeks tightening, his calculations complete and defiance the result; bristling, attack as an option, the best form of defence.

Billy realises their tactics are wrong and no amount of reasoning with Tulip will win out. It's fear he wants to create. Here on this dark and damp balcony surrounded by the Manchester blackness to parley with Tulip, their attempt to convince or to coax and cajole him is nothing without ferocity to back it up. The mere suggestion of it is not enough. Without the fear of consequences he'll strike again at some point and the next time could be fatal and might involve Elsa or Freya, or Tammy, or Martin again. It could be any one of the vulnerable people trapped in the flats between skywalks and balconies and Billy will have failed in his desire to shelter them, his new family. The only way he can think of getting what he wants, to see them safe is to take action, to coerce, no more a spectator in the events unfolding, in the face of Tulip's defiance, in his refusal to cooperate, to act reasonably. There's a look of arrogance on his contemptuous face even as Max takes a step closer to him and withdraws his hands from his pockets. With the fear only momentarily returning in his eyes at Max's change of stance he would have to give him a sample of the deeds behind the words, a taste. A *taste* Billy thinks as though he's a fighter himself. But he's shaking and wants to give it to him not just to warn him off but because he might have the knife. Max is close and he is scaring the shit out him and Elsa and her family and the enclave of neighbours exposed on the skywalk with no protection. And just who the fuck does he think he is to do this to them? This no-mark, fucking crackhead who's screwing things up for everyone, who won't see reason and won't be reasoned with, no matter how rational or reasonable their demands might be of injustice and fairness. Tulip will wield the cosh and brandish the knife and not give a shit for anything or anyone but himself. His kind destroying it for all and denying the liberty of peaceful people, riddling fear in their daily lives. Billy's afraid himself, shaking with fear and anger. Darkness closing in feels like the iron tension of fright. With it something rises from deep inside him, hatred, something vernal and bursting. With it spewing quickly, unconsciously, he feels the splintering, splitting flesh and bone beneath his own fist as it crashes into Tulip's face with as much force as he can muster. It's a force more than he's ever summoned, angled in with his feet well behind him planted firmly on the ground. It's packed with his loathing and disgust of Tulip and of himself at having to bring it to *this*. He hears the brief murmur of Tulip's short gasp before the blow lands and guillotines the sound, the flashing white light of physical and mental shock. The eyes are at once electrified and blank, like the man in the Lancaster Travel Hotel and the hollow knock of his head hitting the hard concrete wall behind him, doubling the impact, the simple physics of the strongest surface, of who or what is hardest in a nutshell. That point in which something must give, the tip of the bullet against Danny face, the tiny micro moment in time when contact is made before all Hell erupts, the explosion in his head, the sensation of little sharp teeth ripping at the soft flesh between Billy's knuckles, mixing their blood like blood brothers. Men caught in violence, the weaker elements yielding to greater powers, the forces vying for supremacy, the irresistible force on the immovable object It's cracking it, spilling and breaking it open, reigning and yielding in a moment that encapsulates winners and losers. Everything else is gone, no more losing, no more Jackie and this, this now for Elsa, it being both supremely satisfying in the relief and joy of victory and yet absurdly and fundamentally wretched.

*

He has a knife.

He can't see it but senses his grip around its handle, hot ribbed against his folded palm. It's lying in wait for them like a scorpion in his pocket ready to strike. The scorpion is a tattoo on his hand. The segments of its exoskeleton are the phalanxes of his fingers, the blade its stinger. He makes it moves when he flexes his fist. He's done it before; it's his party piece. Billy can't remember where he's seen it but is sure he has. There are too many to recall with any clarity. It might have been in the bar in Glasgow, yes that's right, it's the bar in Glasgow. He's the one standing behind them when it all kicked off, when the table went west and the drinks fly through the air. The scorpion is tattooed over his beer gut, the ink blurred and faded. His belly button is the median eye, his hips the claws. He keeps the blade tucked into his waistband with the handle tight on his hip bone, ready for the hipbone claw to seize and whip out at any moment. He keeps the pistols there too and you can see the handles above the waist band. The handles are tattoos the same as Sam Kelly's. She knows him. She knows Nelson too because they were all friends back in the day when she lived on the Estate and Nelson was Elsa's lover. Billy thinks he remembers him but can't place him. He thinks he's the one who gave them the ride into Manchester when Max was all busted up, the one with milk bottle shoulders. He gives no response and Max knows he's just talking for the avoidance of silence and to fend off sleep. He turns against him and Billy notices he's wrapped his brother's jacket around his head, pulled across his eyes and tucked under like a Bedouin headdress. His mouth is open, his throat quickly and rhythmically clucking like there's something stuck there. He glazes over and drifts with the motion and the warmth of the car's heater around his legs, the breeze through the window and finds himself veering into half sleep with half-closed eyes that throw up dark coloured hallucinatory images through the windscreen, some of which are his own reflection, some are Nelson, some are Max. Something's unsettling him, trying to rise through the weight of his fatigue and he thinks it because he can't see the knife. He strikes out his lip and glances at the driver, seeing his hands set around the wheel at ten to two, squeezing the grey foam intermittently, his knuckles drained of blood and the skin on the backs of his hands stretched taught and shiny with the pressure then wrinkled when relaxed, cling film skin and the scorpion beneath.

His eyelids are heavy now, his gritty eyes virtually unmoving at the passing flats on the Estate, fixed to a spot somewhere in the middle distance a few yards on the road ahead at the top of the pool of headlights, transfixed and zombified by the car's rocking motion and the onrushing tarmac disappearing beneath the windscreen in front of him. Max stirs next to him and glances towards the sun-visor and sees a photo held in place behind an elastic band, a Polaroid, a square, grainy photograph of a summer's day; a back yard surrounded by walls and fencing, some climbing roses, a callow young boy of maybe ten or eleven, shorts and shadowed kneecaps, arms straight and hands deep in his pockets. In the distance behind him there is a tall woman in a patterned skirt, her arms folded across her stomach regarding him, a mother's shrewd countenance of pride and vigilance, guarding his innocence. Is it his mother or is it Max's, the one he never talks about he can't say? He stares with a chronic foreboding tiredness, disturbed by the conversion from night into day with the light appearing in strips against the curtainless windows, a glow that illuminates the dingy room of an empty flat on a broken Manchester Estate.

Billy and Max spend the night in the flat having cleaned up in cold running water in its barren kitchen with nothing else working bar the one tap. They exchange few words and share the latter part of a bottle of whisky evenly in two plastic cups. It cuts sufficiently but isn't enough to properly anaesthetise. Sleep follows swiftly for both of them, the drain of adrenalin a toll on their minds and bodies but it's fitful and Billy has the troubles of recurring thoughts, anxiety dreams played on a loop with the same themes; the knife, Tulip, their road journey and round again, the knife, the drivers who pick them up to return the favour for their own hitch-hiking days, Tulips face that looks like a pansy, mean-looking and full of doubt. Several times he wakes, cold and wet, returns to sleep and wakes again, the orange lights through the dirty windows at the rear of the block of flats casting a flat, morbid light on the ceiling and walls, the rectangular shapes where pictures once hung. The flat has a haunted feel of a near dead dwelling having had its rites read, awaiting final demolition.

The morning comes and with it a sense of foreboding. Billy wakes to find Max has gone and can't recall hearing him leave the flat, convinced his sleep has been so restless and not reckoning with the depths of his unconsciousness when it finally came. He tries to lie down to rest again but can't. There's the nagging recollection of the night and he's physically tired and mentally wired and doesn't know what to do or where to put himself. It's as though his body is new to him and he doesn't know how to deal with it. He pulls back the blanket and is fully clothed. He can't decide what's next and paces the flat instead, rolling cigarettes and chain smoking with no desire to step out into the Manchester air with its distant harsh traffic sounds and those of the Estate madness. He watches people go past the window on the balcony and stops his own pacing when they do, pulling at the dusty net curtain, a twitcher the like he's heard the previous owners were. Eventually he pulls on a jacket and steps outside, peering left and right along the walkway, further to one side to seek out activity around Elsa's flat, listening to sounds of life: Marley crying, Kathy coughing, Freya's constant off-tuned Radio One.

There's only silence.

Leaning out against the balcony, smoking once more he scans the green below then the arcs of the walkways, the paths they'd trodden the night before, the scene of their deeds. He tries to work out the location of the flat where Tulip had been pinned to the door but his thoughts are chaotic and everywhere looks exactly the same to him. There's only the pink sofa wedged against the wall behind him and nothing else has moved and nothing has changed, superficially at least.

Around midday Max returns with another half-bottle of whisky and a sandwich, the smell of which turns his stomach though he east and drinks all the same. With little encouragement they agree to a lunchtime drink. It turns into a longer session in the afternoon, parked at the bar the entire time with few drinkers in the pub except an old man of the Estate called Gerald who's cultured with military fictions and a sociable way of exchanging tales and opinions. Max prompts the matter of the previous night, but Billy has no inclination and the subject is left to silence knowing it will come soon enough. The warm sunlight floods the room, the men wrapped in a fug of cigarette smoke and alcohol they know to be transitory with lengthening shadows and a diminishing purse. When Gerald tenders his farewells, Billy finds himself downcast at his impending departure, a growing melancholy relative to the fading sunlight and urges him to stay for one last drink, a desperate attempt to wring the afternoon of its hours. To this, Gerald declines.

In low mood they return to the flats in the twilight with the white strip-lights of the tall flats complex opposite bursting bright light. The familiar doors on the well-trodden walkway are closed and there's no light or life evident from the windows of these flats. On knocking at Elsa's door, a quick flip of the letter box accompanies the recognisable small fingers of Freya ushering their return.

Inside Elsa is sat on the threadbare sofa with Marley in her lap. The baby has been crying and so has she, her lips and the flesh around her nostrils are swollen. Her face has a plucked and puckered appearance, a surfeit of tiny red capillaries colouring her pale skin. With hair matted flat to her head she hugs Marley, clutching him tightly to her and stroking his back and hair, a real-life teddy bear for a grown-up child. Marley's not still and wriggles and squirms in her arms, arching his back and pushing against his mother, away from her with his powerful doughy legs so his head lolls and he looks at the upside-down faces in the room, clear spittle trailing from his lips across his cheeks.

Max stays out of it, on the balcony smoking, a cigarette-length stay of execution. The harsh aroma of the nicotine and smoke follows him indoors in an unseen haze as he enters nipping at his bottom lip with pinched thumb and forefinger to pluck off a strand of loose tobacco he can't get at. He leans against the wall at an angle; his participation accompanied by no desire to sit.

"Where were you?" Elsa asks.

Billy knows he's in the dock but wants to steer a course between his guilt and justification. It's a fine line to walk and his steps are big and clumsy and his response too slow to head off a further enquiry.

"What did you do?" Elsa sighs, elaborating no further to the meaning of her question.

"What did we do *what*?" Billy asks clumsily but without insolence, sitting as far forward on the sofa as he can, his attention mandatory, elbows resting on his knees and forcing his hands together, prayer-like. He plucks at the skin of his palms then laces his fingertips over the knuckles on the other, thereby concealing the wounds there, the marks yet to be noticed or noted.

"It's all over the Estate."

"What is?"

"What you did to Mark Tulip."

A leap of alarm surges into Billy's throat, not shock or disbelief but a movement of apprehension he swallows back down. He takes a deep breath and collects himself once more for the imminent inquest.

"How did you find out?" he asks.

"Everyone knows; and then I had a call from a friend through the infirmary."

Freya sits down next to her sister, a heavy movement that

rocks Elsa and Marley in its wake. Billy's glad to see her, hoping for some levity. "Loads of people know about it," she says but her customary brightness is inappropriate, sensationalist amidst the solemnity. "He was found unconscious in a doorway at the bottom of the crescent, blood everywhere. People who live in them flats found him coming home from the pub and called the paramedics; ambulance came, even cops."

Kathy Kelly is balefully silent, closely watching Billy on his perch and Max stood behind him, impatient with her younger daughter's enthusiasm: "News filters fast through this Estate," she says at last casting a line and hauling her daughter back in. "Whispers on the wires and across the way. The emergency services don't venture this far in unless they have to. The paramedics had police with them for protection, out in force, to guard the ambulance against passing opportunists. When an ambulance arrives on this estate with a police escort you know it's something serious. He's been taken to the Royal in a serious condition; fractured skull, broken nose, broken cheekbone, swallowed teeth..."

Kathy lets the incomplete litany linger, suggesting the possibility of more as though this is not enough.

Freya pulls her legs up, plucks open a can of Coke and works her backside into the sofa, her knees drawn up against her chest. "Teeth all over the walkway." Billy can see the white of her knickers.

"What did they say at the hospital?" he asks.

"What can they say? Another victim from the Estate; another casualty rushed in of a night time." Elsa's mouth is twisted as she speaks in a way Billy's not seen before, an ugliness alien to her that fills her lips and skews her speech. She's trying to retain composure and with it her dignity. Marley, ever restless in her arms drops a large set of plastic keys to the floor and begins to cry.

"How serious is it?"

"They don't know Billy. He may respond, he may not; he was not in prime physical condition in the first place. Time will tell, won't it?"

"What's your experience of it?" Billy asks arresting his frustration in the absence of any quick headlines, sensing his obligation to prize the information out piece by piece as contrived, a deliberate form of punishment. "What are the details from your colleagues?"

"*Details*?" The question's laced with disbelief, a legitimate enquiry for all the wrong reasons; *to protect his own skin?* "It's a linear fracture, a simple break, the most common type that's the least likely to cause permanent brain damage. As if you're concerned about his welfare."

"Too late for that!" Kathy Kelly says. "You should have thought about that—"

"That's as good as it gets," Elsa continues over her mother. "Concussed upon arrival, extracranial hematoma, bleeding outside of his skull. As Mam says, a broken nose and he'd swallowed one of three teeth. The others were missing, maybe still in the doorway where you left him."

"Jesus Christ!"

"You bloody *idiots*!" Kathy says abruptly. "The pair of you. Don't you see this puts you in the same league as him?" Her words are harsh but even, a brittle edge with a thin jagged blade slashing through the air. "You *knew* that, doing to him as he did to our Martin back there; as he did to *me*! *I* didn't want revenge. None of us did. Where's the sense? Where's the justice in that?"

"It wasn't meant to be like that," Billy begins but the sentence diminishes with impotency, its residual weakness in the face of the consternation and rolling eyes before him.

"We had an agreement Billy, I thought we had the trust. We spoke of it not going this far."

"You were meant to frighten him," Kathy continues, "not half kill him. It was supposed to be a warning to him to stop him coming back for more. You were only meant to do that."

Then from the back, pushing off the wall with his elbows Max at last enters the fray with his opening salvo: "*Were only supposed to blow the bloody doors off!*"

Mother–daughter synchronicity, Elsa and Kathy yelp in unison. Billy gets to his feet quickly, looks to the ceiling then down again, Heaven and Hell, nothing in between, not in this here and now.

"That's not funny Max," he says, glancing at Elsa, herself unable to maintain her regard for either of them. Billy appreciates his grounds for reasoning are weak, even more so his ability to put them into words. Only Kathy Kelly herself attacked can speak here before them with the certitude of her personal involvement at the hands of Mark Tulip.

Max kicks his heel hard against the wall, a heavy thud that shakes the cups on the table and makes them all start. "You all got what you wanted didn't you?"

"No, we didn't," Elsa's quick to retort. "Nobody asked for this."

"What you wanted was a fucked up, drug crazed mugger out of your hair and that's what you got so you can all rest peacefully now."

"Nobody said anything about assaulting him," Kathy hisses. "You were supposed to warn him so he wouldn't bother us again. And I never sanctioned that."

"We need your permission?"

"I left it to Elsa and your man here."

"You don't appreciate what it's like living here Max. It's lawless and we've been managing our own safety all this time. You don't go wading into situations with the law of the oppressor. Might is not right. There are many ways of dealing with people without resorting to violence. What he needed was dissuasion, nothing more."

"He got that alright," Max says. "And he's not dead so lose the melodrama."

Kathy gets to her feet unsteadily, her lungs constricting and breathing heavily with the effort. "How smug you are about this," she says overcoming her affliction, the reedy vitriol rasping deep within her. "What you did to him is deplorable and for many reasons. We did not ask for that. We did not ask for you to come here and dish out malevolent justice. Can you not see that?"

"I don't see *him*!" Max says.

"We despised him for what he did to us. We never wanted it repeated. Is this what you thought when you were pulping him, an eye for an eye? The man knows no other way of behaving or he wouldn't have done what he did in the first place. Beating the shite out of him won't have taught him a lesson you fools; it will only have poured more bile into his already black heart. If he gets out of hospital, he'll come straight back here looking for us again. And where will you be then?"

"He's a crack addict," Max says. "He'll go wherever he can to feed his habit."

"And next time more vicious than before! Next time he'll go the whole distance, maybe not on us but on some other poor unsuspecting bastard sitting alone and vulnerable on the estate; God knows there are enough of us around here. I've seen it happen before. He won't want payback on himself, so he'll make sure he does a proper job. And when he does he'll be giving out all the pain and the punishment you two dealt him; straight back at us."

"Not if the job's done properly."

Marley still crying and Kathy moves to pick up the plastic keys, thrusting them back into his grip behind her without thought or tenderness. With the toy in his mitts, she moves closer to Max.

"I knew you were trouble."

"*Little ol' me?*"

"What's your endgame? Why not just remove the problem entirely and just rub him out? Is that how you see it; erasing the problem?"

"You asked us to help you out here and we did."

"But you haven't, have you? Either of you."

"We tried," Billy says. His voice is shallow, an intervention devoid of confidence. He has a hot tingling sensation pulsing about his face and a notion of the recurring themes of being reproached for violence just like they were in Lancaster, be it senseless or justified he can no longer tell. Becca's censure then, Elsa's now; two cuts from the same cloth.

"No," Elsa says on her feet now herself. "No, you didn't try. We've looked after each other for years up here with no help from anyone else. We've had to do it for ourselves. It's our autonomy and our responsibility. What you did to Tulip is just blatant viciousness. There's no responsibility in that, no restraint. I thought you knew that more than anyone, Billy."

"You go and preach," Max says throwing his thumb up over his shoulder, "but spare me the moralising."

"I thought more of *you* Billy," she says ignoring his friend stood behind him. "You shouldn't have done that. I thought I could trust you."

And at once Billy feels an implosion within, a quick series of little collapses that happen inside his head, in his throat and chest and stomach, like lights going out all through a tower block. It's an absence of air from his lungs and with it of all of oxygen that drains out from his body and blood, as though the blood in his veins and brain is thick and dark and congealing. A spectre of helplessness envelopes him and wraps him in an inability to say anything or take any action. He's locked and rooted into the white space within the bright lit room of bare walls with hairline cracks any one of which might open up and suck him into somewhere he'd rather have been than in the stasis in which he stands. A vision of nothingness and nowhere dawns upon him, something akin to Max's professed desire to immediately exit a place upon arrival. His passage would continue on a path unknown and with people unknown, places yet to visit and strangers yet to meet and the thought of these things holds no pleasure or surprise, no appeal or purpose at all as it is with the faces staring at him with a mixture of abhorrence and sadness and disappointment. There will be no new dawning, no sun-up on a new day to cast fresh light on the worn and tired events of today and yesterday. Billy understands the investment he's been making almost subconsciously, piecing together ideas and designs and transformations, an order in which Elsa features prominently and perhaps even permanently. And at once, the disintegration Billy feels is the dismantling of this construct that gives him an insight into the fragility of it, the simplicity of it all, and its futility. From this a deviation will be necessary, a breath drawn and with it, the perception of a new beginning.

And Max, standing behind him, whose hard breathing Billy can hear in his ear, steps up beside him and slowly, in clear and simple words speaks:

"It wasn't Billy," he says.

He clears his throat.

"It wasn't Billy," he says again, louder this time. "It was me."

Billy turns to Max and sees with his head rigid and poise maintained he's locked his gaze directly at Elsa and her mother and beyond them a wide-eyed Freya observing the unfolding spectacle. The effect is that these words momentarily prevent any others. Max rocks his head and shoulders back, inflating his chest as though the increase in size and stiffness of physique adds weight to his words. He stands in front of Billy and speaks again.

"It was me. Billy didn't want a part of it. It was my idea and he tried to stop me, but I wouldn't listen. I couldn't see another way and I thought he was carrying a knife, so I took him out."

Elsa is not sure but in her eyes there is an expanding combination of astonishment and contrition, a dissipating confusion with the relief of a breaking light filtering through widening blinds. She holds her breath as if to breathe will break the moment and stares at both of them, the certitude of her thoughts breaking and disbanding before her, scattering them and constricting her speech. Tears come; a liquefying arrangement of insight and sadness, of respite even. She makes a motion towards them then stops. Kathy next to her maintains her firmness which is encased in an invisible force, her inability or unwillingness to err from the path on which she has chosen are engrained in her features. Stood together Billy marks their similarities; their height, the U shape of their faces, the way Kathy's anger has narrowed her lips into an upturned V shape like a cat, the deep philtrum below her nose shadowed in the bare electric light above her. Kathy, her longer life of greater hardship having moulded her look and weathered her character; wary, sceptical, she remains obdurate against Max and his refusals to be intimidated or outdone.

"Max," Billy begins and stops as his friend turns to him at last, the dark pools of his brown eyes filmy, the faint yellowness of his bruising still about his face colouring his cheeks like jaundice.

"I should go," he says.

Billy grabs his arm and turns to face him. "Max, wait."

Billy sees the muscles in his chin flicker, oscillating pulleys from the pressures in his mouth. He raises his eyebrows, a forced mechanical movement, a prompt for further enunciation or enquiry from Billy but on hearing nothing forthcoming and seeing the faltering shapes of his friend's mouth and tongue, closes his eyes and can't prevent his shoulders from wilting. With a gentle movement he withdraws his arm from Billy's grip. He turns and with a sigh pats down the rear pockets and then the hip pockets of his jeans with both hands. Squeezing the tubular shape of his cigarette lighter between his thumb and fingers his face at once brightens as though its discovery is all that matters to him at that moment and that with it, the key to the gateway to his next adventure is within his grasp.

"Wait," Billy repeats.

"Wait for what?" Max says quietly. He moves closer to his friend, then pitches his head back towards Elsa and Kathy; "We're not welcome here anymore."

"That's not true Max," Billy says softly.

Max smiles then releases a gentle laugh. "Maybe for you, but not me. You know that."

"What about us?"

Max reaches out and takes Billy's hands in his, so gently at first that he doesn't register his touch or any other sensation at all until with the pressure of his fingers against the palms of his hands he's able to focus on him standing before him. By now Max has him in a firmer grip the tight clasp of a valedictory handshake.

"Stay here or come with me," he says. "That's your call, only you can make. Join me if you want to but I don't think you will. Deep down we both know you've found what you're looking for. Are you with me?"

"Where will you go?"

Max smiles, a broad grin that exposes the gap of the missing tooth.

"There's a whole wide world out there," he says and in his eyes Billy fleetingly sees the old Max, the maverick, the indomitable force enlivened by the challenge of the next place to visit, who's always ready to bolt no sooner than he's arrived, bracing himself for the next chapter of chance and gamble into an unchartered future. That future might be anywhere but all the time, wherever it may be, a sense of complete fulfilment will be there tomorrow or the day after, always at the next place, for ever one step ahead. Like the moon on the horizon it will elude him. In the harsh glare of bare electric light, a hard truth quickly takes root. It's solid and resolute and with it a void, a hollowed-out trunk of simple white walls and an unadorned bulb where there is nowhere else for either of them to go and nothing left to say. Max steps away from his friend and is still smiling as he turns and walks out of the door. Maybe it's this look across his face and the optimism that's settled in the rich brown of his eyes that allows a thin sense of comfort to settle. It's a vague notion of truth that Billy doesn't consciously acknowledge but forms around him with a sense that Max will be alright and so will he. It comes from within, not a warm feeling inside but a gentle prickle in his skin, tiny points of soft pressure that come and go in his hands and fingertips. And Billy flinches as he hears the sound of the letter box flap slapping against the frame of the front door and in an instant the feeling disappears. It's only then he recognises the sensation. Now he understands it, strangely by its absence and not during its existence, the remnants of it and the feeling that lingers until it's gone.

Manchester
and Todmorden; early
Autumn 1989

It can't be but two weeks since the letter's arrived and already it's gone missing. Kathy is in a funk trying to find it and musters hitherto dormant energy to fuel the progress in a throwback to the old days when the family were all together as they are now briefly, apart from their Dad. He'd have whirled around the maypole of her ill temper in a dance that would eventually pull back her humour. He had a knack for it and Sam and Elsa, and later Freya would watch it with glee as their Mam's frustration at the smallest things like a misplaced letter would soften to a distant smile she'd try her best to keep from emerging.

"It'll be here somewhere," Elsa says dismissively checking Marley's things to see if he's appropriated it. "It's not like we've got much place to lose anyway."

Kathy will not be dissuaded from conducting an inch-by-inch search that Elsa knows will steadily head towards the sofa where Sam is sat with her feet on its back and head hung upside down reading a book, the posture of her childhood. That she still sits like this, incongruous with her tattoos and make up makes Elsa smile. There's something comforting about it. Less so Kathy's latent friction. It's a part of the way her Mam's always been with Sam, a ploy to move to any ground over which to battle. It's her ingrained spite, a hostile love, mild but enduring. Elsa's witnessed it as often as she can remember over the years and it hasn't changed even when others have. What its source is she cannot say and she's prudent with her words when talking to Sam, who always claims to be a mistake that the Catholic straight jacket opinions of termination and contraception facilitated. Elsa doesn't buy it anymore, and that's based on her unconditional love for her own first child. Whatever, it's why Sam won't be sticking around for much longer despite Elsa's contention that their Mam's declining health has tempered her. Some things will just stay the same and the provocative mechanics of their domestic complexities are too well established to untangle.

"Even when we're rehoused?"

"Even when you're rehoused."

Besides, Elsa has a lover and Marley a father figure now and though she inwardly winces when Billy struggles from time to time with the practicalities of step-fatherhood she also sees that he makes the effort. He's a trier. She feels his love for her as something tangible and solid and there's a real certainty in that. She trusts him and understands these are the qualities she needs and Billy too. Sam has no such desires, always the freer spirit of all of them, perhaps a product of the difficult love their Mam dispensed after all. Where she will go she does not know, but it won't be back to Glasgow for sure. There are too many memories and too much complexity. She's taken by the transitory life on the road both Max and Billy have described. There's a joy to living the ephemeral, a literal flight of fancy that's unprescribed, led by the imagination and the call of dreams. She has her jewellery to trade that can fund her journeying, maybe abroad, somewhere with a sunny climate though she can't take much heat. Wherever it will be, she'll write.

"We'll soon have a new address," Elsa says. She's excited, anxious and wistful.

As Elsa foresaw the letter is soon discovered, the consternation a melodrama. It's been moved to one side of the only surface in the kitchen and piled next to the microwave with magazines and other correspondence such as Freya's school letters and wedged inside a filthy copy of *An Inspector Calls*. It's confirmation of the process of their rehousing, details of the next steps and the timeframe in which it's programmed. The waiting will soon be over. Strange how they'd longed for this moment for years and when it finally comes it's almost an anti-climax, the waiting being a part of the anticipation and the joy of the final news, the striving as much as the prize. Billy says it's like the connection of travelling and arriving, the conundrum that exists between the two, something he and Max had talked of often on their days on the road. She understands that. In some ways the confirmation of their relocation is her arrival.

She looks around the flat that's always been substandard and a contributor to her Mam's ill health. It's crumbling now beyond repair, an embarrassment for everyone concerned and outlived by many of the inhabitants who were promised a better life there. Still the familiarity of it is romantic and resides in the things that survived the deterioration: the dusty light shades, the faded colour of the cupboards, the finger-marked light switches. Growing up she had been intimate with every dark corner, warm cupboard and hiding space then into wider, less cosy realms the Estate offered with loss of innocence, adolescence and beyond. The confirmation in the letter from the Local Authority allows this quiet nostalgia to flourish like a guilty pleasure; her happy childhood days and the family making the most of the inadequacy around them, all in it together until the premature death of her father. Then the birth of her son and the full wheel has turned. Like the declining state of the Hulme Crescents Kathy's failing condition will never improve. The Estate will be bulldozed, and she will be rehoused and made more comfortable by the relocation, but Elsa fears the removal of her focus from what was once her roost however insalubrious will have the opposite impact, like the old folks who quickly decline upon retirement.

She wonders how long she's got, then quickly dispels the morbidity of the thought, a sacking assisted by the exuberance of youth as Freya glides into the kitchen looking for things to eat.

"What's the goss?" she asks. "Why so sad; Billy dumped you already?"

"I'm not sad." It sounds defensive.

Freya is immune to it all, unaffected, just like her father had been when he was alive. It's a great place to be Elsa thinks;

tough, self-contained, amused and amusing, resolute. Freya's a proper Northern girl, a Manchester Hulme Estate girl.

"You going to miss this place, Freya?" she asks.

Freya pulls an expression that silently enquires *have you gone mad*? Elsa's contention is that Freya could actually live anywhere, and her invincible spirit would remain as just that. She's up on the chair, tight jeans that sag at the backside and knees, shaking the tins high on the cupboards for hidden sweets or biscuits. The canister that had John Henry's flat key in it is empty like the flat itself where Billy and Max had stayed. The key can't be found but with relocation imminent it doesn't matter anymore. Besides there are certain connotations of the now infamous night that the flat brings with it and the wider subsequent ripples.

Elsa is careful when talking to Billy about Max, prudent in her enquiries and the timing. Billy's left Manchester to meet him for a valedictory drink; Todmorden, a place beyond the moors. She appreciates there are complex issues of divided loyalties for him, ones over which he has drawn his conclusions and where inevitably there are winners and losers. Sometimes there is just no middle ground that can be occupied and that's the way of it. She's sad for him, for both of them but Billy's choice gives her the certainty that he's in it for the long game. She feels for Max for what she knows he perceives as his loss when the time came to choose and for the reasons her sister has told her about; an added complication she's not sure if Billy fully appreciates. It's something she'll talk through with him at some point in the future, when the time is right. There are other things to be discussed beforehand. She's seen the marks on Billy's knuckles and the swelling there but it's the look in his eye that conceals and reveals so much more. She'll never condone what they did to Tulip but knows that the events of that night are complex. He will be honest with her in the fullness of time she is certain of that. In the meantime, he has unfinished business with Max.

*

The hillside below and beyond blackens in the night with the setting sun, a pure shadowy black that contrasts with the lighter blue black of the clear night sky above it. Definition is sharp. Pinpricks of lights are emerging, sprinkled across the steep hillsides all around; houses and streetlamps in winding rows and the horizon of the hills tapering to the valley to the left in a gradual decline like a reclining Buddha bejewelled and studded with golden trinkets. It could be a Mediterranean resort, an Italian hillside of villages disappearing into a harbour-side of yachts and bars and waiters below it with a canopy of a night sky full of stars overhead. In the balmy warmth of the English late summer night there's a remote hint of a chill disturbing the air.

Billy stares out across the vista from the balcony and imagines it so; more, he wishes it could be and if so, things might be different. He smokes a cigarette; a thick, filterless Continental number of dark cigar-like tobacco from a soft-pack he's bought from the machine in the bar earlier that adds to the impression of foreign lands. Next to the tables on the balcony tall umbrellas have been pushed back against the wall, their use not yet required but soon to be in the autumn when the vista beyond will be just as good but the nights too cold and drizzly for open necked shirts and summer dresses. The balcony's getting busier with punters sitting at the tables or leaning with drinks in hand against the wooden balustrades surrounding the decking. Their conversations and laughter and cigarette smoke all drift up and away into the warm night air and over the valley below, melting into the night sounds of the dark countryside, rustling leaves, nocturnal animals and a passing vehicle on the distant road below.

Billy takes a sip of his drink, looks about him and watches the people with vague curiosity with the residual warmth of the evening condensing under his fingertips against the cold of the glass. He tightens his hand to prevent it slipping and feels the moistures squeeze out from beneath his grip. The group of drinkers to his left, three men and three women are in their teens and all smartly dressed; the lads he notices foremost have an eye for a colourful shirt, floral, patterned and stiff cuffs. They're similarly attired with pointed shoes and bleach-marked jeans, laughing together at common amusements, white teeth and athletic-looking. The young women huddle in a similar stance with colourful drinks, glasses held in one hand, straws stirring or sipping with the other. He wonders to himself why this place and how Max even knows about it. It seems so alien from their usual drinker haunts of the past few months as he watches him returning to their table on the balcony, fresh drinks in his hand, more bulk about him, after only a few weeks, as though the people he's been staying with have been feeding him up. His solidity is not just in appearance; conversation has been strained and slow between them. Billy's waiting for the alcohol to get to work; to loosen their tongues and their thoughts.

Placing the drinks down on the table Max sits and turns to look at the people behind him standing on the balcony or is it the view beyond them, Billy can't tell. He sniffs the night air with an exaggerated pull of his nostrils, tugging at the neck of his T-shirt with his thumb and forefinger, then takes a drink. The shirt falls back to the same position. He dips his eye contact and Billy watches with a growing edginess, nascent frustration at their lack of discourse. Max had written and suggested they meet to talk things through, like a couple in crisis but the conversation has stuttered, and Billy feels strangely uncomfortable in his presence and disturbed by his reticence.

Max is equally phlegmatic.

"This smell of the summer," Billy says. "It evokes things, don't you think?"

Max smacks his lips and carefully returns the glass to the table. There's colour around his face scattered with ill-shaven stubble that makes his eyes appear narrower and his mouth off-centred.

"Like what?" he asks.

"The summers of before I suppose; unnoticed smells filed away somewhere, oblivious to their potency until they return again, triggered by memory."

"To prove you were there after all," Max says flatly. There's a white rim around his lips set against his swarthy features that reminds Billy of an explorer, someone accustomed to a living outdoors, a witness to a hard existence, a life on the move. With his narrow eyes and skewed mouth it's difficult to see whether there's any warmth or humour about him.

He pushes the glass across the table, until it's almost in the centre.

"What are you thinking?" Billy asks.

"About that beardy French guy in the Glasgow squat."

"Belzaire. What of him?"

"That fateful night when you and Elsa first met, he was talking to me about his outlook on life and something called *detournement*."

"What is that?"

"He wanted to blur the distinction between art and everyday life, neither one he took seriously. He said he treated life like art and was happy to just mess about in both; dipping in and out whenever he chose, making mischief when he was bored. He talked about The Situationist's idea of *detournement*; parodies and subversion carried out to hijack popular culture and deceive the masses. He said he'd put on a Galerie de Detournement in the European cities where he'd lived, literally translated as the Gallery of Derailment, the Situationist's weapon of sabotage, a space of no thing. He hated modern artists' desire for fame and money and his Gallery was completely made up but well-advertised with false invitations including lucky golden tickets for free Champagne on arrival. He even made booklets about himself and his art and circulated them amongst other artists, people he said he loathed. They came, saw nothing and left confused, empty handed and empty headed. The Gallery was dismantled and moved to a different city along with its artist to reappear afresh, Paris, Toulouse, London, Glasgow. And so the circus continues."

"Why are you thinking about that right now?"

"I don't know. I guess I liked his outlook. Out of all the crazy people we came across on the road he impressed me the most; you just have to live your life to the beat of your own drum."

"Is that a metaphorical statement."

"For what?"

"For us. For the here and now, for where we are?"

"Perhaps, for where we *were*. It was great when we first hit the road; it felt like we had real freedom, like we were leaving all the banal shit behind us and living life how we wanted to, life in the moment."

"So sorry to disappoint," Billy says more cynically than intended. "But it was good while it lasted, right?"

"Everything comes to an end, and it's all over now you put that mutt Tulip in hospital Billy."

The images still unsettle Billy, in part because he can't fully understand his actions himself. He's never assaulted anyone before, and the feeling of Tulip's pulping face sickens him still and makes his fists twitch and his stomach fold.

"You were a Peacenik," Max continues. "Did I lead you astray? Was it me who turned your head?"

"I don't know," he says. "The guy had a knife and could have pulled it on you."

"Billy boy," Max says. He shakes his head. "We both know it was for Elsa, not for me."

Billy glances over his shoulder again, the crowd next to

their table laughing loudly. He turns back to Max and slowly rocks his head though it's more from his shoulders, the thoughts bouncing within that manifests itself in his body. "Violence changes things and does so quickly."

"I know all about that."

"Yes Max, of course you do."

"And sometimes it works for the better; it got us out of the Travel Hotel in Lancaster, remember," Max says.

"But you made a decision to leave after what I did."

"I made the decision long before that."

There's movement in the air, a gentle breeze that comes between them.

"Why d'you take the rap for me Max?"

"Truth?"

"Always," Billy says.

"It's my gift to you Billy, a gift to show you how much I care; taking the bullet."

Billy leans forward. "You didn't have to do that Max."

"And see Elsa slaughter you for what you did? She'd have kicked you out along with me and that would have broken your poor heart in pieces. And you know it. I lost one brother to a bullet and I'm sure as hell not going to lose another."

"*Max.*"

"It's clear where your love lies. Watching you with Elsa says something to me too; that you say you've been looking for freedom all this time but in truth what you've really been looking for is love. You call it freedom and maybe they are one and the same for you. But that's not for me."

"And that's why you did it; for me?"

"Well, I sure don't want to be on the road with some broken-hearted mope all over again!"

There's both warmth and disquiet in these words that makes Billy twist in his seat, as though he's being simultaneously pushed away and drawn back in. The chair leg wobbles and knocks against the wooden decking, the sounds of his thoughts rebounding in his head.

"What's for you now?"

"I'll leave again, it's what I do. Try find somewhere to stay, someone's sofa for a week or so then maybe go abroad, somewhere nice where the living is easy. What I do know is that I *can*; I'm free to just get on and do that Billy and that is *my* freedom. It's not true freedom because I can't run from myself and I can never escape the loss of my brother as Sam says but you know what, it's as good as it gets."

"I owe you," Billy says.

"Yeah, you do." he says, and shakes the lighter in his hands before lighting a cigarette at the side of his mouth. "No, you don't." His voice is thickened by the smoke.

"You've got to keep in touch" he says, studying his old friend across the table.

"Sure thing, you'll soon be off the Estate with Elsa hitched up and the kid in tow and another on the way and soon you'll forget all about me. You'll quickly settle into a nice family life, Mr Anarchist."

Max smiles infectiously and Billy concedes with a grin to the likely truth of it.

"Thanks Max, but there's a secret I have to keep from her."

Max exhales loudly and flicks the ash from the cigarette

into the ashtray from the edge of the table. "Everyone has secrets Billy; we all have things going on deep down inside that other people are unaware of; me, you, everyone. You'll tell Elsa one day, when things have passed and the time is right." He takes another sip of his drink and keeps it in his mouth for a while as though intentionally, to physically hold his thoughts and words. Eventually he swallows and wipes his mouth with the back of his hand. "I'll remember it how it was," he says at last, softly and quietly, "and you'll remember it differently and once everything is lost in the blur of years everyone will look back on it in their own different way."

Billy sighs. "How strange it is that an episode in life can be interpreted differently by different people."

"It'll be a story recounted with the teller's slant on it. The way you see it is your version, *your* history Billy, and I'll see it my way and Elsa hers."

"And yet we were both there together."

"Yes, we were. But when you recite the story, then retell *that* one, the story changes bit by bit, until what remains are only the main parts, blurry and indistinct and the spaces left in between are filled by interpretation. This will be *my* story," Max says with a broad smile; "and your version will be yours."

"And somewhere between the two," Billy says softly, "is the truth."

Max gets to his feet and Billy does the same feeling suddenly lightheaded, a little unsteady now, knowing Max is about to leave. He steps forward and they embrace each other awkwardly manoeuvring around the table, a chair in the way between the two of them. Then quickly and without looking up Max turns and pats down the rear and hip pockets of his jeans and feeling his cigarette lighter between his fingers turns quickly and walks out. He does not look back.

Billy leaves his drink on the table and strides over to the balcony. It's more of a shuffle and he clutches the wooden handrail with both hands and looks out across the view beyond. More lights have appeared in the hillside now and although the night is truly set, the black horizon is still distinct against the Oxford Blue sky. The breeze from below brings with it a coolness, a freshness to his face that's welcoming and soothing. He breathes in deeply, filling his lungs to their capacity, holding the air for a while; the longer he keeps it there the more purifying its effect.

Exhaling at last he slowly turns around and leans back against the balcony railing, staring back at the table, resting one hand against the surface and holding the other to his chest, as though holding a heavy heart. There is only one chair and his packet of cigarettes, one empty glass on the table; the other stool opposite already taken by the drinkers stood next to them. And Billy has a strange feeling deep within, an instinctive awareness that Max being free to be wherever he needs to be will go and never return. In the weeks they've spent travelling on the road together they've been an equal part of the formation and the flight of a beautiful friendship. And perhaps more, it will be remembered differently as such, but always as a unique moment in its time and place.

The End